CHOSEN BY THE BILLIONAIRE

UNTAMED BILLIONAIRES SERIES

MAXINE HENRI

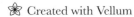

This one is for you, Veronika.
Your Happily Ever After is behind the corner.

PROLOGUE

"I THINK THIS IS EVERYTHING." Carla dropped the last box on the counter at Violet's café. Seeing Carla carrying the pastries brought back memories of their daily breakfasts.

"Thank you for bringing everything over," Vi said. "You've been a great help." She stepped from behind the counter and hugged her friend.

After Carla had moved her bakery to the new location five years ago, Vi hadn't seen her friend on a daily basis like before. Their friendship was strong, but with both of them in relationships and running businesses, they met only sporadically.

Carla pulled away. "It's getting late. You should go and get changed, and I'll finish setting up the buffet table."

Vi smiled wanly, butterflies tickling her stomach.

Only these were not the butterflies of excitement. Their wings carried anxiety, dread, guilt, confusion. They were pesky insects rather than wings of thrill.

She looked around the room that had been her home for years. The end of an era.

The end should really signify a new beginning, and she was happy about her next chapter. But still, the closure of her café felt like a sacrifice.

She twisted the engagement ring on her finger. She was being silly. Just sad about the last evening here. David was her future. Her handsome, educated, perfect fiancé. Her filthy rich fiancé who encouraged her to sell her business because his wife would have many duties. The whirlwind of hosting parties, attending fundraisers and managing David's social agenda was a full-time job for the future Mrs. David. Definitely different from all of this.

"Don't just stand there. Go and get ready." Carla frowned at her, dusting sugar from her skirt. "Everything is ready. It's going to be a great party. Don't you dare get all melancholy on us now."

Vi shuffled to the back room and changed into a simple cotton dress. That morning, she'd briefly considered wearing a new cocktail dress, but this didn't really feel like a celebration. By lunch, she'd wanted to cancel the whole event. Getting together with her friends and loyal patrons for the last evening here had seemed like a wonderful idea a few weeks ago. But now? It felt more like a funeral.

What was wrong with her? So many times, she had complained about the hours, the stress, the constant duties this little operation required from her. Especially since Becca was no longer here to share the burden. And now that she'd practically hit the jackpot and was hours away from freedom, she couldn't shake off this weird feeling that she'd made a mistake.

Her phone chimed with a message. She applied the lipstick and checked the screen. David.

Sweetheart, I'm running late. Important meeting. Enjoy yourself. Love, D.

Vi sighed, checked her reflection in the mirror and returned to the front. Some of her guests had already arrived.

The party took off pretty quickly, mostly due to Carla's enthusiasm. God bless her, the woman didn't let anyone sulk over what had been. She sprinkled laughter around the four walls of the small café.

"I hope you're sad only for tonight. This is a very exciting time. You're getting married. To a millionaire." Carla threw her arm around Vi's shoulder and squeezed. "Wait. Is he a millionaire?"

Vi burst into laughter. "I think so. I don't know. I haven't been *served* the prenup yet."

Carla turned to face Vi, her eyes wide. "Do you think he'd insist on that?"

"I would if he didn't. I'm not marrying David for the money." Vi took a sip from her wine. It was warm on her tongue, and she realized she had been holding the glass all evening.

"Where is he by the way?"

Vi was equally annoyed by David's absence and her strong need to defend him. Where was he? "He's held up at work. I don't think this is really his crowd." She bit her lip, regretting the last sentence.

"Now I'm offended." Carla scowled and put her hands on her hips. Several people turned their heads, but then returned to their conversations.

"He adores you." Vi winked. *And me. He adores me.* "He wanted to be here." Though she wasn't sure who she was trying to persuade anymore.

"I'm sure." Carla's features softened. "Are you going to miss this? All the hard work?"

"My life has been connected to this place. My life *has been* this place. I'll miss the people."

Charlie sauntered over and wrapped his arm around his wife's waist. He and Carla couldn't keep their hands off each other.

"Charlie wants me to work less, so if your work withdrawal is successful, I might join you and become a lady of leisure." Carla chuckled.

Lady of leisure? Was that Vi's destiny? She looked around, remembering the dreams she and Becca had when they had started here. Little of it had come to fruition in the end. Perhaps it really was time to move on. And she had a wedding to plan.

"I want you all to myself, baby." Charlie planted a

kiss on Carla's temple and lingered there for a beat longer, his love palpable to everyone. "Let's go check the back room."

Carla chuckled and swatted at him half-heartedly.

"The two of you. Gross. Don't you dare use my kitchen."

"It's your kitchen for only a few more hours. We're practically trespassing already." Charlie winked and pulled Carla behind the counter.

"Trespassing," Carla whispered, in her typical loud way, and beamed at Violet.

Vi rolled her eyes and turned to mingle with her guests, hoping that whatever Charlie's plan was, it either wouldn't happen or Carla would be uncharacteristically quiet while it happened.

David never did show up, and Vi said goodbye to everyone as the party wrapped up. Carla stayed to help her clean, then she had to practically force her friend to leave.

"I don't want to leave you here alone. I'll wait in the car if you need a moment," Carla insisted.

"We'll wait for you, Vi, no problem, but hurry up." Charlie nuzzled Carla's neck from behind.

"Charlie," she berated him and giggled, leaning into him.

"Okay, lovebirds, you're triggering my gag reflex. Get out of here. I don't want to know what surfaces I have to disinfect."

"I have no idea what you're talking about." A blush spread around Carla's neck.

"Just go." Vi rolled her eyes. "My car is right there across the street. I literally have to take five or six steps after I lock up." She shoved Charlie playfully and wrapped Carla in a tight hug. "Thank you for being here today. I'm a bit scared about tomorrow morning when I have nothing to do, though."

Carla laughed. "Let's have breakfast together at Sweet Temptations. We can do it regularly until you get busy with your duties as the wife of an heir."

"God help me." Vi cackled. "See you in the morning."

Vi locked the front door behind her friends and faced the bakery case for a moment. To say a proper farewell to the place that held so many memories. She might not miss the work, but she'd miss the community, the sense of belonging.

She wasn't sure how long she stood there, but when she checked her phone, she was surprised it was almost midnight. David had sent another message, saying it was too late and he'd gone home.

Violet picked up her purse and walked through the door for the last time in her life. Tomorrow the new owner will take over.

She crossed the deserted street to her car. Searching for her car keys, she was rummaging through her bag when she sensed a movement to her right. She whipped around and yelped.

"Quiet, bitch. Give me your purse."

The stench of alcohol turned her stomach. She wanted to comply with the demand, but her brain gave up. Her mind completely blank, she could only stare at the haunted, dark eyes in an acne-scarred face and a gun in the shaky hand of a disheveled man.

Then she registered a strange tremble, and it took her a moment to understand she was shaking uncontrollably.

"Your purse," her attacker growled and poked her ribs with the barrel.

The contents of her bag rattled as she couldn't control the tremor. The man snatched it from her.

Suddenly, he lifted off the ground as if pulled by an invisible string. Her heartrate slammed into overdrive when the contents of her purse flew through the air, landing at her feet with a clang.

Someone had yanked the man away.

"Fuck off." The voice startled her. Its owner had her attacker in a firm grip, by his collar. "Get the fuck out of here," he growled and dropped the attacker, who hit the ground and collapsed.

The robber scrambled to his feet and ran, leaving profanities in his wake.

Vi was frozen in panic even though the danger was sprinting away from her. The man who saved her squatted to pick up her things. He was practically kneeling at her feet, and she just stared, unable to grasp the situation or figure out her next move.

As he rose, her breath hitched. He towered above her, a wall of muscle. She knew it wasn't possible, but he seemed double her size. His hoodie obscured his face in the darkness, but his ice-blue eyes pierced through her, searing the memory of him into her mind. An inexplicable jolt of attraction zapped through her.

"You okay?" He handed her the purse.

She nodded. He narrowed his eyes and studied her. She wanted to reach out and pull away his hood.

"Can you drive?" he asked, and she nodded again.

He gestured toward her car. It took her a beat to understand he wanted her to get in. She blinked a few times, but he was still standing there. She was not imagining it. The hand tremor returned as she tried to find the keys.

He stood there like a sentry, his shadow comforting and eerie at the same time.

Finally she clicked the key and the car beeped. He pulled the door open and waited for her to get in. Vi stumbled and practically fell into the seat. Questions whirled around in her mind, like balls bouncing off each other in perpetual motion, unable to stop.

"Thank you," she whispered, but he'd shut the door already. She watched his imposing figure disappear, wondering if her heart was having a delayed reaction to the robbery and she should call an ambulance.

She gripped the wheel and lowered her head,

exhaling deeply. Those eyes. Jesus. She shook her head and started the engine but didn't shift into gear. She sat there still. Stunned. Mortified by the event, but mostly mesmerized by the depth of those ice-blue eyes.

1
___

CONFORM
to act in accordance with the prevailing
standards, attitudes, practices, etc.,
of society or a group

SOMETIMES WE MAKE a decision and stick with it even after we've realized it was a mistake. Perhaps we didn't want to disappoint those around us, or we couldn't truly accept our own lapse of judgment.

On paper, it was the best thing ever and our rational mind was cheering our luck and common sense. And yet... deep down, in our heart, we knew. We knew we were heading down the perfect path to inner death.

Violet tried to sweep away the feeling of dread. Today was a lovely day. Unseasonably warm for early spring in Chicago, the air vibrated with premature sunshine, putting a smile on most faces on the street.

The weather didn't put a spring into her step. Today was more exciting than any other day in the last three months. Or years. Which was strange. Strangely unsettling.

There was something seriously wrong with her.

Today was going to be great. She was going to help out at her friend Carla's charming patisserie. A bit of a change in her routine and a wonderful opportunity to escape her thoughts. Two months of purpose.

Vi pushed the front door open and the coffee aroma hit her immediately, bringing a smile to her face. Sweet Temptations was a small place, serving coffee, tea and delicious cakes with a side of inviting atmosphere that transported its patrons to Provence or Italy for at least a few moments.

The white and light gray interior featured tables with mismatched chairs around a wall of windows facing the street. At the far back of the narrow space, Carla presided over the entire operation from behind a small bar of stained white wood.

Cube-shaped shelves with books, cups and lavender pouches lined the white wall. If someone wanted cozy, Sweet Temptations was the place to find it.

Carla hugged Vi hard, squashing her against her ample bosom. She also greeted her loudly, and Vi's face burned a bit. No matter how long they'd known each other, Carla's volume surprised Violet every time.

Carla ushered her behind the counter and explained the basics of running her shop. Vi was experienced enough, so after ten minutes they were ready to enjoy their own morning cup of coffee.

"Not this asshole again." Carla sighed. She rolled her eyes and shuffled to a small table on the side of the counter that effectively served as her office.

Vi followed Carla to her seat and assessed said asshole. A tall mountain of muscles with slightly messed-up blond hair and ice-blue eyes smiled at her as their gazes met, exposing a set of dimples. The top of his hair was longer and hung into his face a bit.

When he shook it away, Vi's stomach tightened and heat spread inside her. Why did she feel like she knew him?

He nodded his greeting and put his large backpack on a chair near the door.

"Who is it?" Vi sat opposite Carla.

"One of those idiots who orders one espresso and sits here for three hours working on his computer," Carla whispered, glaring at him over Vi's shoulder. "He's been coming here for the last few weeks."

"Oh, I hated when people confused my coffee shop with a co-working center," Vi said, but a part of her regretted she was now sitting with her back to him. Regardless of his disregard for the hospitality of

Sweet Temptations, he was pleasant to look at. Well, that was an understatement. He was way more. He. Was. Fucking. Hot.

"Argh. I don't mind if people work from here, but they need to consume. His one stupid espresso doesn't even cover the Wi-Fi charge. And he occupies a table for four with his two laptops," Carla said in a whisper, which in her case amounted to a normal level of conversation heard by any bystander. Vi glanced back, but the tall guy was apparently oblivious to Carla's complaint and proceeded with setting up his computers.

Carla rolled her eyes again and went back to explaining the ins and outs of the daily business. Not that Vi needed the instructions.

Until three months ago, she had owned a café, very similar to the one Carla had been operating for the past five years. In fact, Vi had been instrumental in helping Carla set up Sweet Temptations.

Vi was excited to help her friend. She'd missed running her own business, her patrons, the smell of freshly brewed coffee. Damn it, she even missed rush hour, the endless responsibility and stress.

Or perhaps she just missed having something to do, interacting with people, making someone happy, having something of her own. How did her life become so dull? So not hers?

"Erica here is fantastic, but she leaves tomorrow, visiting her mother for three days." Carla pointed to her employee, a young woman who seemed to reign efficiently behind the counter. "Maybe we should postpone the trip."

"Don't be silly," Violet protested. "You've worked so hard, and frankly I can't wait to find some new activities—any activity—in my life."

"But you should be planning your wedding," Carla said and leaned back in her seat, tapping her long nails on the table.

But I don't want to.

Violet's fairytale started when she met David three years ago. Her prince had it all—looks, career, trust fund and pedigree. The latter wasn't much of an advantage though. At least not for Vi. Old money accounted for a certain level of expectation, and she wasn't exactly checking all the boxes for David's parents.

But they'd reached an amicable mutual acceptance, if not respect. Vi's happily ever after was only six months away and she knew her relationship was envied by eligible women of a certain social status within a hundred-mile radius.

So why was she plagued with emotions that didn't match the situation?

"I'll be fine. When in your life will you have an opportunity to travel for two months? This is the trip of your dreams, and Charlie would kill you if you backed out now. Go and enjoy it. I'm happy to step in."

Carla studied her with narrowed eyes, and Vi feared her friend was able to access the thoughts Vi tried to pretend didn't exist.

"Are you okay, *amiga*?" Carla asked finally.

I should be. I should be. I should be. Vi swallowed hard. "Yeah, it's been an adjustment to stay at home, but..." What was she going to say? It had been a mistake. The biggest mistake. One she didn't know how to fix.

Carla reached over and squeezed Vi's hand. "Once you get married and have kids, you'll be running your own household and things will get more normal."

"You don't believe that," Violet said, her stomach heavy with a lead ball of confusion and disappointment.

"It wouldn't be my choice, but that's me. Things may change when I get pregnant. If..." Carla looked away, her eyes glistening.

Carla and Charlie had been together for five years now, and while she had established a successful business and Charlie had launched his own financial management company, the one thing they still wished for eluded them. Several miscarriages had led to the reluctant acceptance that they would never become parents. It also led to the two-month trip around Europe they were about to embark on.

"It can still happen for you." Vi smiled sadly, and

they sat in silence for a moment. She really hoped her friend would return pregnant from their trip.

Selfishly, she was grateful for their adventure because it provided her with an excellent opportunity to step in and get out of the mess of her life for eight full weeks. And her life was a mess. One that everyone else perceived as a blessing.

"All the phone numbers for the vendors and contractors are on the board in the back. There's also a number for a temp agency in case you get stuck," Carla said, breaking the silence.

"Don't worry. I still have my contacts. I'll be all right." And she would be. This job would give her an opportunity to really understand what was wrong with her.

"Over the last four weeks, I tested different bakers and I've settled on two. Their delivery schedule is in the back. Make sure you taste everything. Charlie wants me to scale back, so I might contract them in the long term."

That was a surprise because Carla loved baking, but Vi didn't delve into it and simply promised to sample everything. She'd need to add running to her schedule to shed the consequences.

"Part of me is really grateful you sold your place. If it wasn't for your charming David pushing you to give up working, we wouldn't be able to take the trip." Carla smiled.

The espresso machine hissed behind them and the tables hummed with quiet conversations.

"Can I ask you something?" Violet avoided Carla's eyes, looking around as if she wanted to make sure the conversation remained private. Guilt plagued her. Could she reveal a bit of her turmoil to her friend?

"You know you can," Carla said in her typical volume akin to yelling.

"Remember how it was when you and Charlie met? How he broke your heart and how you pissed him off and all that drama and passion?"

"I'll never forget that." Carla laughed.

"Is it still there?" Vi almost whispered her question, fearing the answer.

"What?" Carla frowned.

"The passion and drama." Vi's heart thumped as she teetered on the edge of a big secret reveal.

"Of course! How else would we continue to challenge each other? Without the passion and a bit of drama, the two of us wouldn't work. Charlie is my soul mate. I have no doubt about that."

Soul mate? Vi wasn't sure if she believed in the concept of soul mates, but she was sure David wasn't hers. The thought lodged in her throat, making her swallow rapidly.

"Why are you asking, *amiga*? Is something wrong between you and David?" Carla scrutinized her with a look of curiosity and concern.

Vi bit her lip. "More like there is something missing."

Carla raised her eyebrows, and Violet appreciated that for once in her life her friend remained quiet.

The train was full steam ahead from the station. The engagement to David had been announced to society—people Vi didn't know or care about.

At his insistence, Violet had stopped working. She was to marry a man with status and money. A man she didn't deserve. A man who loved her so much he defied his family and made them accept her.

And yes, there were sacrifices—the biggest one being her own little café—but what lay ahead was priceless. Wasn't it? So why had her mind and heart rebelled lately, questioning everything?

A small part of her knew the events of the last night at her café had something to do with the spouts of doubt. She'd faced an attacker that night and was saved by a man whose face she hadn't seen, but whose eyes would forever remain in her mind.

He'd saved her from the robbery, but that night had also prompted her to revisit her life choices. Faced with a gun barrel, she'd realized how short life could be. Too short to settle. But she wasn't settling. Was she?

"*Dios mío*. Are you having second thoughts?" Carla studied her intently and Vi wished she'd never started the conversation.

It was bad enough that the thoughts had an

endless party inside her head. Sharing her stupid, self-ish, ungrateful ideas about the man she was about to marry laced them with unexpected and frightening clarity.

"No, no, I'm not," she lied. "I don't know. I can't have second thoughts. It's too late." But saying the words out loud for the first time, hearing her own life sentence, broke something inside her and Violet started crying. "Oh my God, what am I going to do?"

"*Mierda*! How long have you known?" Carla squeezed her hand.

"The night of the closing party at my café," she confessed, suddenly feeling a bit lighter for sharing the burden.

"That's three months ago! Violet! Why haven't you said something?" Carla clasped her hands against her chest as if her own heart were trying to escape.

"I don't know. At first, I believed I was sad because I closed the business, or traumatized by the attack. Later, I was embarrassed to even admit it. Why didn't I see this sooner?" Vi sniffled and Carla jumped up to get her a napkin from the counter.

"Oh, *amiga mía*!" Carla wrapped her arms around Vi and another wave of crying ruptured, this time getting attention from the customers around them.

"Geez, stop it, Carla, you're making me cry more," she said, but squeezed her friend tighter, relishing the compassion. Confiding in Carla didn't make the problem disappear or even lessen, but Vi could bear it easier.

Carla sat down again and shuffled her chair around the table's corner, closer to Vi. "Three months you've been doubting your future? You have to talk to David."

The easiness evaporated.

"And what would I say? I want to work and I don't think life with you is exciting enough for me? Do you know how stupid that sounds? I mean, I'm marrying up. Every other woman would be ecstatic. And why didn't I see it all sooner? How could I have been so blindly swept away and agreed to all the bullshit? I gave up my business for him!"

"Stop! Right now! Stop blaming yourself. Tonight, you will speak to David. You must. You can't keep dragging this out, unresolved. Maybe once you voice your concerns, things will get better." Carla kept shaking her head. "What a mess. I'm going to postpone the trip. I can't leave you here alone in this situation."

"No! If you stay on my account, I'm going to regret ever mentioning it to you. I promise I'll deal with the situation. I think working here will boost my confidence and if my engagement breaks off, I'll have your coffee shop to keep me busy. You're my savior. Now go and have fun in Europe."

"I don't know… Why didn't you say something before? *Mierda*. Promise me you're going to update me regularly." Carla stood up and walked behind the counter.

Vi followed her. "I promise. We'll be fine, won't we, Erica?" Vi winked, trying to smile, but didn't succeed, the effort too fake. Erica nodded while pouring a coffee for a customer.

Standing behind the counter, Violet felt a sense of belonging. God, she missed having a career. Working the espresso machine felt like being home. She looked around and a jolt of empowerment ran through her. If nothing else, this would be a great way to confirm her own self-worth.

She'd lost something when she sold her business and she needed to find herself again. It wasn't even that she wanted her café back—she wasn't sure her heart had been in it at the end—but she for sure didn't want to idle about and wait for David to fill her social calendar.

Her eyes wandered to the tall computer geek. The tiny espresso cup looked ridiculous in his large hands. He put the coffee down and started typing. Vi gaped at him. She'd never seen someone running their fingers on a keyboard with such speed. "He really works on two laptops at a time?"

Carla nodded, made a sound between disgust and contempt, and walked into the back room. Erica glanced over and her cheeks turned red. A quick sweep through the room and Vi realized that all the women were half-swooning, stealing glimpses of the man. He worked at his keyboard, oblivious to the attention, but then suddenly he looked up and their eyes met.

He smiled and she narrowed her eyes. She was sure she'd never met him, yet he seemed familiar.

"Okay, now I have a mission." She walked into the back to find Carla. Perfectly aware she was ridiculously thrilled about the self-imposed assignment, she couldn't help herself. "I'm going to teach him a lesson. By the time you're back, there won't be any annoying cheap customers," Violet said and smiled.

God, the silly mission was the most excitement she'd had in months. And she was planning a wedding on a limitless budget. She was seriously messed up.

VI ENTERED the café and locked the door. She dragged her feet across the room, turned on the coffee machine and looked around with anticipation. Having this job, if only temporarily, was like a lighthouse in the sea of troubles her life currently floated in.

However, after not sleeping all night, her first day seemed like a punishment. She yawned and walked to the back room. She assessed her face in the mirror—red eyes, tear-stained cheeks, no makeup. She was going to scare all Carla's customers.

David hadn't accepted a potential break-up. He'd insisted there were still six months until the wedding and they could get back on track. The track that would derail Violet's life, one she wasn't willing to ride anymore. Or was she?

Their conversation last night had only confirmed they were both living in a different relationship. Why hadn't she seen it before? What they had, or rather, didn't have, couldn't be fixed in six months, but he railroaded her and she gave him—them—another chance.

A spoiled rich brat, David hadn't given her the opportunity to decide or act. He'd manipulated her to ensure things would progress as he expected.

She'd acquiesced to try to improve what they had, but his attitude last night had only solidified that there was no chance for them. She wasn't even sure if she was going to try.

In the early hours of the morning, she'd given him false hope because she couldn't continue fighting. It was too exhausting. So, really, she had resolved nothing, she'd only made things worse.

Violet slipped her engagement ring from her finger and put it into the pocket of her black jeans. She tied an apron around her waist. Okay, the first order of the business: a double espresso. Caffeinated, she'd be able to face the world.

She unlocked the front door and soon patrons started roaming in. One hour later, she'd served at least one hundred coffees and took care of the breakfast orders for several regulars.

The lack of sleep was getting to her, but coffee and adrenaline helped her cope and move on autopilot. At least with her mind tired but occupied, she couldn't really think about David and the mess of her doomed engagement.

The morning rush cleared and Violet started the dishwasher when the bell above the door chimed. She looked up and spotted him. The two-laptops-one-espresso guy.

Stifling a yawn, she smiled at him, a challenge in her eyes. Well, he didn't yet know she was going to get rid of him, but the idea of the game had energized her.

He smiled back and she swore under her breath. *Dimples! Freaking dimples.* She glared at him as he set up his work station at the same table by the door. He was hot. Really hot. A Scandinavian god kind of hot.

He wore a gray Henley and gray jeans that hugged his muscular legs and ass. *Game on! I'm not letting your looks distract me.*

He approached the counter with a smile, exposing a perfect set of white teeth. "Can I have an espresso, please?" *Stupid dimples.*

"Just one?" She glared, leaning on the counter by the coffee machine with her arms crossed over her chest.

"Yes, I'm alone here." He wrinkled his brow. "You're new."

She would not engage in conversation with him.

She would not join the female groupies swooning around him. Though based on yesterday, he might be oblivious to the attention. "Can I offer you a muffin or a croissant?"

He shrugged. "No, just the coffee. Thank you."

She turned to make the coffee, rang it up, and he paid cash and put a few cents into the tip jar. For whatever reason, this annoyed her.

He smiled again and sauntered to his seat.

Half an hour and several customers later, Violet walked to his table and picked up the empty cup. "Anything else?"

"No, thanks." He stared out the window, not even glancing her way.

Seriously? "Are you leaving then?"

He checked his phone, looked outside again and then at the screen of his laptop. Violet glanced down, but he was using a screen protecting filter.

He raised his eyes and jerked his head backward, taken aback by her presence. "What?" he snapped.

If you want nothing else, I'd suggest you leave the table for paying customers," she said with her best fake smile, her voice laced with pretend sweetness.

"Okay, I'll have a blueberry muffin," he growled and returned to his activity. His eyes kept darting between his phone, his screen and the street.

Violet frowned. He hadn't picked up on her subtle suggestion about his lack of spending during his lengthy stay, which left her strangely deflated. She wanted to teach him a lesson now. Why she was so invested, she wasn't sure.

She stormed back to the bar and scrutinized him with the evilest look she could muster. And then she had an idea even her tired mind appreciated. She took a muffin out of the glass display and put it in the microwave. She nuked it, practically burning it.

An action that got the other two customers sniffing and raising their eyes toward her. The one-espresso guy, however, continued staring outside or on his screens. *Fuck him!* Violet took a saltshaker and seasoned the broiled muffin generously.

She smiled sweetly and sauntered to his table. "Here you go, *sir*, I hope you'll enjoy it."

He ignored her and started typing frantically on his keyboard.

Unsatisfied, Violet returned behind the counter. It was a slow part of the day and with the lack of sleep, she found herself fidgeting. She emptied the dishwasher and tidied behind the bar. She wiped down all the empty tables to keep herself from falling asleep on her feet.

The blond computer geek hadn't touched the muffin. What was he staring at? She scanned the street. Nothing of interest. Parked cars, some moving traffic and the businesses across the street. Was he waiting for someone?

A man in a black suit walked past the café. Hadn't he passed by several times today?

A group of people entered, and Violet welcomed the distraction. They all ordered to go and the burst of activity got her re-energized again. Geez, it wasn't even lunch. She had another coffee, but the fatigue weighed her down.

The man in the suit walked by again. *What the hell?*

She glanced at the table by the door. The muffin remained untouched. The one-espresso dude chewed on his bottom lip, a line creasing his forehead. Thinking? What was he doing?

Violet marched over to him again. "I'm sorry, but if you're not going to order anything else, I'll have to ask you to leave."

For a second, she thought he didn't hear her. His eyes remained glued to his screens. Then he huffed the air with something akin to relief and whispered something that sounded like an accomplished 'yes'. Clearly, the work was going well.

He finally looked up, frowning as he noticed her.

"What?" he barked.

"Are you for real? You can't just sit here all day." Her exhaustion was probably making her less polite than normal, but he was seriously pissing her off. Or she was taking out on him the frustration from last night's discussion with David. She dismissed the thought because it didn't make her feel better. Or reasonable. God, she needed to sleep.

Commotion outside got his attention again. A small group of four or five men left the building across the street and entered a dark sedan parked in front of it. He smiled slightly and leaned back, looking at his screen again. He clicked on two keys and glanced back at her, his expression a mixture of curiosity and annoyance.

"I'll have a glass of water," he said with a shrug.

"Water? Get your water in the convenience store. This isn't a co-working center!" Violet turned and walked away.

She got busy with another rush of customers, almost forgetting the computer guy. Almost being the key word because her eyes kept turning toward his table where he now sat with his arm over the chair beside him, watching her. Distracting her. She glared at him, but he didn't seem affected by her malice.

As the post-lunch crowd cleared out, he finally packed up his computers and stood, leaving the untouched muffin on the table. He hoisted his backpack over his shoulder and put a five-dollar bill on the bar.

"Thank you for the muffin." He smiled at her. *Damn dimples!*

* * *

THE PAIN SHOT from her shoulder blade to her temple, immobilizing Violet. She couldn't force her eyes open for fear of her head exploding. Time seemed a foreign concept, but she'd slept. A win.

God, please don't let it be the morning yet.

Two more days before the quiet, efficient Erica would return and Vi couldn't imagine how she was going to survive work while her personal life imploded in her face.

At least David wasn't home last night when she'd returned. She'd gone straight to bed rather than showering, eating or even brushing her teeth.

She stirred and mustered the courage to open one eye, focusing it on the digital clock on her nightstand. It was only midnight. Thank God! If she didn't tackle the headache now, she wouldn't be able to work tomorrow. She should just get up and take painkillers and drink a lot of water. That would be the responsible thing, but it seemed like too much effort.

She considered her options, as if delaying the trip to the bathroom would in any way award her with more quality sleep. Still, she lay there. Focused on her breathing, she froze as a sinister feeling crawled over her.

She wasn't alone.

2

Vɪ ᴍᴏᴠᴇᴅ her arm to the other side of the bed, but it was empty. Was her aching head playing tricks on her? She tried to quiet her mind as her heart thumped in her head.

Had David returned? She opened her eyes and lifted herself to her elbows.

"Jesus! What are you doing?" She sat up, pulling the covers tight as she moved. Still dressed in her work clothes, she had no real reason to hide. But she definitely wasn't the one acting weird here.

David sat in a chair beside the bed, his forearms resting on his knees, watching her.

"Sorry, darling, I didn't mean to scare you. I came home and you were sleeping and so beautiful. I couldn't help myself." He smiled with sadness in his eyes and Vi's lungs constricted.

She was causing him so much pain. What was wrong with her?

"You should get to bed. It's late. I have a headache. I'm going to take something." She swung her legs over the edge of the bed, avoiding direct touch or eye contact.

"Stay! I'll get you the pills and a glass of water." David scurried out of the room.

It was time to move out. This couldn't continue. She didn't have it in her to save something that had never existed. She wished, for David's sake, she hadn't stupidly fallen for his sophisticated attention. That she hadn't been dazzled by the glamour of his world. It was all fake and she'd let it destroy her, blind her. And now she was destroying him. He was innocent in the whole debacle and Vi couldn't bear seeing him suffer.

David returned with water and painkillers. He was a handsome man. Some of his well-groomed dark hair had fallen onto his forehead, making him look almost common, approachable. He smiled again and sat on the bed beside her.

"My mother is coming over this weekend. She'd like to take you shopping for your wedding dress," he said, hope written all over his face.

Vi's blood boiled. She wouldn't want his mother's help with the dress even if she went through with the wedding.

"David, I have to work this weekend."

"No, you don't. You *want* to work this weekend.

You don't have to." He stood up and raked his hands through his hair.

"Yes, exactly, I want to work and I'd appreciate it if you supported me." She squinted as the pain rippled through her head.

"Women in my family don't work and you had already accepted that." His tone was level, but he huffed out a heavy breath of frustration.

No, I hadn't. But that was a lie. She had accepted, only to come face to face with regret the size of Mt. Everest.

Vi stood up too fast and leaned on the edge of the bed to steady herself against the wave of dizziness. "And it was a mistake. I want to work and if you can't accept that, as I repeated countless times last night, there is no point going through with the wedding."

"You're giving me an ultimatum?" He raised his voice now.

Vi sighed. "I don't know, David. Frankly, I don't think that even you allowing me to work would change how I feel. Our worlds are too different and I'm sorry I didn't see it sooner, but I can't marry you."

"You're just getting cold feet. It's common, I hear," he said and tried to wrap his arms around her, but she stepped back. God, the snub in his voice. Had it always been there?

"You have a lot to offer, and I'm sure there is a woman who would appreciate it greatly. I'm not that woman. We want different things in life. I'm not housewife material." She yelled the last words as if that made them more comprehensible. Her heart pounded in her chest and the throbbing pain in her head nearly blinded her.

"You can get used to it. It's not that hard to manage a household," he shouted, throwing his arms up.

"I don't want to manage your fucking household!" She pressed her fingertips to her temples, trying to compose herself and tame the headache.

"Watch your language," David said, raising his chin.

"I'm not going to fucking watch my fucking language. We've been discussing this ad nauseam since last night and you're behaving like a child. I'm not a toy you want!" Fatigue fought its way through her limbs and aching head.

She spoke softly. "David, you must feel it as well. Things are not good between us. We haven't even had our wedding and we've already been living like a married couple—not even newlyweds, but like a boring old couple. You must expect more from a relationship. You should. I know I do."

"You're being ridiculous. I take you places, buy you gifts, I cherish the earth you walk on. What else do you want?"

He wasn't getting it. Maybe he never would. He was content with her as his future wife, and that was enough for him. Contentment. She didn't want to spend her life content. She wanted joy and happiness. And passion. The world of David and his parents was suffocating, and while she didn't want to hurt him, she had to save herself.

"I'll move out as soon as possible. I'm going to find a place," she said, the will to fight abandoning her completely. She was too exhausted for this, and he was too stubborn to hear her. To understand her.

"That would be highly impractical. You'd have to sign a lease for at least a year, and we are getting married in six months." He shook his head, looking at her as if she was deranged.

"We're not getting married, David. I don't know how else to explain that to you, but I'm not in love with you. I don't think I ever was. I was in love with the idea of us, but that's not enough for a lifelong commitment. I'm sorry. I really am." She slouched onto the bed.

"You're tired. I have to leave tomorrow morning for meetings in London. We'll talk when I'm back." He left the room.

Violet buried her face in her palms and collapsed back on the mattress.

She must have fallen asleep at some point because when her alarm went off at six o'clock, Violet felt oddly rested. She showered and dressed.

The door to the guest room was open and the bed unmade. David must have slept there, but he was gone. She shuffled to the kitchen and found a note:

Good morning, darling, I'll be back late Saturday night. We'll talk then. I love you! David.

Fuck!

Two more days of work without Erica and then she could start looking for an apartment. She needed to move out before David's return. Not that she expected moving would effectively end the relationship. Clearly, David would not let go easily. What a nightmare! How could you refuse a man who had never been denied anything, who didn't know the meaning of 'no' when he wanted something?

With a heavy heart, Violet picked up her purse and made her way to the garage. Her beloved Audi technically belonged to David. One of many things she'd leave behind. Gifts she'd never wanted and yet had grown so accustomed to.

A tear escaped her as she accepted that this was one of the last times she would drive the car. And the car was probably the only thing she would truly miss. Three years of her life! She had lost more of herself than she cared to acknowledge.

Vi parked the car on the side street at the back of the patisserie and got out. When she unlocked the back door and entered the kitchen, the familiar aroma of coffee and baked goods immediately grounded her. It wasn't so much that she loved working in a coffee shop, but she'd done it long enough that it provided comfort. It was something she knew and could trust effortlessly. A place where she could hide. And she'd been hiding in a place like this for long enough to forget her dreams.

Vi leaned into the merry-go-around of the morning chores, accepting deliveries, polishing mugs and glasses, making new orders, straightening tables and pouring the first cups of coffee, grateful the activity kept her mind off her misery.

It was just before noon when the door chimed and the tall computer geek blocked the entrance with his impressive body.

Vi rolled her eyes, but inside she was kind of glad he came. He was the entertainment of the day for her. And today, better rested than yesterday, she was confident she could scare him off forever.

"Hello," he said and smiled. *Keep the stupid dimples to yourself, dick!*

"Hello again. Welcome. I hope today you came for some of our most popular cakes." Her fake smile was so big it almost dislocated her jaw.

He raised his eyebrows and chuckled as he descended on his usual spot and started setting up his computer. Today, he only had one laptop. *Hm?* Perhaps she was going to get rid of him in phases, one piece at a time.

Three women came in and immediately turned their attention to him. Yes, unfortunately, his testosterone attracted women probably even while he was sitting on the toilet. Vi shook her head as all three women giggled.

"May I offer you something?" she interrupted their drooling.

They giggled again and ordered their skinny, extra shot, kids' temperature, half of the flavor, no sugar drinks that Violet wanted to spit in, but made them with a professional attitude and a fake smile that seemed to be plastered over her face permanently today. It took her a good seven minutes to complete the order and the three shameless flirts left finally, giggling like teenagers while stealing glances at the computer geek.

"I'd like an espresso," he said as he approached the counter.

"Of course." Violet turned to make him one. "Anything else?"

"No, thank you." He smiled.

"A muffin perhaps?"

"Are you going to burn and salt it?" He winked and heat rose in her cheeks.

"Are you going to spend hours here?" She smirked, holding his gaze.

"Most certainly," he answered.

She turned to the coffee machine and swore under her breath while prepping his order.

He paid, grabbed his coffee and sauntered to his seat. His jeans hugged his ass, revealing enough to fantasize about. *Stop!*

Before Violet could come up with her plan of attack, the place filled with new customers who kept her busy for almost two hours before she was blessed with another quiet minute. She looked up and met his eyes. His laptop was closed and he'd been watching her. What was his deal?

She walked over to him. "I'm sorry. I didn't have time to come over. Can I get you anything else?"

He looked her up and down and his eyes lingered for a moment too long on her breasts. Not long enough to creep her out, but there was interest there. She hated him.

"I'm going to try my luck with a croissant this time." He smiled.

Vi narrowed her eyes and stared at him for a moment, but his order took away all the lines she'd prepared. She bit her lip, got him the croissant and returned to work.

He didn't touch the pastry, just continued staring at her, following her every move. Now she was pissed not only because he was sitting there, but also because he was making her feel self-conscious.

A tiny part of her that she tried hard to ignore really wanted him to like what he saw. Her body tingled under his intense scrutiny. Shit! She really was starting to hate the asshole.

The rest of the day was a disaster. Violet made coffee without actually adding a new scoop of grounds into the machine, serving a horrible watered-down excuse for a beverage. She made every possible mistake when working the register, resulting in several unnecessary cancellations in the system. She smashed two mugs with a crash loud enough to stop the traffic outside. She burned her hand and mixed up several cake orders.

All courtesy of the staring Mr. Hot Espresso.

She was seeing red by the time his phone rang and he finally stood up and left.

Vi exhaled, watching his broad shoulders disappear. As soon as he'd stepped out to the street, the man in the black suit showed up by his side and they walked away together.

Who was the suit? He'd been walking back and forth several times a day. Was he waiting for someone? For Mr. Hot Espresso? Why wouldn't he come in and sit with him?

Violet shook her head and exhaled. Finally, it was quiet again and she wasn't going to spend it thinking about that cheap bastard.

She pulled out her phone and searched for apartments. An activity that proved even more depressing than her broken relationship or her losing battle with the computer geek. Nothing came up in her price range and she wasn't going to share a place. Geez, that would be pathetic at almost thirty.

Her phone rang and she answered quickly. "Carla, how is your trip?"

"Horrible. I mean, everything is great. Paris is all it should be, but we're jet-lagged, taking it easy for now. How are things there?" From the murmur of activity audible on the line, Vi assumed her friend was calling from a restaurant.

"Things are great. So far, I only broke two mugs and mixed up a negligible number of orders." It was kind of a lie, but well, she would improve the score over the next few days.

"Don't scare away my customers." Carla laughed. "What about David and you?"

"How long do you have?" Vi sighed.

"Oh, that bad? Charlie, I don't want another cocktail! Where was I? Oh yeah, so have you talked to him yet?"

Vi blew out air and leaned against the counter. "I have, but it's a long story. I'm looking for a place to live." She pictured her friend drinking on the other side of the world and, while happy for Carla, self-pity crawled up her spine.

"You can stay at our place. We're not using it anyway and I'd feel much better having you there than the house sitter snooping around," Carla suggested. "Charlie is nodding as well. Let me make the arrangements and you can move in immediately."

"Carla, that's too generous," Vi said, but she couldn't afford to refuse.

"Don't be silly. We're not using it and it'll give you more time to find a new place. I don't want you to end up with something shitty under time pressure," Carla chirped and giggled. "Charlie!" She whispered a warning, and Vi had to smile.

"Okay, I'll let you go now. Thank you so much. It means a lot."

"Just take good care of my work and my home." Carla giggled again and the line went dead. Those two were having a great time. Vi couldn't help but feel a bit jealous.

The outlook for the next few weeks was looking up though. Two months should be enough to find a new place. Staying at Carla's, she could be out of David's house before he returned. Hopefully he would finally get the message.

The door opened and three people walked in. Vi stepped forward to meet them, and her phone rang again, but she ignored it to focus on the customers.

It was another two hours before she remembered the missed call and dialed back.

"Oh, Violet, thank you for calling," said Erica. "I'm sorry, but my mom has been hospitalized and I need to stay. Do you think you can manage without me for a little longer?"

Shit! "Of course, how long do you need? Is she okay?"

"I'm not sure. She's having tests done and, well… I don't know." Erica's voice trembled.

"Listen, take as much time as you need. I'll call the temp agency. All the best to your mom and keep me posted, please." She did her best to sound positive and supportive while fighting the panic.

A group of young professionals entered the café,

immediately grabbing most of the seats. Between them and the other walk-ins, Vi was busy till the end of the day. By the time she called the temp agency, they were already closed, effectively delaying her ability to find a replacement for Erica and giving herself any chance of rest. Especially since she was going to move in the meantime as well.

Exhausted, she rolled the blinds down. She was sliding the keys into the lock when someone shoved the door open, slamming it back against her.

"Hey," she protested, rubbing at the pain in her shoulder.

The intruder locked the door and turned to face her.

First, Violet registered the gun in his hand, and then she recognized his face. "You?"

3

VIOLET STARED at Mr. Hot Espresso, her eyes darting between his gun and his face as her heart tried to escape her ribcage.

"We are closed!" she snapped, but her courage didn't reach beyond those words. Was he going to kill her? Or rob her? She shouldn't have treated him rudely. She shouldn't have salted his muffin.

Oh God, she was going to die over the stupid muffin.

Vi tried to stop the avalanche of morbid scenarios and compose herself, but it was as if her mind grew its own legs and marched around in all sorts of directions.

"I know you're closed. I was hoping you could provide shelter for a patron in need." He winked, but his gaze sprang immediately to the small opening in the blinds.

"Put the gun away. Now." There was no authority or threat in her tone, the fear simply took over.

He narrowed his eyes and studied her for a brief moment that lasted an eternity, but then shoved his gun into the waistband on the small of his back.

Thump. Thump. Thump. Vi couldn't think over the pounding of her heart.

Thump. It wasn't her heart. Someone was running down the street.

Mr. Hot Espresso pushed her to the corner, away from the windows, his body covering her. They listened to the footsteps outside. Or rather, he did, because Vi's ability to think or command any of her senses disappeared as soon as his solid body blanketed her.

He looked down at her as if knowing fear wasn't the source of her quiver. They stood there, staring at each other, the energy zapping with adrenaline and something else. Something Violet didn't want to contemplate.

With every inhalation, her nipples brushed the solid form of his torso, the sensation pulsing in her core.

Voices from the outside brought her back to reality. He put his index finger on her lips to maintain silence. The light touch spread heat through her body. She couldn't make out what was said outside, but whoever was out there gave up and left.

Mr. Hot Espresso listened for a moment longer

and then he spread two slats of the blinds on the door with his fingers. He peaked out and his body relaxed slightly where it touched hers.

Still pinning her to the wall, he looked down at her, his ice-blue eyes penetrating her with aching intensity. A flash of recognition flickered through her mind, bringing her back to the night of the mugging.

She frowned, not believing the odds and simultaneously trying to get her heart to regain its vital functions. Was it really him? Why hadn't she realized that before?

His finger was still on her lips and he slowly slid it down her cheek, sending her heartbeat into overdrive. He was close, too close. Though not really touching her, she still felt his every sinew and it was hard to deny she wanted to feel more of him. As if his body sensed her need, his erection twitched against her stomach, and Vi's breath hitched.

His eyes dropped to her mouth and somehow, outside of her control, her lips parted in anticipation.

What am I doing?

"Go away!" She pushed and squeezed past him. "Why do you even need shelter? Don't bring your trouble here." What was wrong with her stupid body, practically begging him to kiss her?

He raised his brow and his lips curled up. *Stupid dimples!*

"Go away!" she hissed again.

"I heard you the first time." He smirked.

She widened her eyes and raised her arms in question.

"I have the gun, I stay in charge." He cocked his head.

Vi puffed air into her cheeks. "Well…" And no intelligent thought came. "Well… how long are you planning to hold me here at gunpoint? I'm tired and I want to go home."

"I'm not pointing the gun at you." He shrugged. "Not yet, anyway." He walked over to his usual table and sat.

Was he serious? "Okay, I'm going to balance the register as I planned before your intrusion."

"First, give me your phone."

"What? I'm not giving you my phone." She crossed her arms over her chest. The panic and fear dissipated. Somehow she knew he wouldn't hurt her. He'd saved her before, after all.

"Give me the fucking phone," he said, shaking his head as if her reaction was annoying him. He reached for his gun. Well, more suggested the movement than really drawing it.

Vi pulled her phone from her back pocket, and as he reached for it, she walked around and dropped it on the table. And the asshole dared to roll his eyes.

She stepped behind the counter and started working on the register, forcing herself not to look his way. Oddly, being held technically at gunpoint, she felt safe with him. Safer than she ever felt with anyone else. The ice-blue eyes, which she now believed belonged to the hero from three months ago, kept her panic at bay.

With the distraction of Mr. Hot Espresso and his pistol, concentrating on balancing the register proved harder than she was willing to admit, but somehow Vi managed to finalize everything.

His eyes remained on her as she unloaded the dishwasher and put away the left-over pastries. She washed the coffee machine and busied herself with other chores that didn't need to be done, only to avoid him.

The silence was deafening in her ears, but he seemed perfectly relaxed, simply watching her and occasionally checking the street through the blinds.

At last, there was nothing left to do. She took off her apron and looked at him. She was tired and annoyed. And attracted to the man. Even more now, after she realized he was her mysterious savior.

"We've met before." She searched his face for… she wasn't sure what she wanted to see. Did he even remember her?

"I know."

She waited, but he didn't continue. That was it. No reminiscing. Well, so much for her fantasy about the hero who saved her. Fuck it.

"So what now? How long do you plan to stay here?" she asked, crossing her arms against her chest and tapping her foot.

He pinched the bridge of his nose, his eyes closed, and took one deep breath. "For a bit longer." He sighed.

"Why should I let you? You have been the shittiest customer and now you're hiding out here with a gun and asking for my help?" Violet walked over and sat on the chair across from him. She wanted to go home.

A bruise on his cheek stupidly added to his sex appeal. Hopefully, he was in pain!

He frowned. "Why am I the shittiest customer?"

Vi rolled her eyes. "Really? You sit here for hours every day at a four-person table, use the Wi-Fi and electricity and in return for our hospitality, you drink one fucking espresso."

"I don't use your electricity or Wi-Fi." He looked confused.

"That's beside the point! You only order one coffee and sit here for hours!" Seriously? He was unreasonably hot, but clearly he had no social references.

"I only drink one coffee a day. It makes me jittery," he said, searching her face. For what? Understanding?

Vi sighed and shook her head. This conversation wasn't going anywhere. "I guess you'd understand better if I could explain it in binary code, but just trust me on this one. Your behavior has been rude."

"I'm sorry. I-I'm not good at these things. I usually work from home." He looked away.

He wasn't rude, he was absolutely clueless. That wasn't good. She could repel a rude hot guy, but the lack of social skills made him somehow adorable. *Stop it, Vi! He is not adorable!*

"Can we go home now?" she asked, stifling a yawn.

He checked his phone. "Not yet. I'm sorry."

They sat in silence for a moment.

This situation is crazy. Why is he here? Who is after him?

"What's your name?" He broke the silence and looked at her. Somehow, his ice-blue eyes produced heat and Vi had to swallow hard before she could find her voice.

"Violet. What's yours?" She held his gaze, warmth spreading through her bones.

"Art," he whispered. He was feeling it too, she was sure. What was wrong with her?

"Art? Is that short for something?" she asked, the words catching in her throat as she tried to regulate her breathing.

"Arthur." He gave her one of those dimples-on-display smiles.

More like Ar-Thor.

* * *

SHE LICKED her bottom lip and Art's cock twitched. It'd been a while since he was this attracted to a woman. He was even glad of the trouble tonight. It brought him here... with her. The situation with his last project was fucked up, but he didn't want to think about that right now. He wanted to solve the mystery of this woman who smelled like summer and had the most intriguing eyes. *Violet.*

Since the day he'd first seen her, he couldn't get enough of her. The combo of her blond hair and caramel eyes was too unusual to ignore, but there was more to her than that. The way she wore her hair up in a messy bun drove him crazy with the need to smooth it.

Her lips, full and naturally pink, begged him to explore them. He wished they would beg out loud. The curve of her breasts below the black T-shirts she seemed to prefer made him ache.

The caramel of her eyes was sweet on his tongue even when she glared at him. Oh, and glare she did. Watching her was like sitting at the beach when sharks roamed the water. Admiring the view but avoiding the fatal bite.

He didn't believe in fate, but tonight the stars had aligned and brought them together. An unplanned input gathering session. She hated him because he only ordered one thing while he worked from the café. That could be fixed.

Completely oblivious, he was a prick not to have thought of it before. It was like that when he worked. Focused wholly on a project. Now he needed to address the other variable.

"Why did you cry?" he asked. *Idiot!* That was subtle. As if she trusted him enough to answer.

"I don't cry." She cocked her head and frowned.

"You did your first day here," he explained.

Her eyes widened and she let the air out, pursing her lips. Those full lips he wanted to devour.

"That's none of your business." She eyed him sideways as if trying to figure out what was wrong with him. *A lot of things, Vi.*

Well, at least his assessment of her unwillingness to confide in him was correct. Why was he so awkward with her? Generally, he didn't do conversations. He never needed to. Women made themselves available and he enjoyed them. It was his looks, he'd been told, but he didn't care. It worked well. It satisfied his needs.

Violet didn't seem to like him. Though the way her body quivered under him when he'd cornered her earlier, he wasn't so sure anymore that he could read her correctly. Not that he was good at reading people in the first place.

Why did she have to start working here now? If only she'd started two days later, this job would have been done and he wouldn't be coming to the café anymore. Only he had been. This morning he'd come only to see her.

Frankly, he hadn't stopped dreaming about her since the night he'd stumbled on the pathetic robbery. That douchebag's gun wasn't even real. Something in her caramel eyes, on the other hand, was real. Too real. At least in his mind.

"You're right," he said.

She studied him, her expression saying she expected him to continue. Was there more he should say? Did he need to?

He cleared his throat. "You looked sad, and it was your first day."

"How do you know it was my first day?" She pulled a chair from another table and put her feet up. She looked exhausted. He should let her go home. Luca had called him several times. The coast had been clear for a while now probably, but he couldn't bring himself to let her go. Not just yet.

"I'm observant," he said and she chuckled. Her features softened. It wasn't a laugh yet, but the sound pleased him, anyway.

"And here I thought you only see your screens." Her smile spread like fire through him. "What happened tonight?"

"I pissed off some people," Art said, hoping she wouldn't pursue the topic.

She nodded. "You have a gift for that."

"What?"

"You have a gift for pissing people off." She snorted and even that sounded like music to his ears. Weird. He needed to solve her, like a complicated math equation, and get the hell out of there. "So who is the suit that lingers around while you're here? I saw he joined you when you left today."

Art raised his eyebrows. How had she picked up on that?

"Well, Art, you're not the only observant one here."

"Clearly."

Her eyes twinkled now. She was enjoying piecing together the picture of him as much as he was enjoying the puzzle of her. Or was he getting ahead of himself?

"Luca is my friend and bodyguard." Why did he say that? Having a bodyguard opened a whole new can of worms. Issues he wasn't ready to discuss. *Shit!* She confused him too much. This was the first genuine conversation they were having and he'd already dropped his guard.

"So you're a cheap bastard that buys only one coffee, but you can afford a bodyguard?" That was what she got out of the slip-up? Thank God.

"I'm more of an arrogant prick than a cheap bastard," he said, and she burst out laughing. She put her feet down and doubled over, her laughter filling the room and his heart.

Even he chuckled. He didn't do laughter. Not much anyway. And here she was, a blond stranger with lush lips and huge tits and the ability to bring the worst out of him. Or the best?

"That you are, Art, that you are," she finally

managed to say through her giggles and tears. Her eyes met his and she stopped laughing, the energy between them suddenly serious. She studied him for a moment and his heart thumped double-time. What was she seeing?

"Every hundred years, the moon adds approximately 1.4 milliseconds to a day," he blurted out.

She frowned but said nothing. He was going to scare her off with his inability to control his brain.

They sat in silence, and while his heart hammered, the absence of conversation wasn't awkward. It was charged with something, a sense of comfort despite his ability to simultaneously imagine bending her over the table. He hadn't met a woman yet who could share silence with him. Maybe she was deep in her own thoughts, forgetting he was even there. It gave him the opportunity to admire the view.

"Do you believe in soul mates, Art?" Her words startled him.

Suddenly, it seemed like his entire future depended on his answer. Her words hit his stomach like an iron ball and a panic alarm rang in his head. *Abort! Abort! Abort!*

"I believe in body mates," he answered, hoping to divert the conversation. Why was he freaking out?

She giggled and shook her head. "That's called friends with benefits."

Good job killing the moment, idiot. Why couldn't he control his mouth?

"The position is open currently," he said. The woman somehow unleashed his conversational skills. What the hell was he saying, anyway?

"I'm sure there are plenty of candidates ready to apply." She smirked.

"None actually." After he destroyed the moment, he was now desperately chasing it, hoping to rekindle the spark.

"A player and a liar." She stifled another yawn.

"And an arrogant prick," he reminded her, and she smiled as if it was his most endearing quality.

4

VIOLET SIPPED HER COFFEE. She hadn't slept well, but she didn't feel tired. What an evening! Art had insisted on driving her home, but she'd refused. She didn't want him to see David's house. She would have to explain why a waitress lived in Lincoln Park and she didn't want to go there. It was none of his business and she probably wouldn't see him ever again anyway.

If she was honest with herself, she wanted to. He was gorgeous, but that wasn't the main reason. He was also thrilling, mysterious, and probably dangerous. The exact opposite of her luxurious but dull existence with David.

It wouldn't be fair to Art to use him for the fun she was missing in her life. Nothing good could come from that. And her engagement wasn't even officially broken. What was wrong with her? She was fantasizing about the hot arrogant prick while she needed to call the temp agency and look for a new place to live.

A knock on the window startled her out of her reverie. Geez, people were eager today—it was still five minutes before opening.

"Do you have a coffee emergency?" she asked when she opened the door, pretending kindness to mask her annoyance.

"I have a delivery for Sweet Temptations, but I can sure use a coffee," a young courier said and pushed a crate into her arms.

Without the lid, the contents were on display right as she peeked in. Fresh orange gerberas in small vases lined the bottom of the crate. "What is this?"

"Are you blind?" The delivery guy sneered.

"I didn't order these," she said.

"Well, they were ordered to be delivered here every morning for a year," he said. "Are you going to make me the coffee?"

"Sure." She shuffled to the counter. Had Carla decided to have fresh flowers on the tables and forgot to tell her? "How do you want your coffee?"

"Fast. I got to deliver two more things before eight," he growled.

She opened her mouth but decided to ignore his rudeness. Maybe he wasn't sleeping well like her. She poured an Americano into a large paper cup and slid it over to him. "Enjoy!"

He waved his hand and left. Vi picked out one of the small vases and set it on the table. She reached for the next vase and found an envelope with a card.

Sorry to have only drunk one coffee a day. I hope you enjoy a bit of color in your life. Still arrogant, but trying to be less of a prick.

Violet smiled. If only... there was no point in contemplating what it would be like to allow herself some fun. Because clearly Ar-Thor was a man who played and if her body's response to him was any indication, it would be a mind-blowing experience. But she had too much shit going on right now and didn't want another layer of complication.

The way he'd made her feel last night just confirmed that she couldn't trust herself. The only reason she was attracted to him was that he wasn't David. Her mind—or rather her body—was playing tricks and she would not fall for them. She had no future—no job, no apartment—and arguably a crisis of self-confidence after the shitty moves she'd committed. There was no room for a relationship. Not even a casual one.

The door chimed with the day's new customers, and Vi immersed herself in the magic of the café, relaxed for the first time in days. The orange blooms brightened the space and her mood as well. *Well-played, Thor.*

The joy was short-lived as the crowds flew in endlessly around the lunch hour. It was as if all the coffee shops in the city had emergency closings and Sweet Temptations remained the last café on the face of the earth. The front door was propped open as the line stretched to the street.

Sweat trickled down Violet's spine as she tried to serve everyone without screwing up the orders, breaking things or losing customers. She frothed milk for the millionth cappuccino and fought back tears. Desperate and exhausted, she wondered why she ever thought this job was what she needed in her life.

When she'd called the temp agency that morning, they were skeptical about getting someone on such short notice. The threat of running the operation alone on Friday and on the weekend was too real.

"What can I get you?" She faked a smile and a young woman frowned at her.

"I've been waiting for twenty minutes in this stupid line, so maybe you can pack a muffin for my trouble. Here are the keys. I watered the plants this morning, so don't do that for another week." The woman put a set of keys on the counter.

"I'm sorry you had to wait. We're busier than usual today," Vi recited yet again. "I might be overworked right now, but I'm not sure what you're talking about." She looked at the line and stopped short of swearing.

"Apparently, the Da Bonnos decided they don't need me as a house sitter anymore." The woman rolled her lips to the side.

Oh, Carla had organized everything so Vi could move to their place. God bless her, but when on earth would she get her things out? David was returning on Saturday. Or was it on Friday evening? Shit! With no help here, she wouldn't be able to move her things.

"Thank you for the keys, and for waiting. Here is your muffin. On the house." The woman grabbed the brown bag and left promptly.

Vi didn't have time to ponder the house sitter's attitude because a group of hipsters hit her with the most ridiculous and complicated order. Six people who ordered off the menu and all six of them had a minor change to the recipe. Vi glared at the dude who recited the order and considered throwing in her apron and running away. With a sigh, she turned to the espresso machine and took a deep, calming breath to get over her brief lapse in professionalism.

She scooped a portion of coffee, pressed it in and before she attached the portafilter into the brew group, a movement on her right side startled her.

"You can't be here!" she protested as a woman tied her long brown hair into a knot on top of her head while she waltzed behind the counter.

"My name is Lena. I'm Carla's friend." Her eyes darted around as if she was worried about something. "You must be Violet. Carla mentioned you'd be here. It seems you need help. I can't do much, but perhaps I can help at least a bit."

In Vi's experience, someone who knew nothing

about the job would just cause further delays and mishaps, but she was desperate and this oddly startled woman was offering. "There is an apron in the back. Thank you," Vi said.

Somehow, it only took half an hour for Lena to maneuver into Vi's choreography behind the counter and actually start helping rather than hindering. Three hours later, the place had finally cleared enough for the two women to relax.

"I must admit, Lena, for someone who doesn't know what they are doing, you did pretty well. I can't thank you enough." Vi opened the cash register and pulled out enough cash to cover four hours of wages. She handed the money to Lena, who stepped back and stared at the cash as if it was poison. "Come on, you earned it," Vi encouraged.

"Mom, can I have another juice?" A girl, around ten, leaned against the bar.

"Of course, darling." Lena wiped her hands on her apron.

"Oh my God, you had a daughter waiting here for you all this time? I didn't even notice her." Vi looked at Lena and back at the girl.

Lena's cheeks turned red and she bit her bottom lip. She looked utterly uncomfortable.

"What's your name?" Vi asked the girl, who turned to her mother, seeking permission to answer.

"I'm Sarah," she said once Lena nodded.

"Well, Sarah, you're getting juice and cake," Vi

said and smiled when Sarah's eyes widened in excitement. "Sit down and I'll get your mom to serve you your favorite." The girl hopped to her seat and picked up a book lying on the table.

"Thank you," Lena whispered.

"No, no, thank you, Lena. You've literally saved my ass today. Please take your pay and let me treat Sarah," Vi said.

"Thank you." Lena took the money and folded it into her pocket. She walked around the counter. "Sarah loves chocolate cake, like me." She blushed again.

"Two pieces of chocolate cake it is then." Vi smiled and served them the largest slices she could find. "Listen, Lena, I don't want to impose, but if you could help me tomorrow and this weekend, it would mean a lot."

Lena's eyes widened in horror. "Oh, I-I, I'm sorry I can't."

"Oh, of course. No problem." Vi turned to bus the tables.

"Would it be for three days only?" Lena followed her, whispering. "My husband doesn't want me to work, but he's away for the weekend. I could come during the rush hours, but I'd have to bring Sarah."

Vi couldn't hide her excitement. "Are you sure? I don't want to get you in trouble with your husband."

"He wouldn't know, would he?" Lena shrugged.

"Do you mind me asking, why doesn't he want

you working?" Vi didn't want to pry, but Lena was the first woman she'd met who seemed to be in a similar situation to her relationship with David.

"I think it's a tradition in his circles. He wants me to take care of him and the household." Lena stared at the floor, her face red.

"How have you adjusted to that?" Vi asked and Lena clasped her hands in front of her stomach as if shielding herself. "I'm sorry, it's none of my business. It's just that my fiancé, or ex-fiancé, asked the same of me and I couldn't do it. I tried…" Tears pooled in Vi's eyes, surprising her.

"In my case, the alternative… I mean the life before I met my husband was much worse than this," Lena said, her tone almost apologetic.

What life had she had if giving up on a career or her own self-realization was better? But perhaps Lena was busy in her own ways, running charities or getting involved in her community. Was that what David expected from Vi? To find a calling in altruistic endeavors?

"You better eat that cake. Thank you for every-thing today," Vi said and carried a full tray to the counter.

"What time do you want me to come tomorrow?" Lena asked.

"Come around the same time."

At least one problem was temporarily solved. If she packed today, tomorrow morning she could load her things into the car and after she closed the patisserie, she could unload at Carla's and hopefully even return the car to David's garage. She would unpack and start looking for a new place once she found someone more permanent to work at the café.

At the end of the day, and after only one more milder rush hour, Vi started closing the blinds. She was exhausted, but in a good way. It wasn't a post-argument I-need-to-figure-out-my-future fatigue. It was a job-well-done tiredness that shot adrenaline through her veins. She had a few hours of packing in front of her, but somehow she felt like she could rule the world today. By her rough estimates, she probably turned the best daily revenue this year. Carla would be pleased.

The only shadow over today was the absence of Art. There was no reason to expect him to come, but she did.

She pulled the keys from her apron and moved to lock the front door. It opened before she'd crossed the floor, and Thor sauntered in, smiling at her. Her stomach fluttered.

"We are closed," she said, but couldn't help returning his smile.

"Then lock up," he practically ordered.

"I have things to do tonight," she protested but locked it behind him anyway.

"I brought dinner instead of a gun today." He raised his hand, presenting a plastic bag with takeout.

His dimples flashed and her defenses dropped away.

* * *

ART EXHALED in relief when the lock clicked. All day long he'd fought the urge to come over and watch her. He hated that she intrigued him so much. He wasn't sure if her distress—the night of the robbery and her first day here—had awoken some weird protective need in him or if it was simply the thrill of the chase. Regardless of the reasons, he wanted to uncover the values to solve the equation that was Violet.

The timing of this new challenge was dreadful. His last job had caused unexpected trouble and he should be packing up to spend at least a month in the Caribbean. But instead of drinking and fucking his way through a forced vacation, he was dropping all caution and taking unnecessary risks to stay close to her.

"Thank you for the flowers," Vi said, her caramel eyes glittering.

"They complement the stellar service of this establishment." He put the bag of takeout containers on the table, trying to stay as far from her as possible. Her closeness robbed him of logic and he wanted to solve the puzzle of her with his brain in full operational power. That's why Art had come tonight. To eat and talk. Keep things logical. His cock had other ideas.

He was pretty sure that once he understood what her pull was, he could eliminate the threat quickly. Reprogram his mind. And body. The latter could be solved easily with a booty call to one of the ladies he had on his speed dial. The former, however, persisted as a problem and Art loved mysteries.

"Why, thank you. I'm pretty sure a year's worth of fresh flowers covered your previous lack of spending and it was kind of charming. You didn't need to also bring me dinner." She walked behind the counter and disappeared in the back.

Her absence squeezed at his stomach. Was she declining the dinner?

His worry dissipated as soon as she returned with plates.

"Bringing you dinner was purely a selfish endeavor," he said.

"How so?" She did that thing when she frowned and smiled at the same time. It should look comical, but she pulled it off with grace.

"I was sure you wouldn't go out with me."

She smiled and for a moment he didn't want to get to know her and understand her. He wanted to push her against that counter and rip her clothes off.

"That's true. I probably would have turned down your invitation, but the salivating once you mentioned food robbed me of my senses." She smiled again and dropped into the chair across from him.

Art was trying—and probably failing—not to stare at those perfect lips. She was kind and funny today, which messed with his head. He almost missed her usual hostility. It was safer.

She raised her brows. "So what are we having?"

Shit, he almost forgot about the food. He pulled out four containers. "I brought sushi."

"Bold choice," she said. "Many people hate raw fish."

His palms flashed with sweat. "Do you?"

"I happen to love sushi." She peeked into the first box.

"What else?" He unwrapped the chopsticks.

She stood up to reach for a small cup, then poured the soy sauce into it.

"What else do you love?" he repeated. His words came out coarse. He hadn't been nervous in a very long time. Why on earth did he want to have dinner with her? This conversational pressure was stripping him of his cool. Yet he didn't want to be anywhere else right now. Shit! What was going on?

"I'm fairly easy to please when it comes to food. The only thing I stay away from is Indian." She somehow managed to chew and talk and still look graceful.

"Good, so our next few dinners would be easy," he said.

"Are we having more dinners?" She held a maki mid-air, wiggling the chopsticks between them.

"Undoubtedly." He turned his attention to the food to give himself a break. It had been years since he'd last wanted a woman—hell, anyone!—to like him this badly.

She chuckled. "You're very confident."

"Arrogant prick, remember." He grinned.

"Oh, right, with the flowers and this dinner I almost forgot about that. You're doing a pretty shitty job of upholding your reputation, Art."

"I wouldn't worry about that." He stopped eating, preferring to look at her.

She raised her eyebrows in question.

"I'm sure to fuck up soon." Why did he say that?

"I'll be ready." She laughed. "Why do you think you'll fuck up?"

"I-I…" He wanted to get to know her, not the other way around. "I don't do this kind of thing." His mouth was dry now.

"What kind of thing? Holding women hostage at gunpoint and then bringing them dinner?"

He chuckled. "I got myself into a bit of a trouble last night."

"Are you bringing the trouble to my door again?"

Am I? The air between them was charged, or was it just him feeling it?

"No," he said.

He hoped so at least. It had been a mistake to lead

the thugs in this direction last night. He hadn't even started in this neighborhood but somehow found himself here. As if… as if here was the safest place in the world.

Her eyes held his and the moment fell perfectly still. Everything around them ceased to exist. She moved her hand toward his and gave him a squeeze, but then, as if he burned her, she retreated fast and looked away.

"So where is Luca right now?" She sounded hoarse, as if her throat was as dry as his. She kept her focus on the food and he was quite sure it was a deliberate move.

"Outside."

"Are you in danger, Art?"

Only from you. And perhaps a group of criminals. "No, I'm not," he lied.

"Why do you have a bodyguard?" She lifted her eyes to his, studying him intently.

"I've had some threats in the past."

She narrowed her eyes and opened her mouth, but then changed her mind and said nothing. Her attention returned to her sushi.

"Where did you work before here?" he asked, hurrying to change the subject.

"I used to have my own café." A shadow passed over her face. "I'm here helping out Carla, the owner, while she travels."

"What happened with your café?" He could sense

the topic was a challenging territory for her, but perhaps this would lead him to the cause of her crying. He hung on to the need for that information. It would set him free. He could fix the problem for her and finally mind his own business without her dominating his mind.

"I sold the business. An unfortunate decision." She swirled her chopsticks in the cup with the soy sauce, avoiding his eyes.

"Is that why you were crying the other day?" he asked.

"Geez, you won't let it go, will you? I'm fine. You don't need to force the whole knight-in-shining-armor act on me. Why would you even expect me to tell you anything personal when you're avoiding my questions? What did you mean when you said you don't do this kind of thing?" She tapped her foot and any moment now she would cross her arms over her chest.

"There's a precise speed where jogging becomes running. At six miles per hour. Any faster and it's technically running."

She narrowed her eyes and cocked her head. "Are you okay?"

"I don't date." The words barely made it past his throat. He took a sip of water, but the liquid had lost its hydrating properties. His throat scratched like sandpaper.

"Is this a date?" She smirked and there went the arm-cross over those amazing tits.

"Well, at least I delivered on the promise to fuck things up."

* * *

VIOLET ALMOST FELT sorry for him. No doubt he was an arrogant prick, but there was something about him. And it wasn't just the looks. It was almost like he wanted to pursue her, but at the same time was trying to push her away.

He showed her only a tiny part of himself while demanding that she deliver intimate details of her life on a platter. He was annoying, infuriating, and yet there was a certain vulnerability to him. Maybe it was the geeky part, like he was trying to figure out the world around him and not truly understanding it.

"Art, I'm at the place in my life when I need to find myself. I spent the last three years making choices that seemed very right at the time, but I lost my own identity in the process. I have so much to figure out right now and I don't really have room for another person," she said, hoping he would accept it and go.

Though a small—okay, not so small—part of her hoped he would stay. No! She couldn't allow another complication into her life.

He nodded and watched her, obviously not liking what he was hearing, but perhaps fighting a retort. His jaw tightened and she almost reached out to soothe it with her fingers. The stubble would prickle her, probably. She wanted to find out.

With every passing moment, her resolution weakened. If only she were strong enough for a casual fling.

She'd always entertained the idea of a one-night stand, but somehow every previous attempt had turned into a relationship. Starting with David like that had led to an engagement and her own identity crisis. Unfortunately, she wasn't a casual sex kind of girl.

The silence grew uncomfortable, charged with a sexual energy that filled the air and every cell in her body.

"Do *you* believe in soul mates?" Art asked.

"I don't know." She hesitated. "I didn't, but I'm considering it. You know there could be someone who is perfect for you on paper, but it's not enough, so I guess the connection must be one that defies all the odds and expectations. I recently became a believer in that. Though it's hard to put it in words. Words are too logical and I don't think love is."

"I like logic," he whispered.

"Don't we all?" She sighed and started cleaning the table. Art grabbed her wrist and their eyes met again. The ice blue of his eyes melted her insides, sending a direct message to her center.

"Give me one date." He stood up and stepped forward, closing the distance between them. She stared at his chest, unable to raise her eyes. His immediate proximity had all sorts of physical consequences —she couldn't breathe, her heart thumped around like a wild animal, her core tingled, goosebumps blanketed her skin and her mouth became too dry.

Thor was a health threat.

He traced his finger down her cheek and she closed her eyes, trying to block the onslaught of feelings and physical reactions. He lifted her chin and exhaled heavily, as if the weight of the world burdened him. "Look at me, Vi."

She did and those eyes penetrated to her heart. She stepped back, but he was still too close. There was no escaping Thor.

"One date. I'm thirty-six years old and it'll be my first." His eyes pleaded, but also shined with mischief.

She had to save herself.

"No."

5

His expression sliced her heart, compelling her to continue. "Not now. Why don't we wait a month and if you still feel the same about this, I'll give you one date."

"One calendar month or four weeks exactly?"

The curious way his brain worked fascinated her. "Well, today is April twelfth, so let's say May twelfth." His need for preciseness somehow increased his hotness factor. A geek in a chiseled god's body.

He frowned. "What if you change your mind by then?"

"Art, take it or leave it. I'll be in a better place in four weeks, I hope. If I went on a date with you now, it would be a lie," she said.

It would be a betrayal for all parties involved. Art, David, and most importantly herself. A part of her hoped Art would forget about her in four weeks.

"I don't like this," he argued.

Violet shrugged and smiled at him. "You don't think I'm worth the wait?"

He huffed. "You're worth waiting, but that doesn't mean I want to."

"One month or never." She shrugged and took a tiny bit of enjoyment from the torture she was inflicting. Too bad she was also a victim of her own decision. "And now I have to really go because I have things to do and an early morning tomorrow."

* * *

"THANK GOD YOU'RE HERE," Vi greeted Lena. "Look at the mess. The first rush cleared already and I need to tackle the dishes before the second wave arrives."

"On it, boss," Lena said. "I'm sorry I couldn't come sooner. I was dropping Sarah at her friend's. That way I could stay as long as you need."

"Now that just got you two slices of the chocolate cake."

Vi turned to the dishwasher and Lena promptly grabbed an apron and started to clean the tables.

Vi had packed all her things last night. At least she hoped she'd gotten everything. The realization of how little she owned had hit her hard. She'd merged her life with David's and somewhere along the line she'd accepted everything that his lifestyle provided. Now, three years later, she couldn't imagine keeping any of the things he'd given her.

The money from the sale of her business would carry her over for a while, but her current possessions were pathetic. Luxury was surprisingly easy to become accustomed to, and now she felt strangely exposed and vulnerable. She wasn't attached to the items David had bought her, but the packing solidified the mistake she'd made. As she'd loaded two suitcases and one box into David's car last night, an over-whelming fear had enveloped her.

She couldn't—and was pretty sure didn't want to —revisit her life before David or with David. But that left her with life after David and absolutely no idea what that should look like.

Despite being swamped, she found a new appreci-ation for Carla's offer to help. It was like a gift of interim existence so she could explore her future options. Exhausted, she'd fallen into David's bed for the last time and ended up tossing and turning all night. When she had finally fallen asleep at dawn, she'd dreamed darkly arousing, confusing dreams with one hot protagonist: Thor.

"Lena, do you think I can leave you here for about two hours by yourself?" Vi asked and Lena's eyes widened in horror. "No worries, not yet, but around five in the afternoon it's usually quiet here and I'll be back as soon as I can." She wanted to move her things to Carla's and return the car and she didn't want to risk running into David.

"Okay." Lena bit her lip.

"You're doing a great job. I wouldn't even consider leaving if I didn't know the place would be in excellent hands."

Lena smiled timidly. This woman either had serious secrets or an extreme case of shyness and lack of confidence, but she was kind and really helpful. And it wasn't Violet's place to pry.

The bell above the door chimed and Vi forgot all about Lena's demeanor.

"Ladies." Art nodded with a smile, rewarding them with a blinding sight of his dimples. "Can I have an espresso?"

"What are you doing here?" She really didn't need this distraction.

"Having a coffee." He wiggled his eyebrows.

"We agreed—"

"To postpone our date." He winked and a jolt of irritation ran down Vi's spine.

"The idea was to keep our distance to see how we feel. You showing up here is not part of the deal." She dumped the puck, banging the portafilter harder than needed.

"You should have laid out the rules clearer. Or in binary code."

Vi almost threw the used coffee bucket on him.

She made his espresso, giving the machine the aggressive treatment intended for Thor.

"Here is your coffee. Enjoy!" She glared.

"Thank you." He turned to sit and stopped because his usual seat was taken. His shoulders tensed under his black T-shirt and Vi grinned, satisfied with a minor victory. And enjoying the view of his hulking back a bit too much for her liking.

Art recovered and sauntered to another table.

Vi tried to busy herself with a few things behind the counter and then showed Lena how to work the espresso machine, all the while feeling the burn of Art's gaze on her. To take time off later, she needed to let Lena mind the counter alone for a bit, so she grabbed the ledger from the back and walked over to the table Carla normally used for admin work. She focused on avoiding Art, but she could sense his stare.

Shortly after she'd sat, he stood up and ordered several pastries and a tea. Vi jumped up and stomped over to his table. "What do you think you're doing?"

"It was pointed out to me I shouldn't nurse one coffee if I'm staying for hours." He winked. The bastard *winked* at her and returned to his seat.

"If you think this is going to get you that date, you're stupid!" Vi stood by his chair, tapping her foot.

"No one has ever called me stupid. Let's stay with the arrogant prick." He smiled, bright and shiny, including the damn dimples. It was unfair how hot the man was.

"How fitting! The date is off. Don't bother asking in one month," she hissed and went back to the paperwork. She shuffled everything around, so she could sit with her back to him. *That should suit you well, asshole!*

6

Art stared from the passenger seat, the streets blending into a mixture of colors and sounds. In retrospect, it hadn't been a good idea to show up at the patisserie. Violet didn't appreciate his presence even though he'd ordered more than one coffee. The woman was confusing.

It was his job to find vulnerabilities and fix them or occasionally exploit them. But he couldn't fix her because he couldn't figure her out. She wouldn't let him.

Why had she cried? Why did she regret selling her business? Why did he even care? If only she went on a date with him, he'd be able to move on. One month! He couldn't wait one month.

"We have company," Luca said, glimpsing in the rearview mirror.

"Shit!" Art didn't bother to turn and check. Luca

was too experienced to misread the signs. "Can you lose them?"

Luca didn't answer. He continued driving and checking all the mirrors. Art clicked on a traffic map on his phone to help navigate.

As they approached an intersection, Luca slowed the car, signaling left as if he was trying to park the car along the sidewalk. The green light switched to yellow, and just before it changed to red, Luca slammed on the gas and bolted through the intersection.

The trick didn't work though. The driver of the pursuing car must have realized he was made and didn't worry about remaining unseen anymore. The car rammed into the intersection, narrowly avoiding the traffic coming from both sides, but making it through.

"Fuck!" Luca jerked the steering wheel to the right.

"No!" Art howled, but it was too late. They entered a dead-end street, falling into a trap.

"No?" Luca deadpanned. "Something you should have told me before I turned," he added dryly.

The large black SUV closed the distance between them quickly, stopping diagonally to block their only escape route.

Luca turned their car to a similar position. "Stay down."

"Man, there's no point. It's only you. I don't want to have you killed," Art protested.

"Let me do my job," Luca snapped and checked his handgun. He opened the glove compartment and handed another one to Art.

Two men got out of the large SUV.

"Let's hope it's only two of them. I'll hold them off. You get out of the car, stay low and try to reach the building over there…" He pointed to a brick low-rise to their left. "…and pray the door is open. I'll cover you." Without further conversation, Luca reached across Art and pushed the passenger door open. Art jumped out. Luca scooted over to use the same door.

Art should have listened, but he turned toward their attackers. He ducked a bit, so only his head was visible from behind the car. "What do you want?"

Luca swore, but didn't look at him, keeping his eyes on the potential targets.

"To have a word, *Viking*," the taller man said, tucking his gun back into the holster under his jacket.

"Speak then," Art said, feeling like a coward standing behind the car, but then he valued his life and didn't trust the air the thug was breathing.

"The transaction that you facilitated recently. We're interested in buying the data, but let's talk somewhere private," the man said.

Interesting. They were after the data that was not

his to sell. "You have the wrong guy, gentlemen," Art said and stood up taller.

The man moved his arms up, not exactly surrendering, but suggesting he would not draw his gun. Not yet. Luca stepped back to maintain the right angle of vision between the man and his driver. The man approached, now standing by Art's car, and cleared his throat.

"My name is Phil Taworski. I work for Tony Da Bonno." He paused to let the consequences of his connection to the feared mob boss sink in. "There are very few people who can efficiently hack the security of Miller Holding. Many would argue you're the only one. I'm pretty sure I have the right guy. And let me also reassure you that Mr. Da Bonno gets what he wants, but the next time we meet won't be this pleasant."

"As much as we appreciate a good threat, you've got the wrong guy because he doesn't have the data," Luca answered.

Art had known he shouldn't have taken the job. How did this man know who he was? And how come he didn't know Art usually mined data for others? Why would he assume they were for sale?

"Who has the data then?" Phil asked.

"Now, Mr. Taworski, it would be the death of me if I didn't protect the identity of my clients." Art smirked. He caught a glimpse of Luca who rolled his eyes. Getting arrogant under the circumstances was… well… arrogant.

"It would be the death of you regardless, if you don't talk." Phil smiled, subjecting them to the unsavory sight of his rotten teeth.

"Mr. Taworski, you see, I don't know the identity of my client. In my business, we use several layers of protection," Art said. How did Taworski find him?

They all turned at an unexpected, but welcome, sound. Followed by a bell, the yard behind filled up with children of different ages. A school.

Taworski nodded his head to his driver who lowered his gun. Luca did the same, but by his stance it was obvious he was ready to use it very fast if needed. Shit! Having all the kids behind them sent shivers down Art's spine.

Taworski stared at the yard for a moment, annoyed by the interruption, and then cleaned something off his lapel. "You have twenty-four hours to get us either the data or the name of your client, *Mr. Viking*. Or it *will be* the death of you." He turned and walked to his car, his driver following.

Only once their car disappeared into the traffic of the main road did Luca tuck his gun away and the two of them got back into the car.

"Maybe you should have told him you did the job for Uncle Sam." Luca snorted.

"I don't have a death wish," Art said. He pinched the bridge of his nose, but this time it didn't help him focus. He'd understood the risk involved when he'd taken the job, but the possibility of danger was half the fun. He didn't expect this level of interest though. Not outside of the virtual world.

"Can I book the flight now?" Luca asked as he reversed and turned the car.

Art didn't want to leave. He wanted to annoy Violet into agreeing to have a date with him. It was stupid and selfish. Completely driven by his ego. Or by her beauty because the woman was a vision. An angel. In black clothes.

That was another mystery. Why did she always wear black? Was it just for work? He wondered what she'd wear for their date. Red would look good on her, he imagined. Hopefully nothing too tight or revealing because he would end up staring at her tits. He wanted to see them. Badly.

Shit! What was wrong with him?

"Art, you either go into witness protection or you disappear for a while. The longer the better," Luca insisted.

"Witness protection? Are you out of your mind?" Yes, it was on the table. A generous offer from the Bureau. One he never planned to use. The agents had come to him because he was the only one who could do the job. And he took it. Not because of some misplaced patriotic sense of duty. He took it because it was a challenge and it helped erase some of his previous transgressions.

But that didn't mean he was going to give up his life.

Violet asked for one month. Maybe Da Bonno and his butler Taworski had just given it to her.

"Book the flight," he growled.

＊ ＊ ＊

THE DISASTROUS SITUATION at work had its downsides, but there was a distinct benefit. Vi had an excuse not to think about her future. Wasn't that the ultimate recommendation? To live in the moment? But there was no way she'd find a solution to all her problems through avoidance.

Carla's tea kettle clicked off and Vi grabbed it off the kitchen counter. Steam filled the space around her as she poured boiling water into her cup. It caressed her forearms with damp heat. Lately, she was always cold. Cold and lonely despite the warmth and comfort of Carla and Charlie's home.

It had been a good day at work. Lena had proved a godsend. The staffing agency would send someone on Monday. And not just anyone, but a woman who had temped at Sweet Temptations on several occasions before. After a few days, things at the patisserie were starting to look up.

And that meant no more excuses.

Vi's life desperately needed attention, which sent cold shivers down her spine. *When you lose everything and it's arguably your own fault...* That line of thinking wasn't helpful, but the idea of recovery seemed insurmountable at this point.

Perhaps she could just let one more day slip by without thinking, without maneuvering. Her future had been on her mind constantly, lingering there like a reminder of all her failings, rather than an active problem to be solved. One day wouldn't make a difference. She needed to rest because when life got tough, sleep seemed to be the most valuable commodity.

Vi shuffled into the living room and sat down with her tea, then turned on the TV for background noise. She used to love silence, but that was before Rebecca. Since Becca had been gone though, Vi needed the sound to distract her from her grief. And slowly it had become a habit. Silence would invade the corner of her soul that needed to stay in obscurity. The darkness could easily consume her and she fought it with noise. Only then could she smile at the world and enjoy its light.

She sipped her tea. It was so nice to have her feet up. Carla and Charlie lived in a beautiful penthouse that was large and bright. A little too cluttered with knickknacks for Vi's taste, but nevertheless a comfortable home. The living room and kitchen were an open concept with a wall of windows that led to the terrace. It was all cream and beige with various accent colors.

So different from the dark mahogany of David's house.

When her phone rang, she considered not answering, but that wouldn't get her anywhere.

With a sigh, she picked up. "Hi, David." He'd probably returned home and realized her things were gone.

Sounding tired, he said, "Hey, sweetheart, how are you?"

What? She didn't expect a casual chat.

"I'm fine. What do you want, David?" A pang of guilt hit her, hearing her own bitter response.

"Pardon?" he sounded genuinely affronted. "I'm calling my fiancée because I was in an accident."

Shit! "What happened? Are you okay?"

"I appreciate the concern," he said dryly. "I'm fine, but the doctors want me to stay for observation, so I missed the flight. I should be out of here hopefully by Monday."

"Oh God, David. You're still in London?" she asked stupidly. All alone in a hospital. "Do you want me to come?" It was the last thing she wanted to do, but duty and a sense of responsibility called louder. She couldn't abandon him now.

"No, don't be silly. No point in you flying overseas only to fly back. They're only being thorough."

"Let me know if you need anything," Vi offered like a fool, as if she could do anything from this side of the pond.

"I'll call you with an update tomorrow, but no need to worry," he said.

Silence settled for a moment. She didn't know what to say. David was wounded. Or maybe he wasn't, but he called her because she was his person. And with him in the hospital, she couldn't hijack this call and argue she wasn't his fiancée anymore. Weariness engulfed her, as uncomfortable as a blanket made of cacti.

"Well then, sweetheart, good night," he said finally, sounding distant. Or hurt, she wasn't sure.

She hung up, but the aftertaste of the conversation was heavy. God, she hadn't even asked about the accident. Hearing his voice switched her to autopilot with a single goal—to get off the phone.

She'd broken up with him but was still causing this honest man so much pain due to her much too delayed epiphany about their relationship. Maybe he was right. Maybe she was getting cold feet and simply needed to adjust to the idea of becoming Mrs. David Waller and the lifestyle and responsibilities that came with such an honor. And not everything was bad.

She was so confused. And so alone. Ever since Rebecca, she'd been so painfully alone.

Vi dragged herself from the sofa into the guest bedroom. She hauled her suitcase onto the bed and started unpacking her clothes. The sea of black. Becca used to tease her endlessly about her wardrobe. *Why do you wear funeral clothes all the time? Save them for during your period if you need to hide.* The woman was full of life and color. Until she wasn't. The last days in the hospital, she'd been reduced to gray and white. No more color. And ultimately no more life.

Violet sighed and threw her shirts and jeans into the chest of drawers. The guest bedroom featured only a few pieces of furniture, but it had all she needed. A space for her clothes and a bed.

She was about to close the suitcase, but something wiggled inside the zipper compartment. She opened it and found an envelope with a college stamp. She didn't need to look inside. She'd buried her academic aspirations along with Rebecca.

It'd been easy to take classes while they ran their café together, but after Rebecca passed, Vi couldn't abandon the business and continue her education. Keeping the café open in Rebecca's memory took precedence over the scholarship Vi had been awarded. It would have been easier to close the business. Let it go with Becca, but Vi couldn't make that move. It felt like a betrayal. And so she'd soldiered on.

Vi rummaged through the box of her possessions and pulled out a frame. She sagged to the floor and leaned against the bed. Laughing like lunatics—their usual state back then—Becca and Vi had posed for the camera the day they'd opened the café. Becca had inherited it from her great aunt and Vi was more than happy to join in and make the place their own. It was either that or stay dependent on her parents, who never failed to remind her she was a disappointment.

"Oh, Becca, I made such a mess of things," Vi said. She tilted her head back and rested it on the edge of the bed, fighting tears.

Looking back at her life, Vi realized she had made all her decisions for someone else. She started the business with Rebecca because Becca needed help. She kept the business in Becca's honor. Maybe she'd never wanted it, but immersing herself in work had helped her during those first long months when she was left alone.

She'd abandoned the scholarship. And then she'd abandoned the business for David. She'd sacrificed her dreams to please others.

She didn't even know what her dreams were anymore. A single tear rolled down her cheek.

One lonely tear.

Invisible. Sad. Lost.

Vi wiped it away briskly. She'd learned one unfortunate thing this week: running a café didn't bring her joy. Not anymore. Had it ever? Was she one of those people who went with the flow without ever questioning if the choice was theirs?

Her choices led her to this point in her life— homeless, practically unemployed and alone. Pleasing others with her life decisions brought her here.

She reached for the envelope and read the acceptance letter. A scholarship to study as an art history major. A tear dropped on the paper.

Art history? She'd minored in business because she'd always wanted to run a gallery, discover artists and help them speak to people through their work.

Wow! That dream had been buried deep. A flutter of something—excitement or anxiety?—tickled her insides.

Was that still her dream?

God, but she was too old to go to school.

THE HOLLOW FEELING of emptiness persisted. Violet pretended it wasn't there, but that didn't magically heal it.

David got stuck in London for two weeks. The doctors had discovered he'd cracked several ribs and refused to clear him for flying. It was probably a precaution, but he'd stayed nonetheless.

When he was finally released, he was in no hurry to return to Chicago and their relationship hung in limbo. Each time she tried to bring it up on a call, he refused to discuss ending their engagement, and Vi suspected he was staying in London to avoid the whole situation.

The woman from the temp agency had been covering Erica's shifts, which allowed Violet to spend time looking for an apartment, but two weeks had produced no positive results in that area. It was impossible to rent a place without proof of income, which in her case was tricky. Yes, Carla was paying her, but it wasn't like she could show that she had a regular income. She needed to ask Carla for an offer letter or payslip to at least get her foot in the door of some shitty building. But Carla was cruising the Mediterranean and Vi didn't want to bother her with that conversation.

She tried to surf through the days, pretending things were manageable, but it was becoming clear she'd hit rock bottom and springing up required more time. More effort. More will.

She was sitting at Carla's table pretending to do paperwork when the bell above the door chirped. Her head snapped up before her ears recognized the sound. For days now, she'd been looking up every time the damn door opened.

She didn't want to admit it, but part of her was hoping Thor would show up. He hadn't since the day she'd told him there wouldn't be a date. It was for the best, anyway. So why was she hoping? Waiting?

A mess of blond hair doubled her heartbeat, but disappointment settled as soon as she saw the face. She was ridiculous. On all fronts of her life. A poster child for a pathetic woman.

"… oh, you need to talk to the manager," the temp waitress, covering the register, said and pointed at Violet.

The young man with blond hair who was not Thor turned and their eyes met. For a moment, he was looking at her through his glasses as if summoning the courage to approach her. He fidgeted with a large portfolio he carried.

Violet smiled to encourage him. He didn't look like a delivery person or a potential vendor. Sales reps approached her regularly, trying to sell her a different brand of coffee or introduce wine into their menu and many other things that according to them would bring the business to the next level. Most of them were selling an equivalent of tap water, but she was always kind to them. If this guy was a sales rep, she worried about his commission.

He inhaled and smiled, his dimples inducing cold sweat on her spine. *Damn it!* He wasn't Thor by any stretch of the imagination, but the dimples nibbled on the emptiness inside her in a way she didn't want to admit.

"Hello, my name is Chrysal. I'm an artist, a painter. Do you have a moment?" He looked around as if he was sharing a secret with her.

An artist? "I'm not sure how I could help you, but please sit down."

He slid into the seat across from her, his Adam's apple bobbing up and down. He leaned his portfolio against his chair carefully and started speaking while staring at the table. "I was hoping you'd be interested in displaying my art here. I came yesterday and I've noticed that the back wall there, he pointed behind himself, "has space for at least five of my paintings."

"You want to sell your art here?" she asked, peeking over his shoulder to look at the wall. It was empty. Positioned to the right of the door, it was kind of forgotten. Most of the interior was to the left of the entrance, where everyone turned their attention when entering the building.

"I'd like that. You see, when you enter you don't even look that way, but when you're leaving, you see the empty wall. I thought you might benefit from a bit of decorating," he said and wiped his forehead. His glasses were getting foggy.

Vi studied him for a moment and then looked at the wall again. "And your pieces are for decorating?"

"Oh, God, I hope not, but I need money so I can rent a studio. I've got these ideas for large canvases and…" He widened his eyes, probably realizing his creativity was taking over his marketing efforts.

Vi smiled inwardly. It wasn't her place to decorate Carla's patisserie, but the idea of selling the art for this young man stirred something inside her. "Show me what you've got."

He stared at her for a moment as if unsure he'd heard correctly and then pulled up his portfolio. It was too big for the table and in his effort to open it before her he sent some of her paperwork flying to the floor. He jumped up with an apology and his port-folio fell off the table as well.

"Fuck," he muttered and then widened his eyes again. "I'm sorry," he blurted.

Vi wasn't sure if he was apologizing for the mess or for cussing. Regardless, she had to stifle a laugh.

They both squatted down, trying to pick up everything, and their heads collided.

"Ouch," Vi yelped, the impact sitting her down on the floor. When she met Chrysal's mortified expression, she burst out laughing. It felt good and so genuine that even Chrysal joined her with a nervous chuckle. The last time she'd laughed was with Thor.

Hearing the door chime as it opened, she looked up and her gaze locked with David's mother.

Vi's laughter died abruptly.

7

CHRYSAL FROWNED at Vi in concern as all the color leeched from his face. Poor man. It must have cost him so much to approach her.

"Listen, Chrysal," she said, "I have to take care of something. Just wait a moment and I'll be right back."

She struggled to her feet and made a futile attempt to fix her appearance, smoothing her hair and her apron. *Oh, for fuck's sake!* There was no pleasing David's mother, anyway.

"Hello, Margot. What brings you here?" Vi asked, her lips still threatening to curl up from the previous laughter. Especially now when it was clearly causing Margot heartburn.

"You. But if I knew what I would find here, I would have called," Margot said and raised her drawn-on eyebrows. She pulled her purse closer to her body, either expecting someone to rob her or to contract a disease if she touched anything. "We need to talk, Violet."

Margot stepped to the side and looked down at a table. She pulled a white handkerchief from her bag and spread it over the chair before she descended on the fabric.

Violet stared, stunned. The handkerchief deed replaced the initial shock of seeing David's mother, but it was nowhere near the mortification at the idea of having a conversation with Margot. Now. Here.

Vi sat tentatively, connecting with the edge of the chair only, ready to run.

"David has been tied up in London for way too long and the wedding plans have stalled. I don't understand why you feel the need to spend your days here…" She leaned sideways to look at the spot where Vi and Chrysal had sat on the floor. "But you need to catch up on the wedding preparations. I know you didn't want a planner, but I have to insist on hiring one now." Margot pulled out a card. "She is the best. She comes highly recommended. We should be grateful she's willing to squeeze us in on such short notice," Margot said, tapping her long French-mani-cured nails on the golden card.

The air vanished around Vi as she swallowed hard. David's mother had no idea the wedding was canceled. Of course she didn't. David wasn't willing to accept the break-up, so why would his mother know? And Vi had to explain now. Why? She feared the woman under the best of circumstances. *Damn you, David!*

"Margot, the thing is…" she started and swallowed again, her mouth dry as a desert. "David and I are calling the wedding off." *Phew.*

Margot's drawn-on eyebrows shot up even higher than before, surprising Vi with the elasticity of her Botoxed skin. The woman pursed her lips, lifted her chin and studied Violet as if she was a pesky insect. She didn't speak, just stared, and Vi withered under her scrutiny like a plant without water.

The silence stretched for eternity, increasing Vi's dehydration. She put her hands under her butt and then she crossed them over her chest. She dropped them to her side and made fists and then she repeated the senseless actions. The thumping in her temples blocked out the murmur of the patisserie.

And Margot remained silent. *Damn you, David!* But then, Vi deserved this. She'd broken the engagement after all and this was her punishment.

"I'm sorry." The deafening silence finally broke Vi. "I thought David mentioned some—"

"No, he didn't, which proves that you're being delusional. We can't cancel the wedding. Our reputation is at stake here. Whatever is happening between you two needs to be fixed. Immediately." Margot stood up. "I should have known something was wrong with *you* when he kept his membership at that dreadful gentlemen's club."

Violet jumped up, her chair rocking back on two legs before it dropped with a loud thud. Now was her time to raise her eyebrows. "A gentlemen's club?"

"Never mind. It doesn't matter. I'll talk to David today and the two of you fix this. I'll not go through a public humiliation over this. Certainly not after I've defended David's choice of a bride in front of everyone." She looked at Violet with such disgust that Vi stepped back.

She opened her mouth to respond, but before she could speak Margot left.

Vi stared at the door, her senses numb. David had a membership at a gentlemen's club? What club? The way Margot had uttered the words made her believe sex was a part of that membership.

Oddly, the news had a liberating effect on Violet. *Screw you, David!*

"Perhaps I'll come by tomorrow," Chrysal said softly behind her and Vi jumped, startled.

"No, that's okay. I'm in the mood for some beauty. Show me what you've got."

It was a somehow peaceful mayhem of shapes and colors. When Vi looked long enough, she could see layers under the initial abstract depiction—animals and plants. Nature. Hidden behind geometry and color explosion. There was a story there on Chrysal's canvases. She wasn't sure yet she could read it, but the intrigue was part of the genius.

The door chimed and Lena entered with Sarah in tow. She narrowed her eyes when she noticed Vi standing and staring at the back wall. She looked that way as she closed the door and smiled.

"Hello," Lena whispered, as if making sure she wasn't interrupting. She came to stand next to Vi. "These are wonderful."

"I think so. A young artist installed them this morning. I've already sold one," Vi said. She was really pleased about that. Not only because Chrysal needed money, but also because after the longest time she'd felt accomplished again.

The door opened once more and they had to step aside to allow the customers in. From the new angle, on the side of the counter, the paintings came to life differently.

"There is pain and hope in these, but they bring joy. How refreshing. You know, so many artists depict their own suffering on the canvas. Or hide it there. I'd dare them to relate joy without being clichéd. And this artist is obviously capable of that," Lena said and cocked her head as if uncovering another layer of the picture. "What a wonderful idea to lend this wall to the art. I'll be happy to look at these when I'm here. So much better for your patrons than staring into their screens. People have lost the ability to look, to really see. We only scan and scroll nowadays."

Vi turned to her, not even ashamed of gaping. This was the longest the woman had spoken. "You are an art connoisseur?"

Lena tilted her head backward and laughed. Another first. "I wouldn't go that far. I love admiring it. Art supplements for me the beauty I don't always see in the world. Like a reminder. It also reminds me of the suffering and as much as I hate to admit, it makes me feel better just… knowing I'm not alone." She shrugged, but a tiny smile remained on her face as she admired Chrysal's paintings.

They stood there for a moment in silence. Whatever this woman's life was like, she was able to find solace where others would give up. Vi admired the quiet confidence Lena exuded. And understood too. For a long time, art used to be her safe harbor.

"I enjoy going to galleries. It's the best form of relaxation," Lena said.

"I used to also." The memory lingered bittersweet on Vi's tongue.

"Why did you stop?" Lena stepped closer to one of the paintings.

Because I used to go there with my best friend. We'd escape from home—each of us running away from a different level of dysfunctional—to relax and dream in the vast spaces filled with emotions rendered into valuable pieces of art. I couldn't do it without Becca. Galleries are too silent.

"I don't know. I guess I've gotten too busy," Vi said instead.

Vi's phone vibrated in her apron. She looked at the display and sighed.

"Hello, Mother," she answered and stared at Chrysal's colors, hoping his art would help her like it used to when she was still a teenager.

"Why is it that the first time Margot Waller finally acknowledges my existence, it's over the phone to reprimand me for my lack of parenting skills?" Vi's mother spat.

No hello. No how are you. No concern over Vi's feelings since she'd obviously heard the wedding was off.

"Could you explain yourself, Violet? You called off the wedding? First time in your life you were doing something that made sense and you decided it wasn't good enough for you?"

Vi rushed to the back room, her mother's voice too loud for a private conversation, turning a few heads in the vicinity. Tension, inexplicably heavy, compressed her chest and Vi tuned out the words, focusing on her breathing.

In. Out.

In. Out.

"Violet?" her mother shrieked.

Apparently, the monologue was over and it was Vi's turn to speak. She forced the words past through the lump in her throat. "I'm sorry you and Margot are disappointed, but there will be no wedding. I don't love David. And more importantly, I don't love who I am when I'm with him." Nausea clenched at her insides.

"Get over yourself, Violet. Do you think you could do better? I was so proud of you for landing David. Whatever doubts you have, they can't be real. Let's have lunch and discuss this." Her mother must be desperate—this was the first time she wanted to have lunch with her daughter.

"Mother, I'm not marrying David. No amount of threats or pleading will ever change that. Goodbye," Vi said with all the calm she could summon and hung up.

She barely made it to the corner before the contents of her stomach splashed all over the old industrial sink.

The condescending voice rang in her head, finding a comfortable crevice to haunt her from. *Do you think you could do better? I was so proud of you.*

Vi rinsed her mouth and washed her face. The cacophony of coffee brewing, register ringing, milk steaming and hushed conversations out front convinced her to leave the dimness of the cold storage room. She trudged over to the counter and put her mind into the automatic motions of familiar work.

With her head down, she didn't notice Lena standing on the other side of the bar until she felt a warm palm squeezing her hand. She looked up and stupid tears threatened to break free. Vi blinked a few times.

"Perhaps you should start visiting galleries again," Lena whispered and somehow her words made everything slightly better. And worse at the same time.

"Lena, I don't want to overstep here, but I got a feeling your life is not... ideal, but somehow you make it work," Vi said, feeling that Chrysal's art had forged an unspoken bond between the two women.

"You're not wrong. I make it work because of Sarah." Her words soft, Lena blushed and looked at her daughter.

"How?" It wasn't loneliness, Vi realized. She was being crushed under the enormous weight of being lost. Utterly lost in the world. "How do you do it?"

Lena looked at her through her lashes and smiled. "One day at a time."

8

The sunset on this side of the island was ridiculously beautiful. If he took a picture of it, no one would ever believe it wasn't photoshopped.

Art had stared at it every evening for almost a month, but he didn't see it. Any time his sight and mind weren't on his computer screen, they were on Violet. He hadn't seen her in four long weeks.

Well, that wasn't exactly true since he'd hijacked the CCTV system on the patisserie's street and watched her arriving and leaving.

An annoyingly persistent voice in his head kept telling him she would be less than pleased if she'd known. His thoughts routinely competed in a race, stampede, regatta and free fall, so ignoring that voice was easy.

The first week he'd been in his villa in the Dominican Republic, he'd talked himself out of following her further, but it hadn't lasted. He was the best in his field and since he'd hacked her phone after that first evening they'd spent at the café, it was the easiest thing to find her at home.

Though he doubted it was her home. Somehow, it didn't fit her. She moved around with a certain care or hesitation like she was only visiting. Perhaps she was house sitting. Just as she was taking care of her friend's business. Back-ups were important in his work and it seemed Violet was a back-up for her friend. Not for him. Definitely not a back-up. She was the primary source of air.

The apartment she lived in had state-of-the-art surveillance. What a joke. It took him two minutes to access the cameras. He wished they had them positioned better, so he could see her more clearly, but then, if he was consulting them on their security, he would place them exactly the same. After all, you didn't install security for voyeurism. That was exactly what he was doing.

He wished they had audio, but he'd settled happily for a visual. She seemed okay. She'd cried only a few times.

Why was he so consumed with the need to console this woman?

There were days when he'd stayed away. He'd gone to the beach. He'd had a drink with a willing woman, usually in a tiny excuse for a bikini and… well, he'd gone home. He'd lost interest in fucking. It didn't matter how beautiful and at times even smart the woman was, no one intrigued him.

Violet Holland had ruined him even before he had her.

She had a grip on him and he didn't like it. Now, there was a thrill in it for sure. Watching her or staring at the red dot that told him where she was or rather where her phone was. But he'd never been obsessed with a woman like this. In all of his thirty-six years, he'd never felt like this. It was a foreign feeling. A variable.

Unknown made him nervous. Unknown made him angry. Unknown made his muscles twitch and his heart race. And not in a good way. That's why he'd spent his life venturing into the darkness, searching, uncovering hidden secrets. At least virtually.

Tomorrow would have been their date. Art wondered if she'd sorted out whatever was bothering her. He'd hacked into her phone, but he had the decency not to snoop around. He'd only used the geo location features. Knowing where she was provided him with a strange comfort.

He hadn't gathered any intelligence on Violet. He hadn't even searched her name online. He didn't care about her digital footprint. He wanted to get to know her. He wanted *her* to let him in and choose what she would let him see. A lot, he hoped. Everything.

God, it wasn't like him to dream. *Shit!*

"I made a few phone calls." Luca walked from

inside the house with two bottles of beer. "No arrests have been made at Miller Holding."

Art snapped his notebook closed and sat up on the lounger, shaking his head. He had forgotten he was on the patio by the pool.

The warm breeze skimmed the water of the pool. However, no amount of harmony and beauty could ground Art.

"Are you okay, man?" Luca was observant. They'd known each other for long enough. Art didn't understand relationships, but he understood that the longer people spent together, the better they knew each other. Luca had stuck with him for too long.

"Sure, I'm fine." Art took the beer and pinched the bridge of his nose. "No arrests. Fuck!"

Luca settled on the second lounger. The infinity pool lay abandoned in the dusk. On a normal trip, they would have women here, mixing cocktails, swimming, having fun. This time around, Art preferred solitude and Luca had accepted that. Art wondered if his friend's observation skills stretched enough to see that Art was pining for a woman he'd met fewer than three times.

"I think you either call Agent Scully or we need to figure out a more permanent move," Luca said, staring at the sea in the distance.

"You know, referencing *The X Files* makes you ancient." Art took a sip of his beer. "And I love my house. I'm not moving." *Not before I get my chance with Violet.*

"So what are you planning to do? Until the Bureau closes on the Millers, there will be people after you to get the data. Da Bonno's found you and it's only a question of time until the others do."

Luca wasn't wrong, but at the same time, Art's privacy and his whereabouts had never been compromised. Someone had successfully doxed him. Why hadn't he thought about that before?

"How did *they* find me is the question, though."

"There is only one person who knows who you are and where you live." Luca turned to face him and Art shuddered.

"She wouldn't," he said a bit too quickly. *Would she?*

"Yeah, dickhead, she totally would if the price was right. Or just to hurt you. Wouldn't be the first time. And as much as you want to believe otherwise, deep down you know it." Luca took a gulp of his beer. "I know change is hard for you, but I think it's time to relocate."

Simone Lacroix was the only woman who knew what his online alias and his real-life coordinates were. Simone had also betrayed him on many levels and still hadn't had enough. He should have moved a long time ago, to make sure she couldn't find him, but he'd opted for the known, for the comfort of his home.

Growing up without one did that to him. He valued his stupid house too much.

Could she have ratted him out to the Da Bonnos?

"Simone would more likely try to steal the data, not tell on me to some local mobster," he tried to reason, but the variable of the Da Bonnos finding him remained unanswered. He stood up, grabbed his laptop and walked toward the house.

"Where are you going?" Luca asked.

"Research the Da Bonnos and call Agent Scully," Art said and entered the cool kitchen.

"Now who is old?" Luca's chuckle reached him, but Art was already immersed in accessing the readily available information about the Da Bonno family. The more hidden stuff would come next, but first the phone call.

Art leaned against the counter. He liked this house. Perhaps he could move here. He came here often enough. The property had been his for years now, so why not? It was secure and comfortable. It was known. Familiar. He could do that.

The last of the sun's rays danced on the cool rustic tiles of the living area. With the glass wall completely opened, this room was a shaded extension of the patio. Suddenly, he really wanted to show this place to Violet. He needed to know if she liked it.

Shit! He dialed the number.

"Mr. Smith," Agent Rossio answered with the usual irony reserved for Art's alias. When they'd spoken the first time, she'd suggested his name unimaginative, but Art had never understood why bother with inventing an interesting fake name if all the parties knew it was a fake. John Smith was a perfectly respectable alias as far as Art was concerned. No mystery in it.

"Mrs. Rossio," he greeted her and waited. She must know why he was calling.

To her credit she lasted almost half a minute on the line before she gave up. "Okay, *John*, do you want to tell me why you are calling?"

"I think you know."

"You're wondering about the status of the case, I suppose," she said.

Fucking games. On the off chance he ever decided to work for Uncle Sam, he knew they were going to screw him over. *Assholes.* "I have a pretty good idea of *the status of the case.*"

"Well then, I'm happy to inform you that your file with the Bureau is closed and… shall we say, lost permanently. Erased as we agreed. And as much as I'd like to believe the Bureau's cyber security is bullet proof, I have an inkling you validated your current *upstanding citizen* status yourself already. So why are you calling?" She sounded almost bored.

Agent Rossio was in her fifties, a mother of two and a career bureaucrat. She might have been in the field at one point in her life, but Art had lost interest in her and never bothered to find out. She had approached him because he'd allowed her to find him and had given him an offer he'd accepted. Not to erase his unresolved cases with the Bureau as much as for the challenge of breaking into Miller Holding's impenetrable cyber world.

Officially, some loser hacker was going to be arrested and the data would be *accidentally* discovered. This step was to circumvent the illegal procurement of the data in the first place. The detained hacker would get undue fame for breaking the unbreakable empire of Miller Holding and the Bureau would get the credit for bringing down the company involved in money laundering, illegal gambling, extortion and much more.

"I'm calling because people interested in the data have threatened me," Art admitted.

"Well, *John*, I'm sure you can take good care of yourself. It took me three years to find you and I don't even know what you look like or where you live, so a bit of cyber mobbing is something you can take care of easily. But to make you understand, my bosses want a hacker who goes by the name Venus arrested for this." Her words punched him in the guts. "They want to make sure the story is airtight. He's the only other person who could have done what you did for us."

Yeah, probably not, and also he is she.

"It'd be a big win for us to arrest him. Feel free to help us find him. Isn't virus hunting one of your specialties? This shouldn't be different," Rossio said. "Goodbye, *Mr. Smith*." She hung up.

"Fuck me," he murmured.

"What's up?" Luca strolled in. "What did she say?"

"They want to arrest Simone for the data breach before they bring Miller down," Art said, suddenly feeling slightly lightheaded. He stumbled toward the tall chair by the breakfast counter and leaned against it. Simone was the death of him, but was he ready to send her to prison? The woman had made his life miserable, but he wasn't a snitch.

Luca put his hands on his hips, shaking his head. "Well, fuck me right. What are you going to do?"

Art tried to evaluate the situation quickly. There must be a way to get out of this without sending Simone to prison. Though God only knew she belonged there. A part of him wanted to know if she was the one who'd sent the Da Bonno family after him. Yes, the mafia organization should be the first step.

"Art, you know she would take the chance to bring you down if the situation was reversed," Luca insisted.

"Let me think for a moment," Art snapped and Luca shook his head again and walked back out.

Art turned to his laptop and started researching the Da Bonnos. He couldn't concentrate, however. And to his shock, it wasn't Simone—so intricately linked to his immediate safety—but Violet who monopolized his mind.

His fingers danced on the keyboard for a second and her curvy body appeared on his screen. She'd just come home and put her feet up. He wanted to rub them for her.

Tomorrow would have been their date.

* * *

"ARE YOU SERIOUS? Dude, I can't believe that." Chrysal raked his hands through his thick hair. "You really sold them all?"

They were sitting at the same table as the first time two weeks ago. Soft music with the underscore of coffee making played in the background.

Vi laughed. "Yes, and I want more. I should show other artists, but if you have more to fill the wall, bring it, Chrysal."

"I will. I can't believe it. I was so freaked out to even approach you. It was my girlfriend that pushed me and… oh, man, this is awesome." He kept his hands in his hair as if trying to stop his head from exploding.

"Here's your profit share." Vi pushed an envelope toward him.

He looked inside the envelope and his jaw dropped, but no words came out. Chrysal raised his eyes to her and narrowed his eyebrows. "It's a mistake. We agreed I'll get fifty percent."

"Exactly," Vi said, enjoying the moment. "I took the liberty of raising the prices." She winked at him.

"Sick! Thanks, man! I mean, ma'am." He clasped the envelope to his chest. "I'll get you five more paintings tomorrow. I'll come to install them before you open."

"That sounds good. And stop with the dude, man or ma'am. Call me Vi." She couldn't help but grin at him. "Chrysal?" She bit her bottom lip. This could go both ways, but she had to try. "I'd like to take your work to a couple of galleries in the city. I can't promise anything, but—"

"You want to make money from my art?" he asked. Frowning, he jerked his head backward.

"Well, I want more people to see your amazing work and yes, if we both make money in the process, that's great. But more importantly, you're very talented and I don't think you should discount any opportunity. The way you express yourself is inspiring. I can't promise anything, but we have nothing to lose if we try," she said, her palms damp and her heart pounding. She hadn't realized how much this opportunity meant to her until she'd breached the subject with him.

"You think I'm talented?" He cocked his head as if searching for signs of mockery.

"Of course. Why would I sell your work in the

first place?" She took a sip of her coffee. His vulnerability paired with the wall of protection he maintained around himself was kind of adorable. He hadn't yet discovered his ego and she was sure it was only a matter of time with everything he had going for himself. It would probably bring his art to a whole new level. Vi had a surprising desire to guide him on his road to fame and immortality. Because he could easily achieve it. There was boldness in his artistic expression and she couldn't quite put it into words, but she knew he would find success.

"I'll think about it," he said. *Smart boy*!

"That's all I'm asking." She smiled at him.

She watched him leave and the day got slightly better when a familiar face passed by him and entered the store.

"Erica! Please tell me you're back." Vi didn't try to conceal her excitement. "I mean, I hope your mom is well, of course. Are you back?" The words came out like a plea.

She didn't want to admit it, but Vi desperately needed time off. She needed to regroup and find her own place already. She also wanted to stop thinking about Thor, but she figured it wouldn't be possible while she was here every day. Sweet Temptations would forever be associated with him.

Today would have been their date. Vi hadn't seen him for a month and she didn't think she ever would. Yet the weeks passed hadn't changed her desire to spend time with him again. She wanted to tell him about Chrysal and his art. She wanted to share her excitement with him.

Vi wasn't into signs and fate, but it didn't escape her that a man called Art had shown up in her life at the same time she'd rediscovered her love of art. She wouldn't tell him that, of course. He would think she was a lunatic.

Over the last few weeks, she'd actually talked to him in her head a lot. She could almost hear his short, exasperated answers when he tried to look cool but had no clue what was happening.

How could two meetings impact a person this much? She knew nothing about him. And what she did know and had guessed should hold her off. Yet here she was, having imaginary conversations with him.

And talking wasn't where her fantasies stopped. That's what her loneliness brought on. She dreamed about a man she didn't even know.

"My mom is all well and back home and yes, I'm back," Erica said and Vi almost bounced with relief. "Tomorrow is Friday, shall I take the weekend shift? You look like you need some time off. I'm sorry about bailing on you."

"Please, Erica, you didn't do it on purpose. Do you really think you can take the weekend? I'll come tomorrow morning and open up. There is an artist coming to install new paintings," she gestured to the wall, "but I can use a few days off."

"Paintings, nice," Erica said, but didn't seem interested. "Good. We can discuss the work schedule for the next few weeks tomorrow morning, but I'm ready and kind of excited to work through the weekend. The hospital coffee was poison. I missed this place."

The vision of almost three days off helped Vi sail through the afternoon without a worry. Or a thought of Thor. Not exactly true, but close enough. In the last week, she'd trained herself not to look up when the bell above the door chimed. She had failed miserably at first, but she got better. Today was her most successful day.

It was the idea of a work-free weekend that helped her focus. The first in a month. And a David-free weekend. The first in probably a year.

David had ended up staying in London. A new business opportunity had surfaced and he'd decided to pursue it. Vi hoped it was a good sign, that he'd started accepting the break-up in his own complicated way. As Vi steamed the milk for a cappuccino order, she realized he hadn't called her since his mother had been here.

The door chimed and her heart skipped a beat. She didn't have to look, she sensed it. With her back to the door, she was somehow sure.

The boiling milk burned her through the stainless-steel jug and she almost dropped it. Her heart performed an arrhythmic gymnastic choreography in her chest.

She poured the foam into the cup, swirled it, but failed to create a clear design. She wanted to turn around and confirm her senses didn't fail her, but she feared the disappointment. The absurdity of being attuned to someone she didn't know hit her hard and she almost laughed.

"Skinny cappuccino," she called the order and turned to face the room. The world around them slowed down and went mute. With shaking hands, Vi put the cup on the counter.

"Hi," she said. Or at least she thought she said it.

He was tanned, his hair bleached by the sun, and he was definitely hotter than she remembered.

"Hi," he replied. He smiled and those dimples shot a direct line into her stomach, fluttering around like fairy wings. "Ready for our date?"

9

VIOLET INSPECTED her behind in the mirror. They had agreed to go out on Friday. Art was picking her up in half an hour.

She'd spent all day pampering herself. In the morning, she'd helped Chrysal install the new canvases and handed over the patisserie to Erica. With a goofy smile on her face, Vi had spent the rest of the morning shopping. She hadn't bought a new dress in a long time. And yes, she'd had a few cocktail dresses she'd worn for David's functions, but she wanted something new. For herself. She'd had a very hard month behind her and she deserved a reward.

Who was she kidding? She wanted a new dress for Art. The black bodice hugged her upper body snugly. The square neckline covered her cleavage decently, but still accentuated her curves. From her waist, the soft fabric fanned out into a flirty asymmetrical shape with handkerchief-like points hanging playfully around her knees. The red heels she'd bought were outside of her comfort zone but complemented the black dress in an elegantly daring way.

She had avoided color for years, since she was a teenager and her breasts had popped up large and heavy. The sudden addition of curves at the age of fifteen had brought unwanted attention from her classmates, resulting in many advances, a lot of kissing and some make-out sessions. It didn't take long to realize that all the attention was a part of a bet of who would see her tits first.

And so she'd covered herself in baggy black clothes, hoping for invisibility. Since then, she'd upgraded her wardrobe to look more feminine, but remained loyal to black. She'd grown used to it and still believed it helped her blend in enough for people to ignore her. Or her boobs.

Vi put on the red shoes and immediately felt taller, prouder. She'd never realized that the right shoes lent confidence. She needed some tonight to handle this anxiousness. Yes, she was excited, but also nervous. She wanted to make an impression. Or get laid. Frankly, she wasn't sure anymore. But damn if she wasn't going to try to live some of the fantasies she had about him.

With him.

Unless he'd be his typical asshole self during the dinner. In that case, she would be free to continue her life without the constant nagging memory of his eyes, dimples, and that insanely hot body.

She didn't know where they were going. God, what if she was overdressed? Art had said he didn't date, so he'd probably go with a dinner scenario. Safe. Somewhat boring, but normal. Perhaps they could go dancing afterward. He didn't seem the dancing type, though. Okay, she was overthinking it.

She put on a simple thin golden chain. Understated, yet classy. While her cleavage was decent, she didn't need to draw attention to it with too much jewelry.

Her phone rang. Arthur Mathison. Vi smiled at the name. He had put it in her phone yesterday when he stopped by the café. So very official and proper. She'd change it later to Thor.

"Hello," she answered, her voice breathy. *Damn it! Pull yourself together.* She sounded too eager.

"Hi. I'm downstairs," he said and Vi imagined his dimples. The flutter of butterfly wings in her stomach intensified as she moved the curtain and looked down.

She knew little about cars, but she was pretty sure Art was leaning against a red Ferrari. Oh, she wasn't overdressed and her shoes couldn't be better for this ride. He wore a navy-blue suit that had to be tailored because there was no way he could buy a jacket off the rack that would fit his muscles that well. His blond hair was messed up a bit as usual. God, he was perfection.

"I can see," she said and he looked up, scanning the windows and finally finding her. She was too high to see his expression, but she was sure his face lit up with dimples.

"Come down now!" It was an order and she obliged hastily, almost forgetting to lock the door on her way out.

The elevator ride took twice as long as usual. Vi wondered if she should have worn her hair in a classic updo, but it wasn't like she could go back upstairs and change it, anyway.

She stopped herself from running and sauntered out of the building, trying not to run or trip as she walked toward him. Art looked up and raised his eyebrow, a smirk on his face.

"A bit overdressed for burgers by the lake," he said. He licked his lower lip and it did things in her panties. Shit! Maybe they should skip the dinner.

"This is the first joke I've ever heard from a computer geek." She smiled. "But this ride suggests I might be under-dressed. Is this your car?"

"No, I stole it," Art said, his eyes scanning her up and down.

"What?"

"And now you've heard the second joke from a geek." He grinned, but quickly turned serious. He stepped closer, making Vi's breath hitch. His heat on her skin liquefied her core. She swallowed hard when his ice-blue eyes pierced through her, weakening her knees. He was too close.

He reached out and tucked her hair behind her ear, dusting her cheek with his thumb. Just for this feather-like contact she was glad to wear her hair down.

His Adam's apple bobbed a few times. He cleared his throat. "You're beautiful."

The words could sound trite. It was a first date after all, but he said them with a conviction that took her breath away.

"You look quite nice yourself," she whispered, barely able to speak around the anticipation building up in her throat.

His hand traced down her arm slowly until he reached her hand and squeezed it. Without thinking, Vi leaned in. Her chest touched his as she looked up, mesmerized by the effect of his presence. They stared at each other, and Vi swore their breathing and heart-beats synchronized. She couldn't imagine they would ever step away.

"I'm not an expert here, but the kiss should come at the end of the first date," he rasped.

"Something tells me you like to break rules and defy expectations," she said, surprised at her eloquence.

A corner of his mouth curled up slightly, not yet showing the dimple, but accepting the dare.

Had she just challenged him to kiss her? He was

so close that all coherent thought had abandoned her. He cupped her face with his large hands, tracing her bottom lip with his thumb. Her lower belly clenched in delight and anticipation, but he didn't move, simply drank her in with an intense look.

For a moment, she feared he wouldn't do it. That he would refer back to the proper dating protocol, but as soon as she got distracted with that stupid line of thinking, he closed in.

His mouth connected with hers, soft lips tasting her slowly at first. She opened up for him and he deepened the connection, his tongue meeting hers. He uttered an almost painful groan, wrapped one of his arms around her waist like a vice and then pulled her closer. She was crushed against his hard body and sighed with delight.

He moved his hand from her cheek, cupping the back of her neck and turned his head slightly to gain better access. Their tongues explored each other in a dance that took off with its own choreography as if they had practiced for years. So new, yet so familiar. Soft, yet demanding. Hot, yet grounding.

When their mouths finally parted, Art rested his forehead on hers, not letting her go, holding her tight against him. She found his gaze and smiled. If this was the appetizer, she couldn't wait for the entrée and probably wouldn't survive the dessert. His smoky, woodsy scent ignited her core in a way she hadn't known was possible.

"Better than I imagined," he drawled. "Much, much better."

The very best.

Art pulled away and she immediately felt the loss. Holding her hand, he walked her to the passenger side of the car and helped her get in. They both ignored the tent in his pants, but Vi felt a jolt of satisfaction. She did that to him. He liked her at least as much as she liked him.

"Ready?" he asked when he got in, but before she could say anything, he sped off, breaking all sorts of rules again. But who cared about traffic laws at this point?

* * *

As Vi spoke about the artist she'd discovered, Art had a tough time focusing. He was interested in what she said. In fact, he was really interested, but his mind was pulled in another direction.

They were eating dinner in a private yacht club. To be on the safe side, Art had become a member that morning after confirming that nobody associated with the Da Bonnos frequented the place. Luca was having drinks at the bar, but Vi didn't need to know that.

He had been a pain in ass, protesting Art's use of the Ferrari. Stubborn prick. As if it mattered what he drove when they try to kill him. Luca's point that the

Ferrari drew attention was reasonable, but it was his first date with Violet and that was the overriding argument.

His knees had literally buckled when she came out of the building. That dress was pure temptation. It wasn't sexy in a seedy way. Not at all. Yet it was the hottest dress he'd ever seen. Black again. He needed to ask her what was with the widow dress code. *Shit. Is she a widow?*

He should have checked. No. He didn't want to mine the net for information on her. He wanted her to tell him.

He scanned her up and down, trying not to gape. The red heels would be the reason he suddenly developed a shoe fetish. He had a vision of her bent over naked in just those shoes, but he tried to tame it. This was their first date, after all. Already going better than he'd expected.

Especially after that kiss. He wanted another one. His entire force of will had gone into stopping himself from jumping her on several occasions.

Her laugh during the ride every time he sped up was music to his ears. Thank God he hadn't listened to Luca. That car delivered.

"Are you listening, Art?" Vi cocked her head.

"No," he said and her eyes widened, a blush tingeing her cheeks. He smiled and she fidgeted in her chair, frowning. She started tapping her foot and it did things to his insides. "The moment you stepped out of the house, my ability to think or listen moved down to my pants."

"Art," she gasped.

"Your fault." He shrugged, loving her reaction. "You're the hottest woman on Earth."

The blush came back, skimming her throat, disappearing into her neckline, daring him to take a peek at how far it went. That dress was way too decent, which made it more indecent, leaving too much to his imagination.

"You have the ability to annoy and please me at the same time." She took a sip of her wine.

"I'm planning to do a lot of pleasing." He took her hand and kissed it softly. Today she didn't smell like summer but was instead sweet and warm, like the caramel of her eyes. Her scent affected him more than he'd anticipated, and for the second time tonight, a hard-on pushed painfully against his pants. "I need to warn you though that I'll probably annoy you equally."

"This might be the longest sentence you've ever said to me." She left her hand in his.

He took a sip of his wine. It was a fine Chianti. Okay, a point for Luca. Not driving would have had its benefits. "You make me horny and chatty."

She laughed. "Oh, poor Art, perhaps we should take advantage of that," she purred.

"I'm sure they have a room available here."

He leaned closer, the warmth of her breath

caressing his skin and allowing him another intoxicating whiff of caramel. Delicious. He wondered if the choice of perfume was deliberate.

She giggled. "I was talking about chatting more." She licked her lower lip and he gave up and pulled her closer, seizing her mouth. She moaned and opened for him.

When they'd arrived, the waiter held a chair for him opposite her, but Art ignored it and sat beside her. Grateful for the access he'd granted himself, he gripped her chair with both hands and jerked her closer. With her seat between his legs now, Vi's closeness unleashed something in him and his kiss turned desperate.

Almost violent.

Not a show this pretentious place would appreciate, but he didn't care. And lucky bastard he was, Vi didn't protest either. She bit his bottom lip and a groan escaped him as his dick twitched.

Someone nearby cleared their throat and Vi pulled away. She kept her eyes down as she hastily moved her chair back to her spot. The fucking waiter came to refill their glasses. Idiot. Next time, he'd book a private dining room. He should have done it tonight as well.

"Are you going to represent the young artist?" he asked, trying to fill the silence and pick up the conversation.

"You were listening!" She seemed surprised and

pleased. "I don't know. I have no connections in that world or experience doing such a thing. I feel out of my depth. I don't even know why I offered it to him."

"But you offered, so make connections." He couldn't quite understand her hesitation. Clearly, it was something she wanted to do.

"Yeah... I wish I had your confidence," she said.

"That would make you an arrogant prick and I think one is enough." He winked and she laughed.

This was the best date ever. The best time he'd had in so long. He wished he was here with her only to enjoy each other's company. But he wasn't.

The research last night left him unsettled.

Vi was connected to the Da Bonnos.

10

COMPUTERS WERE SAFE—WELL, not for society at large, but for him they were—but people were complicated and unpredictable. And as much as he wanted to trust her, the facts were perturbing. There must have been a reasonable explanation. And that was why he was here.

Vi's thrilling presence made it too difficult to focus on the task. He used to trust Simone and she wasn't half this exciting for him. Was he making a mistake tonight?

"How long have you been living in your place?" There—that was an appropriate first date question, right? He hoped the answer would put his worry to bed.

They were strolling around the marina, the lake whispering alongside. It was a warm night and, strangely enough for the city, the stars glittered above them with the Big Dipper dominating the sky. He was considering sliding his hand into hers, but he needed to clear her first. Damn it, he even felt guilty for suspecting her.

"Why do you ask?" She hesitated and stopped, searching his face.

Fuck! Not the reaction he'd hoped for.

In the distance, Luca sat on the patio of the club's restaurant and Art could almost feel his judgment.

Her gaze locked with his for a long moment, his heart pounding against his chest. Those caramel eyes reflected something, but it wasn't guilt. Or was it just his wishful thinking? Technically, she worked for a Da Bonno. The extent of her work was the bothersome part. He really didn't want the suspicion to taint their date. What he wanted was to drown in those brown eyes and kiss the hell out of her.

She spoke finally. "Look, Art, this is kind of embarrassing, but it's not my place." Her face took on a new shade of pink. "I'm kind of homeless at the moment," she whispered and scrunched her face as if the admission caused her physical pain.

A flood of relief—probably premature, the devil on his shoulder insisted—poured through him. "We should find you a place to live then." He turned and continued walking.

Silence followed as she remained standing behind, but then the *click, click, click* of her shoes brought a smile to his face. "It's kind of hard right now because I don't *really* have a job."

He whipped around with a frown.

She swallowed hard and focused on the yachts rocking on the lake, avoiding him. "I'm helping my friend Carla, but it's not an official, regular income any rental office or landlord would like to see."

"Okay, that can be fixed," he announced and she stopped again.

When he looked at her, tears glistened in her eyes. Without thinking, he closed the distance between them. He wrapped his arms around her tightly, and his lips found hers.

She felt so good. He was getting addicted to caramel, her scent robbing him of all logic. Her body fit perfectly against his. She was shorter, meeting his mouth voraciously on her tiptoes.

"I'm really embarrassed. The last thing I want is your pity." She whispered against his face, warming his cheek with her sweet breath.

He couldn't get enough of that face. So many different expressions—fierce, pissed, sweet, shy—she morphed unexpectedly, unknowingly encouraging his intrigue. And he really hoped all of it was guided by honesty.

He traced his thumb on her chin and lifted her face to meet his eyes. They were lighter tonight in the moon's glow. "I was offering help, not pity."

She quivered and he lowered his lips to hers again, this time softly brushing, tasting her. Delicious.

He took her hand and pivoted them back toward the club. "How do you know Carla?" he asked. He probably should investigate why she was homeless and unemployed, but she seemed shaken enough by the confession itself. But unless he clarified the Da Bonno connection, Luca might force him to abandon the mission.

"Her bakery used to be next door to my old café," she said and stopped, pulling him close for a quick peck.

She smiled and shook her head, raising her intrigue score higher. He wished there was a manual for women.

"Your dimples are too distracting," she clarified. "Anyway, we became friends. Then she started dating Charlie and he helped her open Sweet Temptations. She's my best friend. My only friend, really. So when they decided to travel, I offered to take care of the business. They are kind of isolated, you know. Carla has no family in the States and Charlie... well..." She stopped and looked around, ready to share a secret. "He's a Da Bonno. But he cut all ties with the family when he met Carla. Sometimes he hangs out with his cousin, but *the* Tony Da Bonno hasn't spoken to him in five years."

He smiled at her and tugged her in for another kiss. He really liked this story. But could he believe it?

His instincts screamed to trust her, but his mind needed concrete proof.

"Thank you," she breathed.

"For what?" He kept his hand on her waist and held her close, drinking in her scent, her beauty, her warmth.

"For offering help instead of judging why my life is in such a shitty place." Her eyes pleaded for acceptance and he really wanted to shut up the persistent doubt in his mind.

He kissed her and she wrapped her arms behind his neck, the tips of her fingers tickling his nape. There was no way he was driving her home tonight.

* * *

Vi couldn't catch her breath but leaned into the kiss anyway. Blissful suffocation.

They had reached the patio but stopped to the side. Inadequately shielded by large potted plants, they had been kissing for the last fifteen minutes.

Art's hungry hands roamed up and down her back, while his gorgeous mouth sucked, licked and teased her lips, her jaw, her ear. She sighed and let her head fall back. He immediately seized the opportunity and nuzzled her neck, finding the hollow under her ear that had a direct line to her channel.

A loud moan broke out from deep within her, probably scandalizing the patrons on the terrace. All reason and propriety had abandoned her under the thorough lips of the computer geek. *Is he even a computer geek?* He was the best kisser in the world.

He groaned against her skin and pulled her closer, grinding his hips against her. His erection rubbed her stomach and the spot between her thighs wept for attention.

"Can we continue breaking the rules?" he whispered into her ear and she shivered under the velvet of his voice.

"What?" was all she managed.

"We kissed before the date. Please, let me take you upstairs." His voice, strained and desperate with want, was music to her ears.

"Hurry," she purred and before she blinked, he dragged her across the patio. And instead of protesting, she giggled, stumbling to keep up with him.

The concierge procured the key to a suite almost immediately, assuring them it was available for the entire weekend. They kissed their way to the elevator like horny teenagers.

Art snuggled her under his arm and pulled out his phone.

"What? Are we going to take a photo?" She giggled into his chest.

"I'm letting Luca know we're staying the weekend," he said and sent a text.

"Your bodyguard was here with us?" she asked

before his words sank in completely. "Wait, we're staying the whole weekend?"

"Of course."

Seriously, this man was the Oxford dictionary definition of a man of few words.

"I have no change of clothes," she protested and he hit her with two perfect dimples.

"You won't need any." The elevator stopped and he grabbed her hand, pulling her down the corridor to their room.

Disjointed thoughts roamed around her head. *What about David? I don't know this guy. This is too soon. I should play hard to get. This is wrong and so right at the same time. And too fast. Geez, I need faster.*

Art twirled her around and pressed her against the door. He captured her lips, his tongue attacking her mouth like his life depended on the connection. And all her thoughts evaporated.

"I need you naked," he rasped, exploring her neckline with kisses.

"Then maybe open the door," she urged. There was a beep, then the door swung open and she fell back with a gasp. In one graceful move, Art lifted her, kicked the door closed and crashed her against the wall.

Vi wrapped her legs around his waist. Between his fire and the wall's chill, between the pounding of her heart and his panting, between his hard cock and the burning ache in her channel, the sensory overload drove her crazy.

"Clothes, Art, clothes!"

Her voice stopped him. He lowered her to the floor and pulled her into a hug. The energy between them soothed from frantic to sensual. He held her for a minute and she was grateful for the break. Part of her needed the carnal animal connection, but at the same time she wanted to savor the moments without painful urgency.

He took her hand and led her farther into the room, the carpet soft under her heels. Neither of them took time to look around—their need lured them directly to the bed. He stopped there and their eyes locked. Fire.

He walked around her slowly, like a predator assessing his prey, and Vi's heartbeat reached her temples. This was seriously hot. Anticipation rippled through her, depriving her of the ability to think, breathe or act. She was just standing there, feeling vulnerable and crazed with desire.

He stopped behind her and swept her hair over one shoulder, exposing her neck. She quivered as his fingertips brushed her skin, tracing the hem of her dress between her shoulder blades. He was slow, inflicting the pain of yearning.

Then he changed the pace as if his own hunger were too much. In one swift move, he unzipped the dress and tugged it over her shoulders. Before she could react, it pooled at her feet. Art's hand dusted her butt cheeks and hips as he moved to step in front of her.

Still wearing her black lace bra and matching thong, she felt naked, bare to him. His ice-blue gaze left a trail of goosebumps as he admired her from head to toe. Vi bit her bottom lip and shivered. From desire. From want. From angst. This was too much. Too good. Too hot. Too everything.

"You're perfect," he rasped and she reached for his tie and pulled him closer.

She loosened it and yanked it off. He hissed and licked his bottom lip. He skimmed her hips with feather-like touches as she slipped his jacket off his shoulders. God, those muscles were lethal even while still covered with the shirt.

He kissed her shoulder. "You're perfect."

"You've mentioned that," she teased. She leaned back to allow herself access and fumbled with the buttons of his shirt. He helped her and shrugged it off, tossing it to the floor.

"Thor." God, did she really say it out loud?

He raised his eyebrow and smirked. "Thor?"

She bit her bottom lip. "That's what I call you in my mind."

He tossed his head back, laughing. "Let me show you the thunder then." He scooped her up and tossed her on the bed. Vi giggled, but her laugh died on her lips when he again shifted the energy. No thunder. More like the quiet before the storm.

His eyes never left her while he pulled a stack of condoms from his pocket, toed off his shoes and socks, then took off his pants. At the sight of the bulge in his briefs, Vi opened her legs involuntarily.

He gave her a sexy, lazy smile. "Good girl." That voice was a promise of velvet and darkness. Her stomach fluttered and her swollen lips ached for release.

Lifting her foot, he brushed his fingers over her leg as if he was playing an instrument, completely immersed in worshiping her. He took off her shoe and kissed her foot, finding her eyes. He caressed her other leg and took off her other shoe.

"We'll use these later," he promised and dropped her heels beside the bed. "Take it off. Take it all off," he ordered.

Vi lifted her hips and shimmied down her underwear.

"Blond." He sighed with a smile.

She pushed herself up and unclasped her bra. She wished she could keep it on. This man was perfect. It was unfair how beautiful his body was and she suddenly felt very self-conscious.

"Go on, babe, let me see them." He met her hesitation with tenderness in his voice.

She took off her bra and her breasts bounced out.

"Fuck me," he drawled and Vi instinctively hugged herself, covering. Protecting.

Art took off his boxers and pounced. "Don't you dare deny me these two beauties," he growled. Pushing her back to the mattress with his weight, he raised her arms above her head and gripped both wrists with one of his large hands. "I've dreamed about your tits, babe."

Yeah, you and every male since I was fifteen. Vi tensed.

"For the record, we'd be here if you were flat-chested," he murmured, nibbling at her jaw.

She suddenly needed a hug, and he released her arms before the thought turned into movement. For a socially clueless man, he could read her like a book. He held her for a moment, stroking her head.

Tears threatened. She was pathetic. Instead of jumping this fine specimen of a lover, she was having a breakdown over her unresolved image issues. *Great timing, Violet!*

"I don't understand what your relationship is with your spectacular boobs, but they have just become my best friends. I need a taste, woman," he teased and she giggled. "Besides, my dick will fall off if we don't proceed."

"Asshole." She leaned back, allowing him access.

"That's someone else. I'm the arrogant prick, remember?" He winked and his mouth found one of her nipples, tugging gently. He cupped her other breast in his large palm, his thumb brushing the pebbled peak. The tickling pull between her legs erased the remaining hesitation.

Vi gripped his hair and sighed. His tender care intensified quickly and the dynamics changed yet again. He lapped with hunger one and then the other breast, pulling and squeezing, sending vibrating sensation through her body. Vi moaned, feeling every contact in her core, craving him. No one had ever ravished her breasts with such dedicated honesty and lust.

He twisted one nipple and bit the other hard. Vi's hips bucked off the bed. She gasped.

"Greedy," he growled, smiling against her skin.

"I thought your dick was falling off," she almost yelled as he repeated the delicious attack.

The explosion of sensations running through her body and culminating between her legs was maddening. She was like an instrument under his touch, playing a beautiful symphony of lust and acceptance.

He trailed a hand down her hipbone and then slipped one finger between her swollen lips. "Yes," she gasped.

"Oh, you need me, babe," he mumbled. "Open for me."

She obliged and he teased her opening gently before sliding one finger into her channel. She contracted, begging him to stay there. He pulled out and impaled her immediately with not one, not two, but three of his large fingers.

Vi screamed and fisted the sheets under her, terrified of how much more she wanted. He sucked on her nipple while pounding his fingers in and out in a rhythm of desire that spread heat through her body. She was falling and arching with every thrust, wanting more and almost unable to take it.

"Art!"

"I know, babe, I know," he said darkly and crooked his fingers on the last push while flicking her clit with his thumb. Vi's toes curled as she convulsed around him and shuddered with an orgasm that shook her core and pushed tears into her eyes. *Fuck!*

He carried her through, his magical hands pumping and his talented mouth kissing her everywhere.

He knelt above her, one thumb still circling her bud while he searched for the condoms with the other hand. Or that's what she thought he was doing because she was lost to reality. The sound of a wrapper and an acute lack of his touch brought her back and she lifted onto her elbows.

Art gave himself a couple of rough strokes and rolled the condom on. This was the first time she'd got a proper look, and holy shit! She'd found Thor's hammer.

"My turn finally," he said as if to himself and lowered himself on top of her on his elbows.

"Arrogant prick." She giggled. This man was infuriating in the most thrilling way. Or she was completely unreasonable after weeks of anxiety and exhaustion.

"You remember now." He grinned and reached between them. He swiped his cock through her lips and they moaned in unison.

The muscles of his shoulders and arms hardened under her palms as she reveled in discovering every beautiful inch of him, bracing herself for the next round of his attack. He lifted himself and brought her knees to his shoulders, then in one swift move he entered her.

Burn. He was huge.

The moment of stillness cracked something inside her. The surrounding air sparked with unexpected intimacy. They were no longer just fucking. Her breath hitched as their eyes locked. Right there and then she couldn't imagine being anywhere else, with anyone else, and it soothed and terrified her at the same time. The moment made little sense, yet it required no reason. It was charged with something beyond comprehension, heightening her senses, finding depths.

His Adam's apple moved up and down several times and Vi was sure Art's protective walls cracked as well. Not yet completely broken, but a connection was established that ran beyond their bodies. The overwhelming need to surrender won and she wiggled her hips a bit.

"Let me in, babe," he rasped, one finger circling

her nipple. Somehow she guessed he wasn't talking about his dick only.

She obliged, circling her hips again and spreading her legs wider. He groaned and seized her nipple, relaxing her further. Delight rippled through her body.

He pulled out and slid back in and she accepted him with another loud moan. She closed her eyes, letting her body enjoy the ride. They moved in perfect unity.

It wasn't gentle or tidy. They were panting, skin slapping and the bed banging against the wall, but it was the perfect score for their connection. He pumped into her as if his life depended on it and she was sure hers did. She would die if he stopped, but she was probably going to die if he didn't.

"Look at me," he ordered and she forced her lids open. The intensity of his gaze consumed her completely as he carried them to a release that broke her apart and made her whole at the same time. She clenched, her walls squeezing every last jerk of pleasure from him and for him.

He collapsed on top of her, gifting her with gentle kisses on her face and neck. He stayed inside her, pulsing with the aftermath of their mutual satisfaction and kept kissing her. Her body liquefied beneath his, completely spent and unreasonably happy.

* * *

SEVERAL ORGASMS and three showers later, it was the lack of condoms that forced them to stop. Art had to give it to her—she took him with eagerness and desire that left him spent and wanting more at the same time. He should have been gentler, less demanding with her. It was their first time, for God's sake. He must have hurt her.

His stomach constricted at the idea. Not that she complained, but the beast she'd awakened in him rocked him off balance.

He rested his head on the pillows while he admired the view. Vi, her hair all messed up and cheeks still flushed, sat opposite him, leaning against the footboard.

She was munching on French fries and he found himself jealous of the finger food. Idiot! She'd demanded food earlier and fussed when he declined the pre-dawn snack. He didn't want to move in fear of disturbing the fluid, lazy joy around them.

She was edible. And right now she was just too far from him, which he planned to remedy momentarily because unbeknown to her, room service delivered another set of condoms.

She was wearing his shirt and while it looked good on her, it seemed unnecessary. "Are you cold?" he asked.

"No." She frowned with a smile. "Why?"

"Get naked," he demanded. Why was she trying to cover herself? There was the moment at the beginning of their extensive session of lovemaking when he'd realized she wasn't completely comfortable with nudity or with her body. Had no man before shown her what a goddess she was?

She focused on the fries as if they suddenly required utmost concentration. "I-I don't like to display…" A blush rose to her cheeks.

"Display what? That amazing body of yours? Take my shirt off now."

She widened her eyes. "Bossy!"

"Explain," he prompted and she stood up to carry the plate to the table. He couldn't deny that she looked very sexy in his shirt. It was way too big for her and offered a delightful promise of curves hidden. Yet, he preferred her naked.

She fidgeted by the bed when she returned and he couldn't take it any longer. In one smooth move, he hauled her over and pinned her under him. She half gasped and half giggled. Smoothing the hair away from her forehead, he kissed her, tasting the salt and oil. She moaned and parted her lips in invitation. Their tongues tangoed and his cock awakened, demanding attention.

"Explain," he demanded again.

She exhaled. "I hate my boobs. The attention they got me when I was a girl traumatized me. It feels like men are only interested in my chest, not me."

Now that was fucked up. "I failed then."

"What? How is this about you? Geez, Art, I tell

you one of my-my… I don't know… I confide in you and it somehow bruised your ego?" She pulled away from him, but he didn't let go and wrapped her even tighter, turning her on her side. They faced each other, her head resting on his bicep while she glared at him, but she didn't move away.

"I failed to show you how beautiful you are. That you're way more than your—and it has to be said—gorgeous tits."

She continued to glare.

"And I repeat: we'd be here even without them."

The glare softened a bit.

"Though I'm not going to lie, I adore those babies," he added and a ghost of a smile lightened her face. "But they are not worth waiting for an entire month. You, on the other hand…" He studied her, trying to memorize every line on her face.

"Me, on the other hand?" She cupped his cheek, her warm palm calming him.

"The jury is still out," he teased.

"You." She laughed and slapped him gently. Even the slap felt like meditation. "Have you realized we spent our first date talking about an unknown artist and the Da Bonnos instead of us?"

Fuck, he could have gone without hearing about Da Bonnos. He kissed her forehead. If this was supposed to be the conversational part of their date, he was suddenly too tired.

"You said *blond* when I took off my underwear.

Why?" she asked and he exhaled. Okay, he could work with these topics.

He took a strand of her hair, silky between his fingers, and inhaled the scent of her. "I'd been wondering if you're a natural blond."

"You thought I bleached my hair?" She looked appalled.

Her hair smelled like a meadow and sex, and a bit like his deodorant. For some reason, he liked that he claimed her this way. "Your eyes are dark caramel. It's confusing."

"I look confusing to you?" Shit. Perhaps there was no safe topic. He was bound to fuck up.

"Confusingly beautiful." He kissed her forehead. "In my defense, less than half a percent of blond people have brown eyes."

"And of course you'd know that. You, Arthur Mathison, are very refreshing company. Your turn to ask a question." She snuggled closer and he turned to lie on his back, her body fitting perfectly around his. The only downside of the whole situation was her need to converse.

"Why do you work at a café if you love art—not capitalized—so much?" Her passionate tale of the young man and his paintings had uncovered a new side, sparkling through her in a contagious way.

The satisfaction of his work had always come from the challenges it presented, so he couldn't quite grasp why she was wasting her time serving coffee.

Though thank God for that because he wouldn't have met her otherwise.

"My parents are assholes." Her honesty surprised him. "Art museums were where I'd escape their expectations and fights. I met Rebecca there. Her parents didn't have time for her and we bonded over our love of silence. Because it was the silence that pulled us to the museum at first. When we were eighteen, Rebecca inherited a coffee shop from her aunt.

"We dreamed about making money and studying art. Art history in my case. I'm not very creative or talented. We worked hard and had a lot of fun. Come to think of it, we were planning to display art in our café too. But then she got sick. Breast cancer. Stage four."

Vi's voice became strained, words coming out on a verge of choking. He didn't want to interrupt her, so he held her closer, stroking her arm.

"She died and I simply continued what we'd started. I felt responsible for carrying on her memory." She sighed and wrapped her arm around his chest, holding on to him.

"I'm sorry," he said. He was pissed at her parents for hurting her and at her friend for dying on her, but even he knew not to say that. Shit, there was no safe topic between them. Or perhaps it was just his unwillingness to disturb the peace their physical connection brought him.

They lay in silence for a while. Eventually, he slid

his hand under the hem of his shirt, roaming mindlessly over the smooth skin of her back and ass. In an oddly non-orchestrated synergy, she was drawing circles on his chest.

"Okay, my turn," she said and he rolled his eyes because she sounded too excited. "How did you get this beautiful body?"

He laughed. She lifted her head, her chin on his chest, facing him. "I'm serious. I'd expect a computer geek to have a belly, courtesy of a poor diet, and ketchup stains on his shirt, while wasting away in a dark basement."

"Fair enough." He smirked and kissed her forehead. He couldn't stop touching her. With his lips. With his hands. And hopefully soon enough with his cock again.

"But you're not. You're very healthy and sexy." She poked his chest.

"Obviously." He flexed the muscle to tease her.

She giggled. "So what? You realized the gym was a good place to pick up chicks?"

"Now that's an idea." He slapped her butt and she bit his shoulder. "But I bought the Ferrari for that." He rolled her onto her back and nuzzled her neck, biting gently. She laughed and protested half-heartedly while allowing him better access. He undid the only button she'd fastened and found her breast. She wiggled under his weight.

"Come on, Art. We're talking—" A moan took the words away from her.

"Take the damn shirt off and I'll answer," he ordered and pulled it off her shoulders. She helped him out and lay back, spreading her arms above her head. He paused. This was a disarming gesture of trust and suddenly he wished he'd let her keep the shirt.

"My brain never shuts up," he said quietly. "Never. I read something and I remember it. I'm constantly solving puzzles. It can get pretty crazy and overwhelming. Only extreme physical exertion helps me balance that." He grazed her breast with his palms, the motion giving him strength to speak.

Her breath hitched under his touch. "So you started working out?"

"I don't like gardening or construction." He claimed one of her nipples with his tongue.

"So I simply assumed you're a computer geek. What is it you really do?" She raked her hands through his hair.

"I have a mouthful here right now," he mumbled against her skin and bit her nipple to make his point. She squealed and arched her hips.

"Come on, Art. I doubt you'll ever say sentences of this length and substance again. Your thoroughly fucked brain is working in a refreshingly chatty way. I need to take advantage of that." But she held his head to her chest anyway.

"Okay, one more question and then I'm taking advantage of you." He rubbed his cheek between her boobs, enjoying their lush softness.

She laughed. "Then answer."

"What was the question again?" He cupped her breast and simply held it. He wanted to use them as his pillow. Just holding them was a treat. He was in love with Violet's tits. How could she be ashamed of them?

"What do you do?" She snapped her fingers and pulled his hair playfully.

"I'm a cyber security consultant," he said. Technically the truth.

"Why would an IT guy need a bodyguard?"

"Hey, woman, I'm not *just any IT guy*." He bit her nipple and she squealed again. "And Luca is not only my bodyguard. He steps into that role when required, but he's more my friend and colleague. I'm good at pissing clients off, so he's a buffer. We go way back. His wife was killed in a car accident and he was lost. I was lost at the same time and we somehow helped each other survive. I employ him as my, I don't know, manager."

"Why were you lost?" Those caramel eyes cut right through his soul.

Fuck!

"I'm lost generally if you haven't noticed. Outside the binary code."

She pulled him in for a kiss but ended it way too soon.

"Your turn for the last question." She put his hand on her breast, as an incentive and a promise.

"Are you a widow?"

Her eyes widened and she pulled away. "What?"

"I've only ever seen you in black."

Enough already with the talking. His cock was screaming for attention. He should be tired, but he wasn't. She was like a selection of candies and he hadn't yet tasted all of them.

"Oh. It's simply a choice." She licked her lip and looked away.

"A poor one," he said matter-of-factly.

She glared for a moment and then shook her head. "And to answer *your question*, I'm not a widow. I've never been married. Have you?"

He pounced. "Let's fuck."

11

_____

AND FUCK THEY DID.

Vi was sore. And so happy. She was satisfied and, if she was honest with herself, a little attached.

It was Sunday and they had just had lunch on the balcony. Since Friday, they hadn't left the room. Art was on his laptop and Vi was simply sitting there, watching the seagulls above the lake, the yachts swaying on the water and—most of all—studying Art.

God, he was gorgeous. He was wearing his black boxers, but the chiseled triangle of his upper torso was enough for Vi to feel the familiar tingle between her legs. Geez, she'd spent almost the whole weekend with him and still she hadn't had enough.

Vi snuggled in her soft white bathrobe and returned her focus to the water glistening on the horizon.

The elegant luxury of the room had dawned on

her at lunchtime yesterday after she'd woken up. Art had slept peacefully and she'd taken a long bath in a large corner tub, surrounded by white marble, a variety of beauty products and soft, fluffy towels. Along with the common toiletries, she'd even found a face mask and a special hair oil treatment. The place was stocked with expensive products.

The room was simple but screamed of money. The three years with David had taught Vi to appreciate things that were tasteful, elegant and outside the reach of most people. She loved it here.

What if that was part of the attraction? Was she really that shallow? She'd fallen for David, dazzled by things and places he'd shown her. But with Art? Did it matter they were here in this beautiful and expensive club?

Everything about this weekend was off-the-chart perfect, culminating in this moment right now when they just were. Together in comfortable silence. She'd never had that with David. In silence, she'd either searched frantically for a new conversation topic or she'd worried she'd say something inappropriate. Or David had talked about himself. She hadn't realized before how much he'd talked.

She wished Art would talk a bit more, but enjoying a long silence so early in a relationship was a good sign. Were they even in a relationship? They didn't need to define it. Part of David's appeal was his money—or rather what it represented—but in this case, she'd sit like this with Art even homeless under the bridge.

Shit! She *was* homeless. Vi stood up.

Art lifted his gaze from the screen and frowned. "Where are you going?" he growled.

"To get my phone. I should check the classifieds. Carla gets back in three and a half weeks and I need a place," Vi answered, but he grabbed her hand.

"Sit down." He pulled her back to the chair and turned his screen to her. "Apply here."

A picture of a bedroom with a large terrace and a beautiful bathroom covered the screen. The exposed red brick gave it an industrial feel. Vi clicked to the next picture. Oh, the bathroom! It had a gray stone sink and a walk-in shower that seemed larger than her old café. Copper fixtures complemented the chocolate tiles. The next picture featured an open concept living room with a kitchen—brick walls, concrete floors and high ceilings decorated with exposed pipes. The natural light from huge industrial windows filled the entire space.

"It's beautiful," Vi said. Art brushed her forearm with his fingers, a smile on his face.

She clicked out of the image gallery and checked the details. Located in an artsy neighborhood, this place would be perfect.

"There is no way I'd get approved in this place, but thank you for the effort." She stroked his cheek, the stubble tickling her skin. She liked him with the two-days growth, though her skin might need a special treatment later. His eyes flickered with mischief.

Oh, he was so out of her league and not understanding her situation at all. The latter was her fault. She wasn't exactly forthcoming with details. She should explain why she was unemployed. And tell him about David. But she didn't want to burst the careless energy between them. Not yet. Tomorrow. Maybe.

"Thank you." She kissed him softly.

"Apply," he said.

"Art, there is no point." She kissed him again.

"You have nothing to lose. Apply." He nodded toward his laptop.

"Art—"

"Apply," he ordered.

Vi sighed. Stubborn man. Infuriating. She clicked on the application and Art leaned back in his chair, practically humming with content.

"You're so infuriating," she murmured.

"And you're beautiful."

She smiled. Her body temperature was now regulated solely by the intensity of his gaze.

"Here, done. Waste of time for me and certainly for whoever is reviewing applications, but at least you're happy." She pushed the laptop away on the table.

"I'd be happier if you took off that robe." He wiggled his eyebrows.

"Not happening. I need to get back to the city. I work tomorrow," she said.

"No." Art stood up.

"What do you mean, no?" She followed him inside.

"No, we're not leaving yet." He stopped by a small round dining table and faced her. His eyes darkened. He was pissed. What the hell? His jaw moved as if he was trying not to show it. Or deciding something. What?

"Art, I don't want to leave, but I have to. I have a responsibility. I have to open the patisserie tomorrow morning. I need a change of clothes and frankly a good night's sleep to plow through a twelve-hour shift." She crossed her arms over her chest.

He glared at her. Every man had to behave like a boy once in a while, she supposed. Or all the time. Vi closed the distance between them and ran her hands up and down his arms.

"Come on, Thor, you'll show me the thunder tomorrow evening again."

His tongue darted out, he licked his lip and heat spread through her veins. She could spend two more hours. It was still early, wasn't it?

"Take off the robe, Vi." Something in his voice confirmed this was not a request to refuse. Her breath hitched and she didn't know if it was arousal or anxiety that nipped at her nerves.

With shaking hands, she slipped the robe off her shoulders and Art hissed.

"Put on the shoes." Again, he left no room for argument. Or her mind was liquified permanently and things didn't make sense anymore.

She frowned. She stood there naked, but his intense glare bared her beyond the flesh. Utterly exposed. The vulnerability of the moment deprived her of oxygen, tingled in her fingertips, fluttered in her stomach, squeezing it, but in her core brewed desire. A dark anticipation that scared her even as it called to her like a siren's song.

"Put the fucking shoes on, Vi," he rasped, a warning and a promise in his voice.

She found her stilettos by the bed and put them on, returning to stand in front of him. Her heart hammered against her chest and the air seemed to avoid her lungs.

Art stepped closer. Tension between them pulsed with angst and lust. This was so wrong. And so right at the same time. The fine line between angst and desire was completely blurred.

He fisted her hair and pulled aggressively, tilting her head. A gasp escaped her before he seized her mouth, biting and sucking like he wanted to kill her with a kiss.

"Art," she breathed against his demanding tongue.

As if her voice snapped something in him, he jerked her hair again and twirled her swiftly, her back now against him. His dominance heightened her arousal to a new level she'd never before experienced. She was teleported into a new dimension where darkness was appealing. Where bad felt better. Where boundaries dissolved.

He traced his fingers down her neck and over her shoulder. She quivered. Where did all the air go? His grasp hurt her skull, but the pleasure his touch evoked overrode any other sensation.

Pain and pleasure. Another line blurred.

"You wanted to leave?" he asked darkly. His voice was familiar, yet foreign to her. God, this was hot. And a bit scary. She wanted to run away and stay at the same time.

"Answer me," he snapped, pulling her hair, so he could see her face, towering above her.

"Yes," she whispered. He smiled, pleased with her answer. Whatever this game was, Violet's body vibrated with a need too strong to rebel against. This was wrong. So wrong. So wonderful.

He kissed her softly and the honesty of the touch dissipated all her remaining hesitation. She moaned and before she had a chance to react, he lurched forward, bending her over the table and spreading her legs wide. He leaned over her, his torso covering her back. The cold table squashed her breasts, its edges dug into her hipbones.

"Are you sorry you pissed me off?" he whispered in her ear, the warmth of his breath attacking her senses, stripping her bare to his desire. She should fear him and perhaps she did, but she wanted him way more.

"Yes." The word pushed through the lump in her throat. She'd never been dominated like this and the intensity of her thirst terrified her.

"I'll have to punish you, babe," Art said with tenderness and Vi sighed. At that moment, she trusted him completely. She wanted him to carry them into a transcendent release. Because that's what his touch promised.

With his erection hard against her back, he didn't move for a long moment, his breath warm and damp on her cheek. He gently pushed her hair from her face, smoothing it slowly, with care. She was pinned under him, unable to move. The anticipation was unbearable and despite his aggression, Vi wanted to beg him to fuck her. This was so confusing.

"Do it." She hoped the words were audible because she was sure she no longer was in command of her vocal cords.

He kissed her shoulder and lifted off her slowly, dusting her spine with the back of his hand. He traced the curves of her behind, his touch so light she thought she imagined it. And then he slapped her so hard it took her breath away. The sting seared through her skin directly into her core, that now wept for attention.

She looked over her shoulder. Art was focused,

caressing her behind again gently. It was all too much. The forbidden contrast between pain and desire destroyed, Vi closed her eyes, the sensory overload too much to bear anymore. Art slapped her again and she yelped. He let out a deep growl. The bastard was enjoying it. Hell, she was too.

His touch was now light again. Vi trembled in anticipation of another spank, but he moved his hand, cupping her between the legs. He slid his finger between her swollen lips and hissed his approval. She needed him to fill her. To make her whole again. The painful desire was too overwhelming.

He pushed his finger inside her and she moaned, but he retrieved it too quickly, moving it to her other opening and circling slowly there. Oh God, what was he planning?

12

"ART," she gasped, unable to articulate her protest. Was she even protesting?

"Shh, shh, babe. Trust me." He slipped his thumb in the opening between her cheeks and she clenched. She expected... well, she wasn't sure what she'd expected, but it wasn't this. She needed him, wanted him to take her.

"Relax, Vi," he ordered, but there was an undertone of care in it and she did.

He lifted one of her thighs and pushed it onto the table, spreading her wide for him. He entered her in one deep thrust while pumping her ass with his thumb.

She screamed, burn and pleasure interlaced. Only a moment earlier she'd wished he'd take her and take he did. He pumped her without finesse. Hard and so good. The table chafed her hips, her breasts ached against the solid surface, but never had she lived through thrill like this.

Before she realized, an orgasm crashed through her with the force of a military aircraft. She clenched around him and Art followed her. The intensity was transformational. He pumped her, riding them both to oblivion, jerking every last pleasure out of the feral act.

VI STIRRED and sighed into Art's warm chest. Interesting how such a solid body turned into a comfortable pillow. She fit perfectly in the hollow of his shoulder. It was almost unnerving.

Yesterday had shocked Violet. He'd shown her a dominant side and she didn't know what to do with that. Because as much as it was wrong and dirty in her mind, what had happened last night was incredibly satisfying. Pure raw pleasure. Soul-shattering experience.

She didn't know she'd enjoy sex like this and now that he'd initiated her—without warning—she wasn't sure she could go back. Not that all the lovemaking they'd done this weekend was the gentle, vanilla kind of sex. They'd fucked hard and unforgiving, but still the last union had left her bare. Confused. Satiated.

Art had kissed her and hugged her for what seemed like hours afterward, inspecting her body for potential hurt and kissing every minor bruise. He'd ravaged her body and then he'd worshiped it thoroughly. Where did one go from there? She hadn't been this Zen for years.

She was at a stage of her life when she needed to redefine herself. To find herself. And instead she'd found an *arrogant prick* who barely talked and he'd turned her world upside down in two short days.

"Did I hurt you?" he'd asked last night, studying her face in the darkness of the room with an intense ache. She wasn't able to answer, because he did and yet he didn't. The emotions crushing her body were too much to put into words, so she kissed him. Hungrily. With all the pain, lust and passion she had. And he'd made love to her. So tenderly, tears had broken when they'd come in unison.

Vi cuddled in closer and Art moved his other arm around her, hugging her tightly. He was asleep, fast asleep based on his breathing, and yet his body reacted with care.

It was the worst thing for Vi to fall into a relationship right now. No home. No work. No future.

The way Thor had painfully claimed her last night—first dominantly and then tenderly—left her lost. Completely, utterly, perfectly lost. He didn't really hurt her last night, but she was sure there was no way to recover from Arthur Mathison. At some point, she would get hurt. She wasn't certain about much in her life right now, but she was sure of that.

For fuck's sake, she didn't even know the man. He shook the ground under her. A part of her wanted to run, but all the other parts outvoted the tiny annoying voice of reason.

The two of them had crossed an invisible line and jumped into intimacy too fast. So fast, they'd forgotten the condoms last night. It was the last thought Vi had before she'd fallen asleep, but she was too spent, too liquefied, too happy at that point to even bring it up. She was on the pill after all.

The heat of Art's body was like the best drug, so potent in getting her high. The fall would be fatal. She couldn't even imagine leaving him to go to work.

Shit! Vi sprang up. It was six in the morning.

"Art, wake up. We need to go." She scrambled around, grabbing her clothes.

Squeezing herself into her little black dress on Monday morning before work felt naughty. She smiled inwardly. *I like naughty.* She stumbled over to the bathroom to fix her hair.

"Art, wake up. Now. I'll be late for work."

A groan from the bed confirmed he wasn't even contemplating getting up. Vi rushed back to the bedroom and shook his shoulder. "Come on. I swear I'll take your Ferrari and drive myself if you don't get up."

He pulled her to him and kissed her somewhere between her cheek and her eye, clearly still half-asleep. "I can't go anywhere," he murmured.

"Fuck, Art, I need to get to work. Don't be an asshole." He didn't seem to be present enough to even understand what was going on. He was drifting back to sleep even as he spoke. Who could blame him? Vi was tired to the core of her bones.

"Luca is waiting for you in the lobby," he mumbled and swatted his hand, trying to grab her. He ended up squeezing her arm and dusting it with his lips.

Vi sighed and kissed his cheek. A jolt of envy that he could continue sleeping flared inside her with a pang of loss. Geez, she was only going to work. *Pull yourself together, Vi!*

Luca was indeed waiting for her downstairs. "Good morning," she said. She thought he nodded a response, but he walked out without a word. Awkward.

Vi followed him, the stupid shoes echoing on the tiles. A walk of shame at its best. Why didn't Art wake up and drive her? Bastard.

"Sorry you had to get up on my account. I-I couldn't wake up Art," she said as she buckled her seatbelt. They were in a large, black SUV with tinted windows. Luca's chilly disposition increased her nervousness. "How did you even know—"

"Art arranged that late last night. No need to apologize. I'm a morning person. Unlike Art." His eyes remained focused on the road.

Art had called Luca to make sure she'd get to

work. Tears pooled in her eyes. Every time the man pissed her off, he'd make up for it with something that took her breath away.

"Where do you want to go?"

"The patisserie, but would it be okay if we stopped at my place first? I need to get changed. I didn't plan to stay the whole weekend. But I wouldn't be able to work in this dress. Or the shoes. God, the shoes are hot, but useless for work, or walking, or anything really. They're the kind of heels you just put on and hope you'll sit the whole time. You know, like get to and from the car and then I don't know, have dinner. I think I'm going to be late, but I need to change first, regardless." *Stop! Stop talking now!*

"Where do you live?" he asked, unimpressed.

She gave him the address. "It's my friend Carla's place. She is traveling right now, so I-I…" *Shut up!* "I've been house-sitting."

He nodded. They drove in silence. Not the pleasant kind of silence she'd enjoyed with Art. This was an agonizing silence. One that drilled into her brain.

"So… Art says you're not only his bodyguard," Vi said, desperate to break the tension.

"We're friends. He's been there for me when I needed him and my skills are useful to him, so we stuck together," he said, no emotions in his words, simply recounting facts. To repulse her? Stop her from prying further?

"How long have you known each other?" She wasn't going to stop. The silence was a fatal alternative.

"Since we were kids."

"Oh, wow, so you went to school together?" Was she going to find out more things about her private arrogant prick.

"No," he responded and Vi pouted inwardly.

"So you know the Da Bonno family?" Luca's question surprised her.

"I know Charlie and Carla. Why?" This was a weird pivot. How did he even know about them?

They stopped at a red light and Luca turned to face her. "No reason. You must know Phil Taworski too." He glared at her.

She frowned. "I've never heard that name. Who is he?"

"Just someone who works for the Da Bonnos." His eyes narrowed on her before they had to move again.

"Oh, you got it wrong. My Da Bonnos have nothing to do with *the* Da Bonnos. Well, Charlie is Tony's nephew, but he cut ties with them five years ago after he'd met Carla. Why would you think I knew a mobster?"

Was he profiling her? For Art? Or out of a friend's loyalty? She thought his morning animosity related to the early hour. Or he was annoyed to be her driver. But maybe he didn't trust her and was protective of his friend. While it created a difficult air between them, she was kind of glad Art had someone to look after him.

"I see. My bad. I didn't know there were Da Bonnos who could be trusted," he responded.

They pulled into the parking lot by Carla's building and Vi ran out to get changed.

"I know this might sound impulsive, but I care about Art. I want to get to know him better," she said when she returned to the car. She knew it was just words, but as she was getting changed upstairs, an overwhelming need to defend her feelings for Art encompassed her and she decided to be honest with Luca.

"He cares about you too," Luca said.

Vi's heart somersaulted in her chest and a warm feeling spread through her tired body.

*   *   *

"VIOLET HOLLAND SPEAKING," Vi answered the unknown number, annoyed her daydreaming about Art was interrupted. Their first date could officially be declared a failure. At least by the general expectations. Not only had they kissed before dinner, they… oh, well, it was wonderful. It was the best time she'd ever had with a man. Everything they did and felt was premature, but nothing had ever seemed so right.

But now, standing in front of the espresso machine, she hated how desperately she was hoping he'd stop by. She'd already eaten several pastries and kept drinking sweet lattes, though those were partially because she needed energy to survive the day after the marvelous exertion of the weekend.

Anxiety was also leading her to indulgence though. Why did she have to leave so early? They didn't get a chance to say a proper goodbye or make plans. He'd wanted one date with her. That's what he'd said a month ago. What if that was it for him? Had he sent her with Luca so he didn't have to say goodbye?

"Ms. Holland. This is Esther Schrodinger from Distillery Avenue Place," a pleasant voice on the line said. Who? The *Place* sounded familiar. "We received your application for the apartment 7B this weekend and I'm very pleased to inform you it's been approved."

Wait? What?

"Oh," was all Violet uttered.

"Usually we have an in-person interview, but the board was so pleased they approved it immediately. We're looking forward to having you as our neighbor. When can you come in? I can imagine you travel a lot, but ideally we would like to have the condo rented by the first, which is in two weeks. Do you think you could come in this week?"

A man waited to make his order, glaring at Vi impatiently. She smiled and raised her finger to suggest she'd be a minute and rushed to the back room.

"Mrs. Schrodinger, I'm kind of busy at the moment," she started.

"Violet, can I call you Violet?" She didn't wait for the answer. "I understand you're busy. If you think you could move in two weeks, which would be really *preferable*," she said in a tone that limited the options, "I can courier the paperwork to you and we can save each other's time. I mean, of course, I'd like to meet you at some point."

The man up front cleared his throat loudly and the door chimed, announcing new customers.

"That would be lovely. Please send it to me," Vi said, her heart pounding. How the hell did she get this lucky? Why did the woman think she was traveling a lot? Oh, God, what if it was a mistake and her application got mixed up with someone else's? She definitely wanted to get the paperwork mailed. Hopefully, they wouldn't realize their mistake before she moved in.

Esther Schrodinger confirmed the address and hung up.

Vi dashed back to her customers, barely able to concentrate. This was so unusual. But so damn cool. Her homelessness could be resolved before Carla returned. She'd have to find a job to pay the rent. That place was expensive, but so amazing. Shit. She wasn't sure if she was thrilled or terrified. Art was right. She had nothing to lose by applying and lose she didn't. A smile played on her face for the rest of the afternoon.

When the time to close the patisserie finally arrived, Vi could barely stand on her feet. She was exhausted. It wasn't just the lack of sleep, it was the torture of not knowing when—or if, let it not be if—she'd see Art.

Again, she'd fallen into the habit of raising her eyes toward the door every time it chimed. The constant rise and fall of expectation nibbled at her mood, turning her cranky and irritable. The number of calories she'd inhaled hadn't helped. This was not healthy. She needed to retreat and pull herself together. The freight train of Arthur Mathison left her needy.

Vi finished cleaning the coffee machine and turned on the dishwasher. She looked at the street, hoping to see him. *Stupid!* She locked the back door and exited the café through the main entrance, locking it behind her. God, she needed to sleep.

When she turned, her heart thumped for a moment in a chaotic rhythm. A large black SUV was parked across the street, Luca standing on the sidewalk. Was Art in the car? She smiled hesitantly and crossed toward Luca.

"Violet." He nodded.

"Hello. Is Art in the car?" she asked, hating how needy she sounded.

"No. He asked me to drive you back to the yacht club." Luca opened the passenger door.

The club was outside the city. It'd take them another hour at this time of the day to drive there and then she'd need to wake up early in the morning to come back. As much as she wished for a sleepless night with Thor, she needed to sleep and recover. And more importantly, to think. The two activities seemed to have an unfavorable correlation. The lack of sleep equaled the inability to reason. But then, too much thinking prevented the much-needed sleep.

And why the hell would he send Luca? Why didn't he come alone? And what's with the club?

"Luca, I need to stay in the city and get some sleep. I want to see him, but I can't tonight," she said and Luca rolled his eyes.

"He'd come by himself, but he couldn't." Luca interpreted her hesitation—well, not exactly incorrectly.

God, she wanted to see her arrogant prick, but she had to slow this speeding train, find a way to transfer onto a more scenic ride. "I'm going home."

"You need to tell him yourself." Luca raised his eyebrow.

Vi stared at him for a moment, contemplating if she wanted to make the call here in front of him. She was exhausted, the fatigue licking at her like poison.

Luca broke their staring contest first by pulling out

his phone and dialing. "I have Violet here with me." He passed her the phone.

"Hi," she whispered, her stomach fluttering. Luca leaned against the car, clueless to her need for privacy, so she stepped away.

"Get your ass here, babe." Oh, just hearing Art's voice melted the anxious knots she'd knitted with such dedication all day.

"Art, I'm not coming tonight." The words rasped through her throat like broken glass.

"You're mad about yesterday. I scared you." It wasn't a question. He whispered, but the pain and anxiety in his voice screamed across the phone line.

"No. The entire weekend was the best first date ever. It really was. If anything, I worry I disappointed you. You wanted only one date, after all." The lump in her throat swelled. Screw it! She should give up and go to see him.

"I need to see you, Vi." Hurt dominated his voice.

"I'm exhausted and the club is so far. I work tomorrow," she said, regretting her excuses as soon as she voiced them.

"When can I see you?" he asked, unimpressed.

"I have Wednesday and Thursday off."

"Okay, Luca will pick you up tomorrow evening."

"Art, I know you don't much care or understand how these things work, but it'd be nice if you came yourself."

"I can't. I'll wait for you here."

She sighed. She didn't understand, but she didn't expect him to explain further, so she just stood there. Cars passed by, pedestrians moved about their day. Vi's ability to absorb her surroundings shrank to a minimum, all her tired senses focused on the man on the other end of the line.

She missed him so much. They stayed silent, unable to disconnect. She wished she could hug him.

"See you tomorrow, Vi." He hung up.

Seriously, having a conversation with him was like sledding on grass.

The phone beeped with a message and she returned it to Luca. He checked it and smiled. "Give me your phone."

Vi frowned, but she didn't have the energy to question him.

"You've got the same phone as Art?" Luca shook his head, typed something and gave it back to her. "I saved my number there. Apparently I'm your driver now."

* * *

VI WALKED INTO THE APARTMENT, toed off her shoes and found her bed without bothering to undress or shower. Both would help her feel better, but they required insurmountable effort. She fell asleep before she hit the pillow, only to wake up two hours later, shivering.

The short snooze refreshed her enough to get up and take care of a proper bedtime routine. Showered and feeling a thousand times more human, she returned to bed and picked up her phone. She hesitated for a moment and then typed a text.

Vi: Are you sleeping?

She waited for a moment and almost put the phone away when a reply came.

Art: No.

Geez. She smiled. He could type like a machine, yet his texting was worse than his conversation skills.

Vi: What are you doing?

Art: Texting. Why?

She laughed. This short way of speaking had infuriated her at first. Now she found it entertaining. She'd uncovered other layers of the man over the weekend. Or was it all in her head? The idea of him.

Vi: Trying to have a conversation.

His reply came almost immediately.

Art: I'm thinking about you.

That's better. She smiled to herself.

Vi: I miss you.

She hesitated for a moment, but then hit send. There was no point in playing games, hide the feelings.

Art: You should be here.

Vi: I want to, but I have to work.

Her phone rang. "Not into typing much?" She giggled, delighted he called.

"It doesn't come with your voice."

The smile wouldn't leave her face. Just hearing him again relaxed her. "You like my voice?"

"Obviously."

"What else?"

"I'll show you when you're here." Seagulls argued in the background.

"Are you at the yacht club?" Had he kept the room even without her? What if he invited another woman now? David's membership in a gentlemen's club—one she'd never suspected—messed with her head and ballooned her insecurity.

"It's lonely here without you." She could almost picture him rolling his lips.

"Art, do you live there?" It wasn't like she could judge, not really having a place of her own.

"Currently yes." He didn't offer any further explanation. Not that he owed her any, but she wasn't sure if he was evading or simply being his usual man-of-few-words.

"Do you have a yacht there?" She pushed herself higher, leaning against the headboard.

"I can get one if you want." She couldn't be sure, but he sounded serious.

She laughed. "No, don't get one on my account."

They stayed silent for a moment, the distance between them leaving Vi cold.

"I miss you," he said and her temperature leveled up.

"Me too," she said, smiling. "Guess what? The apartment you found? They approved my application. It's all weird and I think there must be some mix-up, but I'm so excited."

"Good." A trace of satisfaction laced his voice.

"Thank you," she whispered.

"For what?" She could hear the door sliding and the seagulls' shrieks disappeared.

"You pushed me to apply and it paid off." These one-sided conversations were harder over the phone, but even the snippets of his voice were enough to light her up.

"I'll see you tomorrow, Vi," he said.

He wanted to end the call. Deflated, she said goodbye and hung up. She wanted an evening to think, so why was she so disappointed? And what did she want to think about? With the apartment hope-fully taken care of, she needed to focus on a job. That's what she'd do. She'd enjoy her time with Art while it lasted. No more overthinking.

13

———

"I DON'T THINK you should show your face in the city. Not until we confirm the Da Bonnos are the only people who know your identity. And not until you find Simone and get this thing sorted out," Luca said as he started the car.

"Duly noted, man," Art responded. He felt like an idiot. He'd acted like one too, but he hadn't seen Vi for two days. And yes, she was coming tonight, but he had to see her. He was going nuts, stuck at the club.

She consumed his every thought and he couldn't look for Simone or deal with the Da Bonnos if his brain was fried by Violet. He needed to sort the mess out, so he could fully focus on her, but it was impossible. Catch twenty-two.

They had been together for three weeks now. Three amazing, torturous weeks. Since he'd had to lie low, he'd rented the room at the club for the two of them indefinitely. It was located outside the city and a regular check of the records would alert him if any Da Bonnos decided to join. It wasn't ideal, but it was a good enough hiding place if he wanted to stay close to Vi.

She teased him about his living situation occasionally, but she hadn't pressed the issue or the fact they were only meeting there and she had to add the commute on her busy workdays. It was the best he could think of for now, mostly because he couldn't think.

Luca liked to mock that he was "high on Vi." And it wasn't untrue—Art spent his days waiting for her to return, unable to concentrate at all or with very inefficient, sub-par results.

Their first weekend had left him unsettled. He'd hoped that spending time with her would diminish his obsession, but the exact opposite had happened. She became his lifeline. It felt like they'd known each other forever.

She'd asked him if he believed in soul mates. Now he did. He didn't need to get to know her better. He trusted her, which was completely illogical. And he didn't understand illogical. He didn't participate in illogical. But that didn't apply to Vi.

She was the variable that suddenly didn't need solving. As long as she was with him, he could live with the unknown for the first time in his life. It was terrifying. Immobilizing. Dangerous. And the best thing that had ever happened to him.

"You have it bad for that girl, dickhead." Luca snorted. "Are you sure she's worth the risk?"

Art nodded, though it wasn't true. He wasn't sure. Nothing was certain when it came to Violet, but the uncertainty was acceptable. Easier to live with than to live without Vi.

"For what it's worth, I don't think she's involved with the Da Bonnos. Or at least not the ones that matter. I've talked to her several times in the car on the way to and from work and I believe her," Luca said.

The traffic on the highway stood still. Art bounced his leg and typed on his thighs with his fingers, pretending it was a keyboard. Coding always calmed him.

"That's good." They didn't have any proof, but he also believed Vi's connection to the mafia family was pure coincidence. He'd even calculated the probability of such coincidence, but the result didn't put his mind at ease, so he ignored it. Ignoring data wasn't smart. But being with Violet was way better than anything else, so fuck the statistical analysis.

"That leaves us with no lead. And even if you find Simone, it won't eliminate Da Bonno's interest in the data. Your best option is to leave and wait for the Bureau to arrest Miller. The data would have no value then," Luca urged, sitting casually with his elbow on the window.

"That could take years," Art said.

"So, what? I don't think the Da Bonnos would chase you outside of their territory. You can simply move."

"I need more time." Art pinched the bridge of his nose, squeezing his eyes tight. He wished Luca wasn't so annoyingly reasonable. Art was new to the unreasonable sphere of life and it would be easier to adapt if he wasn't being constantly reminded of the right choices. The safe choices. The choices that would protect him. He should have never taken the job. But then, he wouldn't have spent time in the patisserie or met Violet.

"More time for what? You've spent a few weeks with her and you're risking your life by sticking around," Luca said.

"What if I gave the data to Da Bonno?" Art asked.

"Now, this is the first time since I've known you that you've said something stupid. Could you ask your brain to get out of your dick?" Luca hit the steering wheel with his palm, shaking his head.

"Do you remember that night in the Dominican when you told me how you felt about Samantha?" Art asked.

Luca's wife had died in a car accident. Art was at a terrible place in his life at the same time and the two of them had nursed their wounds by the pool with a lot of whiskey and pot. Luca had told him that he didn't know how to live after his ability to breathe died with Sam.

"Yeah." Luca exhaled sharply.

"That's how I feel," Art said. Like he could never breathe freely again unless she was around.

"Then let's go back to the island and take her with us."

"I don't think she's ready to leave with me." Art stared out of the window, willing the stupid traffic to move.

"Just tell her everything. Or a version. She'd understand."

"And put her in danger?" Art shook his head.

It's not like he could really tell her the whole truth. Would he ask her to sign an NDA? Honesty would be the best thing for them.

If only *she* were honest with him. She'd told him a lot, but there was more to her current life situation. He was sure she'd tell him in time and he didn't want to pressure her. But time wasn't something he had right now. At least not if he stayed in town. And if she didn't trust him yet completely… could he trust her?

"She knows something is up since you, stupid prick, barged into that café with a gun. So tell her it'd be better to go on vacation," Luca suggested.

"I don't want to scare her. I need more time. She doesn't trust me yet," Art insisted.

"Art, you're not a person who fully opens up to anyone, which is the basis of building trust—"

"We'll wait." Art didn't need to hear this. He wanted to open up to her, but even as the clueless idiot he was when it came to relationships, Art knew it was too early for that level of honesty. The attraction, the connection, the need was strong, but... Even if he felt as if he'd known her forever, their time together was insignificant. Still, so significant. Shit!

"Simply tell her it's a vacation. What woman doesn't want to go to the beach?" Luca tried again.

The Violet kind of a woman who, despite having some sort of life crisis, gets up every morning to help in her friend's café. A loyal, dedicated, and perhaps a bit foolishly responsible Violet. "We'll wait," Art repeated.

"Let's hope you survive it." Luca sighed and Art agreed. Not so much because of the threat his latest job had spawned, but because of the woman who now consumed his thoughts and feelings.

They arrived at the café and Luca gave him a stern glare. "I'll keep an eye on the street. Keep your phone in your hands, and I'll send the vibrate signal if something is off. Call me before you leave. I might pick you up at the back."

Many years ago, Art had designed an emergency app. By pressing an icon, the partnered phone would vibrate. An efficient way to alert of any trouble without wasting time dialing, calling or explaining.

"Thanks, man." Art squeezed Luca's shoulder. His

friend was right, they should leave. Art hoped the squeeze delivered his appreciation better than his words would. Luca nodded.

Art rushed across the street and stopped in front of the window. The patisserie was full of white-collar walk-ins getting their mid-morning caffeine fix. At first, he couldn't even spot her through three suits who blocked the space around the counter. Lucky bastards.

Then he spied her hair. Tied in that messy bun on top of her head, it jumped around as she danced behind the bar. She moved in some choreography only known to her, efficiently serving her customers and freely bestowing her astonishing smile.

Even watching her work did things to his cock. And to his chest, strangely. Because, to his shock, he realized he could go without fucking her, but he couldn't survive without seeing her, hearing her laugh or voice. He was lost and unable to code his way out of this problem.

She served a cup of coffee to an elderly gentleman and laughed at something and Art wished he was the recipient of her attention. The crowd cleared out and Vi started cleaning the tables. As if she could sense his eyes on her, she looked up and he wanted to taste the caramel in her eyes. She widened her gaze at first, but when he smiled, her face lit up and Art's chest constricted, his heart hammering against his ribcage.

He entered and she dropped the washcloth, wrapping her hands around his neck and kissing him gently. *Home.*

"Someone couldn't wait till tonight?" Her eyes glimmered with joy.

"I came for coffee."

Vi giggled and swatted at his arm. He stole another kiss before she stepped back and glanced around the room surreptitiously.

Some of the regulars occupied a few tables. Art recognized them from his two-week work engagement here. He took a seat with the best view of the counter.

"Not sitting in your usual spot?" Her smile alone improved the quality of his life.

"Better view from here."

She lowered her lashes and blushed. How was he going to sit here without touching her?

She seemed to have the same predicament. Vi leaned down and kissed his cheek. That didn't solve the problem, but it made it better.

"What can I get you?"

He let his gaze glide from her face to her toes and back, savoring and aching for his fingers to follow his eyes. "The sweetest thing available, please."

Vi bit her lip and sauntered away. She retrieved a slice of cake from the glass case and carried it over, not breaking eye contact. Coming here was self-inflicted torture, but he didn't want to be anywhere else.

"Caramel swirl cheesecake. My favorite." She put it in front of him.

He crooked his finger, beckoning her closer, and she leaned in. He could happily live off her closeness, scent and warmth.

"The sweetest thing available here is your pussy, babe," he whispered and her breath hitched.

"Arthur Mathison, you're a dirty man." Her hushed words spread heat down his spine. Just the tickle of her breath created a domino reaction in his body, finishing between his legs. His cock twitched against his pants.

"I'm a lucky girl," she cooed and he had to grab the edge of the table to stop himself from bending her over right there.

He groaned and jerked backward. Distance. "So this is the artist." He gestured toward the wall displaying the paintings. Any topic would do to remain decent and keep his hands off her. The art was actually good. A bit raw, the strokes lacking confidence, but it held promise.

Vi sat down across from him. He'd timed his visit to enjoy her during the quieter hours.

"Yes." She beamed with pride. Talking about art lit her up more than any other obligation she'd buried herself under. "I wish I could help him break out."

"You can." He believed it. Her phone buzzed in her apron and she pulled it out. With one glance, she got paler and refused the call. She smiled at him and dropped the phone to the table.

"You really think I can?"

He nodded, taking her hand and kissing the back of it. Her quiver vibrated through him and he wanted to urge her to close the place immediately.

The door announced a new customer and Vi stood up, her hand still in his. When she looked over, she clenched her fingers. Her whole body tensed as she stepped back. Art stood up, not really knowing why, but sensing she needed support. She dropped his hand and it felt like a slap.

What the hell was going on?

The man who'd just entered met her eyes. His haughty chin and immaculate three-piece suit screamed money, manners and entitlement. Who was the pompous dick?

"Violet, we need to talk," the man demanded.

"David, this is not a good time or place." Her voice trembled.

"Believe me, sweetheart, I find it distasteful we even need to have this conversation. Or that I had to come to this place..."— He looked around with disgust. "But you haven't behaved very maturely lately. Where are you even staying? This nonsense must stop now. We have a wedding to plan."

Sweetheart? Wedding? What the actual fuck? Art looked at Vi whose eyes glistened with tears. She shook her head slightly, trying to communicate something to him, but he couldn't interpret any of it.

Anger blinded him.

She walked behind the counter and opened a drawer, then closed it with her hip and returned to hand something to the man. David? Her fucking fiancé! Art followed the movement, and a shiny glint caught his eyes. A ring. Fucking engagement ring! Ire replaced the marrow in his bones.

"Violet, enough is enough. I gave you time and space so you could pull yourself together. Your commitment lies with me," David said. "You accepted my proposal and you're going to follow through. I'm sick of this absurdity. You have an appointment to try your wedding dress tomorrow."

"Fuck off, asshole. Now," Art growled.

David widened his eyes and Art stepped forward. The threat worked, pushing David to retreat to the door. "Violet?"

"David, go, please," she said through tears, her face burning red.

David shook his head, looked at the ring in his palm and raised his gaze to Vi. Art could sense her trembling next to him. David put the ring into his pocket and left, taking with him the feeble trust she and Art had built in the last few weeks.

Art couldn't even breathe. His blood boiled. "You're fucking engaged?" He shook his head, grabbed his phone and stormed out.

14

HE COULDN'T FUCKING STAND the bullshit. This was the grand secret she kept from him? Now he regretted ever wanting to know what she was hiding.

"Let's go," he barked at Luca, sliding into the seat and buckling up.

"What the fuck, man? I told you to call me before you leave. You really don't give a shit about your security, do you, asshole?" Luca started the car and merged into traffic.

"Just drive." Art closed his eyes. The engagement ring. Sweetheart Violet. The wedding dress. *I gave you space and time.* She'd never broken off the engagement. She was figuring things out. Tasting the buffet before she settled down.

"What happened?" Luca asked after a while.

Art couldn't answer. He didn't want to say the words.

Just because he was an idiot, he didn't need to voice it out loud. He'd almost punched the dickhead fiancé in the face. He would have killed him. He would have.

"Do you want to go box? We can spar at the club's gym?" Luca always knew what Art needed.

The tears threatening her face. The tension in her body. The paleness of her face. Fuck, maybe he should have stayed.

He needed to release this anger before he did something stupid. After the gym, he'd call her and sort things out. Fuck. Was she okay? That first day he'd seen her, she'd cried. Was David the reason?

Damn it! He needed to talk to her. He grabbed his phone and swiped. Nothing happened. *Fuck! Fuck! Fuck!*

"Turn around," he yelled.

"What's wrong with you? I can't turn here. The exit to the club is only a few miles away. What the fuck is going on?" Luca hit the gas and the car sped up.

"I grabbed Vi's phone. My phone is back there. Unprotected." Art raked his fingers through his hair. "Fuck!" He punched the dashboard.

"Call her," Luca said and steered to another lane, whizzing past law-abiding cars.

"It would be easier to hack my phone while in use."

"Your phone is un-hackable," Luca countered,

zipping through the lanes accompanied by outraged honking.

"When it's on me. My firewall alerts me anytime someone is trying, but I'm not by my phone now. If someone is looking like they have been over the past few weeks, they'll find it soon enough."

"Your laptop is behind you, asshole, don't just sit here," Luca snapped and took the ramp to exit the highway.

Art leaned over and pulled his laptop from the backseat. He booted it up and checked the activity on his phone. "Someone's in. Fuck!" He opened another window and a map. It took only a minute while Luca cursed at the red light and Art grabbed Luca's phone and dialed a number. "Please pick up."

* * *

VI PACED AROUND the small space behind the bar. She checked the phone several times, but Art hadn't tried to call her. She couldn't get into his phone. Why had he run away? Why had David shown up?

"Excuse me." A customer approached the counter. Not now! She couldn't deal with work. *Damn it, Art, why couldn't you wait and let me explain?*

She gave the woman a weak smile. "What can I get you?"

"I have someone on the phone for you." The

woman looked as if she'd just found evidence that Earth was flat. Vi grabbed the phone from her hands.

"Hello." *Please be Art.*

"Vi." There was relief in Art's voice.

"Art, why did you leave? You took my phone. I don't know your passcode. I need to explain. It's not what it looks like," she blabbered. "I know I should have told you—"

"Vi, shut up," Art snapped, stealing words and breath away from her. "Close the shop and get out of there now."

"What? What are you talking about?"

Two men in suits entered the café, scanning the premises. One of them stepped behind the counter, invading Vi's space. He shuffled around her, inspecting everything.

"You can't be here," she said.

One suit pulled out a gun and stepped into the back room.

"What are you doing?" she protested weakly, the words lodging in her throat. The sight of the gun brought on the memories of the robbery, invading her mind and releasing the anxiety she'd stored away in the days after the mugging.

The suit came back and shook his head. "There's a back door." The other suit joined him and they exited to the street behind the café.

Heart pounding in her temples, Vi remembered

she was holding the phone and whispered, "Art, what's going on? Two men—"

"Are you okay?" If she was concerned before, his urgency caused her to panic.

"Yes. No. I don't know." Her heart still pounded in her temples.

"Can I have my phone back? We should call the police," the woman said, packing her laptop.

Vi rushed to the back and locked the door.

"Vi, are you hurt?" Art yelled into the phone.

"No. I locked the back door," she said, gasping.

"Good girl. Now leave. Destroy my phone. Break it with a hammer and nuke it in the microwave. Leave." The panic in Art's voice froze her to the spot. If he was panicking, things were bad.

"Why?" she asked irrationally.

"Vi, it's Luca here. Listen carefully," he said as if he was a teacher explaining something to a small child. Somewhat condescending, but calming at the same time. "Get out of there. Get rid of the phone. There is a Salvation Army store half a block from you. You know it?"

"Yes." She wasn't sure if she said it out loud. Her eyes darted between the street, the back door and the woman who kept her hand in Vi's face, demanding her phone.

"Good, get to the store and wait for me. Okay?"

"I think so."

"Ten minutes and we'll be there. Stay in public." Luca hung up.

As soon as Vi lowered her hand, the woman snatched her phone away and marched out. Vi took Art's phone, grabbed her purse and took a breath to ask everyone to leave, but the place was empty. All the patrons had left already.

She stepped out and looked both ways before locking up. No guys in suits. She paced down the street and then she remembered Art told her to destroy his phone. Should she go back?

She threw the cell to the ground, stomping on it. Nothing. "For God's sake." She looked around but didn't see any rocks. *Damn it!* She stomped on the screen again, inflicting a tiny crack. *Seriously?* She scanned the street desperately and dashed into a boutique a couple of doors from Sweet Temptations.

"I'm sorry, do you have a microwave?" Sweat trickled down her spine. She checked over her shoulder to make sure no one had followed her into the store.

A woman with fake eyelashes and an even faker smile raised her eyebrows. She assessed Vi from head to toe. "You work at the bakery," she said.

This was not a fucking social call.

"Do you have a microwave?"

The woman shrugged and walked to the back. Vi blinked a few times, but then decided to follow. With one hand on her hip, the woman pointed to the corner in the small room. Vi beelined for the appliance and yanked its doors open. She threw in the phone and set it for three minutes.

She didn't bother waiting and dashed to the door.

"Thank you," she called.

"Wait, isn't that dangerous?"

Vi didn't care. The door closed behind her, swallowing the woman's protests.

Her eyes darted around. Every man in a suit jump-started her heart, pushing her toward cardiac arrest. The half-a-block distance stretched into infinity. Had the ten minutes passed? Was Art waiting for her?

Finally, she reached the shop. She didn't run, but she was out of breath by the time she made it inside. The musty smell attacked her nostrils. She walked through the aisles, brushing her shaky fingers across the garments on the long racks.

Her pulse thumped in her head and her legs trembled. All her essential body functions were stressed out to the point of collapse.

She was going to faint.

Or suffocate.

Air wouldn't fill her lungs.

Vi focused on the inhale and was pretty sure she breathed in, but the air didn't reach her. She doubled over, panting, her hands on her thighs. The oxygen didn't make it past her mouth or nostrils. She needed to inhale. How?

"Let's go," someone said right next to her, and she yelped.

Two muscular arms pulled her up and she was crushed against a wall of a man. Her animal brain didn't recognize his scent or voice, and she felt paralyzed in fear as he walked her out of the store.

She wanted to stop, to see who was making her leave, but she couldn't clear her vision. Everything was blurry. She should scream and she was sure she was screaming, but she couldn't hear herself, so perhaps she wasn't.

Just like breathing, screaming didn't seem possible. She stumbled and almost fell, but the arms kept her upright as they left the store.

Where were they taking her?

15

Luca finally emerged with Vi and Art jumped out of the car. He opened the back door and helped her in, joining her immediately. He'd barely closed the door when Luca was pulling onto the road.

Violet didn't seem to know or understand where she was. She was shaking uncontrollably, panting for air. Fuck! He had done this to her.

"Vi, babe, it's okay. You're okay," he whispered, pushing the hair away from her face. He cupped her face, trying to catch her eyes.

"Art." She sobbed and buried her face in his chest. *Home.*

"Shh, babe, I've got you now. You're safe," he whispered and stroked her head, trying not to squeeze her too much while unable to loosen his grip at the same time. She wrapped her arms around his waist and sobbed.

"I don't think they're after us, but I'm going to drive around for a while to be sure we don't have company," Luca said and checked the rearview mirror.

Art nodded.

Vi shivered in his arms and he wanted to kill the fuckers who'd scared her. But then, he didn't think he'd leave her ever again to execute such a threat. There wasn't much he could do right now, so he settled for running his hand over her head, her silky hair under his palms calming him down, providing him with as much comfort as he was trying to offer. As her breathing calmed, her sobs transformed into hitched breaths, eventually slowing down until sleep claimed her.

"How did you know someone would hack your phone?" Luca asked.

"Someone has been trying for a while." Art pinched the bridge of his nose and closed his eyes.

"Didn't think to mention it?" Luca stopped at the red light and turned to face him. "It's her, isn't it?"

"It must be." Art closed his eyes, blocking the outside world. Right now, Vi was his only priority. But the shit that had brought them to this point required attention.

Art inhaled. "My usual firewalls got cracked the night the punks pursued me, and then again when that fucker Taworski found us. I was too distracted to notice. Stupid." He shook his head and coiled a strand of Vi's hair around his finger. She fidgeted and made an adorable sound, nestling against him.

They drove through a residential area, obeying the speed limit. Kids shot basketball in a driveway. A man carried groceries from his car. A woman played fetch with a Labrador. So normal.

Never before had he considered normal. Not like this, but suddenly, with Vi in his arms, he wished this was them.

"Okay, but you've noticed, and we haven't had company since," Luca said.

"I've installed an additional layer of protection on my phone and computer. The attacks didn't cease, but I was able to interrupt them."

He leaned back, suddenly as exhausted as the woman who'd suffered a panic attack because of him. He kept stroking her hair, unable to stop.

"But how did they know it was unattended?" Luca asked.

"They didn't. The code attacking my phone was trying constantly, it was automated. It was smart tracking, learning and improving, but I blocked it every time anyway. Leaving the phone unattended helped them discover the location."

"Okay, so who came to search for you?"

"My theory? Someone created a code to penetrate my cyber security and sold it to Da Bonno along with the information about Miller's data," Art said.

"Not someone. Simone did. But why the Da Bonnos?"

"Perhaps her code depends on the proximity. Come to think of it, I didn't have the problem on the island. It only started again when we returned."

"So the Da Bonnos were the most probable buyer for her *Art trap app*. I've been replaying things in my head and you know what I realized? Taworski asked you if you're the Viking."

"As if confirming it?"

"Exactly. He didn't know what you look like or your real name," Luca said. "She might not have doxed you. She might have just given them the ability to track the Viking."

"So now, Taworski and God knows who else knows about me, and if they're not stupid, they'll connect Violet to me." Art exhaled.

"Maybe yes, maybe no. Why didn't you completely block the tracking app or whatever it is they're using?"

"I haven't had enough time or the ability to focus," Art admitted and planted a kiss into Vi's hair. She smelled like caramel and coffee.

"Fair enough. Maybe you need to work more and fuck less." Luca smirked.

"Asshole. Where are we, anyway?"

"I don't know, but I think it's safe to return to the club," Luca said.

* * *

"Vi, babe, we're here." The soft familiar voice invaded the darkness.

Vi opened her eyes and squinted, surprised it was still bright outside. Her heart fibrillated before she focused on the blue eyes. The sight immediately calmed her.

"Hi," she rasped, her throat dry. The car wasn't moving anymore. "Where are we?"

"At the club." Art kissed her gently on her forehead. She cuddled closer to him.

"I'm hungry," she said and he chuckled.

"Let's feed you then." He opened the door and got out, pulling her behind him. "Are you all right?" The concern in his eyes was palpable.

"I'm sorry I didn't tell you about David." It wasn't their only problem right now, but all the other problems could be tackled as long as he was by her side.

He pulled her closer and held her tight. "Are you still engaged, though?"

She groaned against his beautiful chest. "No. I'm not. I've been trying to break it off for more than a month."

"Okay." He slid his fingers through hers and they walked to the club, straight to the patio. Luca joined them and they ordered dinner.

They sat in silence. The seagulls shrieked, other guests talked, laughter echoed.

All of it drove Vi crazy. Why was everyone acting normal?

Their drinks arrived and she downed her vodka-soda in one gulp. "Who were those men?"

Art rubbed the spot between his eyes and Luca turned his phone to her. On the screen was a photo of a man in a dark suit.

"That's one of them," she confirmed. The silence at the table sent her heart racing again.

Art grabbed her hand and held it as if worried she would run away. Would she? What was going on?

"That's Phil Taworski. He works for Tony Da Bonno," Luca said and she snapped her gaze to him.

A million questions roamed around her head, but she couldn't catch any that made sense, so she settled for, "Why?"

Art puffed out his cheeks with a sigh. "I did a data mining job recently, and it seems the Da Bonnos are interested in getting their hands on the data." Art pulled his chair closer to her.

"Why don't you go to the police?" she asked and she was sure that Luca snickered.

"I did," Art said.

The fright from earlier must have clouded her mind because she wasn't understanding. The unanswered questions broke free. "Why did they come to the café? Did they just miss you? Are they following you? Are we safe here?"

The oxygen was evading her again. Art stood up

and pulled her to him, wrapping his arms around her, holding her tight. A good thing because her legs stopped working.

"We're safe here," he said and she inhaled finally. "Nothing will happen to you."

"Okay." Her voice wasn't steady. The waitress brought another round of drinks and Vi untangled from Art's embrace to take a generous sip. She slumped back in her chair. Art sat too, observing her with a look that suggested he expected her eminent collapse… or perhaps that she would cause a scene.

"To answer your questions, or some of them…" Luca looked at Art who nodded, giving his permission.

Art held her hand and continued watching her like a hawk, his eyes worried.

"They are following him. Not him, rather his phone. When he had it on him, he could easily rebut the attempts to locate him, but today he left his phone behind, so they hacked it and went looking for him. The police won't help us."

Vi swallowed hard. "So what's the plan?"

"I think…" Luca started, but an almost invisible shake of Art's head stopped him.

"What were you going to say?" She frowned.

Art's Adam's apple moved up and down a few times and then he answered with a sigh. "Luca believes I should leave town. Get away from the Da Bonnos forever."

"Oh." All the previous anxiety culminated into this moment. "Wouldn't they find you anywhere?"

"I don't think they could find me anymore with my phone destroyed," Art said. "Also, they're local mobsters. I doubt they would cause trouble elsewhere."

"Can't you simply give them what they want?" Strange numbness claimed her limbs and mind. She wanted to sleep, to be held by Art and then wake up into a new day where none of this existed.

"No."

"Why?" Seriously, now wasn't the time for his short answers.

"It's not that easy, Vi." Frustration laced his voice.

"Explain," she snapped.

"The less you know, the better," he retorted and she crossed her arms over her chest.

"Bullshit. It's a bit too late for that, don't you think?" She tapped her foot, the adrenaline shooting through her.

"Babe, I'm only trying to protect you." He sighed and reached for her, but she pushed her chair away, turning her head toward the lake.

Tears threatened to escape and she didn't want to show weakness again. What did it all mean? If he was going to leave, would he ask her to come with him? She couldn't suggest that; it was too early to broach such a significant commitment. And what if they didn't work out? She couldn't simply abandon everything for him like she had for David. But then, she didn't really have anything to give up right now.

The waitress brought their meals and they ate in silence. Luca tried to engage them in a casual conversation about the weather and the yachts, but Art just growled his answers and even Vi fell into one syllable responses. She polished off her food and ordered a caramel cheesecake, the two men staring at her as if she'd grown horns.

"What? I eat my stress," she snapped and dug into her dessert.

Art and Luca lowered their sunglasses and watched the sun rolling above the horizon of the lake. Art peeked at her occasionally, as if assessing the level of her insanity.

Today's events sat heavily in her stomach, wearing her out. David showing up, Art leaving abruptly and then the suits and her own escape from—from what exactly? Emotional exhaustion blanketed her tired limbs.

Her eyes sought Art's. The shadows of remorse painted his face and darkened his ice-blue eyes. He clenched his jaw so visibly that she worried he would crack a tooth. There was too much shit going on around them, outside their control. It was obvious they were unable to gift each other with complete honesty, regardless of the reasons for it. Sadness joined the clusterfuck of emotions draining her of energy.

But there was one place they were honest.

Vi pushed her chair back and Art jumped up, his eyes haunted. "Let's go upstairs," she said. "Good night, Luca."

Art followed her. They remained quiet in the elevator, but for the first time the silence was thick with anguish. Art tapped his fingers on his thighs and she smiled inwardly. He did that when he was overwhelmed or stressed. Her poor man, hiding so many things.

"A moment is a medieval unit of time. The movement of a shadow on a sundial covered forty moments in a solar hour. The length of a moment in modern seconds was not fixed, but on average, a moment corresponded to ninety seconds," he recited from the vast reservoir of random facts his brain housed.

Vi smiled and slipped her fingers through his and he let out a long breath, holding her hand as if his life depended on it.

They entered the room that had become their home in the last three weeks and Vi jumped at him, wrapping her arms and legs around his solid body.

He stumbled but quickly found his balance as her lips captured his. She attacked him with all the frustration and fear of the day behind them. Art squeezed her ass and twirled them. Her back hit the wall, supporting her and freeing one of his hands. He pulled her hair, turning her head so he could get better access, licking and biting her jaw and neck. Responding with equal urgency.

"Art," she whimpered. She needed to find honesty between them without the words. For now, it was all they had.

His eyes, full of desperation and ache, met hers. She cupped his face and smiled at him, letting him know it was going to be okay. The electricity zapped both of them, and they shivered together with the need for release. With the painful need for connection.

"Make me feel better," she whispered.

Heat passed through his eyes, but he froze, panting. He dropped his forehead to hers and remained still. They held each other with agonizing affection for long minutes. The intimacy of the moment was almost too much. The last straw in the emotionally draining day and the only way to recover at the same time.

Pinned to the wall, she quivered against his body. Or maybe he was shaking. She wasn't sure, only knew that they had found synchronicity.

Art kissed her gently and walked them to the bathroom. He turned the shower on and pulled her shirt over her head, then kneeled and removed her jeans and panties in one swift move.

His large hands slowly traced up her legs, leaving a trail of quiver in its wake. He blew a warm breath onto her sex and something between a sigh, a sob and a cry shook her lungs. He tugged his shirt off and unzipped his jeans. His crown beaded with pre-ejaculate already.

Unable to move, Vi trembled, a combination of anticipation and the ordeal of the past hours. His mouth brushed her collarbone while he unhooked her bra, but he didn't take it off immediately like he usually did. He was obsessed with her breasts, but today, he stayed still, just inhaling her skin. She felt protected, leaning against his solid muscles.

The running water warmed up the air, the steam misting their skin. He held her and didn't move, giving her a chance to find peace. She craved him, desperate for release, but at the same time she was grateful for the painfully slow tempo he favored this time.

Vi didn't know this was what she needed, yet he led them through the experience at the right pace, with the perfect care. Art dominated in the bedroom, but always with the exact level of tenderness—or roughness—she craved. And she wanted nothing else anymore but to let him carry them both to the dimension where the outside world no longer mattered.

He stroked her hair and stepped away, her bra falling to her feet. He dropped his pants and boxers and took her hand, guiding her to the shower. It was a walk-in with two glass walls, but they clung to each other, barely using the generous space.

They kissed, lost in the intimacy under the warm

water, almost unwilling to pull away for a breath. Art toyed with her nipple and she moaned against his mouth. With no warning, he picked her up and pushed her against the tiled wall. She brushed his shoulders with her hands, marveling at their masculinity. Like a Greek statue. Perfection. He aligned his crown at her center and impaled her in one thrust.

She yelped. He was too big for her. He lowered his head to her shoulder and waited, allowing her to adjust, to let him in.

She circled her hips and Art pulled out slowly and plunged back in again, filling her to the hilt. They both gasped and he started moving in and out leisurely, nuzzling her nipples.

"Art," she moaned. "I think Luca is right."

He froze and looked at her, never breaking the connection.

"I think you need to leave," she whispered.

16

"Not without you," he rasped and Vi lost her mind, claiming his lips, sucking and biting. The relief of his words sparked an onslaught of desire she couldn't control anymore.

Art smiled against her lips and responded, riding her hard and fast, bringing them both to a shuddering climax. They went over the edge with an intensity that brought tears to Vi's eyes. She'd never felt this close to him. To anyone. She'd been broken by the events of the day, but here and now with this man of few words and many actions, she was complete.

Vi opened the door and gave him that smile that pumped the blood into his heart at double speed. She fisted his T-shirt and pulled him in, raising on her toes and kissing him. *Home.*

She looked positively delicious, wearing a pair of denim shorts and a black tank top. He wished he could taste more of her, but for now he settled for her lips.

She'd come to her friend's apartment earlier to pack. He was going nuts at the club and decided he would come and help her with the move. Luca stayed downstairs, allowing them privacy.

"You should have stayed at the club. It's not safe for you to be out and about." Vi wrapped her arms around his waist tightly. *Home.*

The lingering danger, or the perception of it, created an additional layer of intimacy between them. As if there was an expiration date on their time together and every moment could have been the last one. Art had never lived in fear—with caution, but not in fear—and now he kind of enjoyed the urgency in her touch, kiss and her presence overall.

"I wanted to help." He leaned into the kiss. His cock twitched against his jeans and he hissed, pulling away while he still could. This was someone else's house, after all.

"Is this all?" Art asked, pointing to the two suitcases alongside the wall. Had she left everything with that pompous prick?

Instead of answering, Vi walked away. He

followed her through a short hallway into the open living space with the kitchen to the left.

"Are all your things still with him?" he asked, leaning with his back against the kitchen island.

"Do you want a cup of tea?" She put the kettle on and didn't look at him.

"I want you." He pulled her between his legs, her wonderful tits bouncing against his torso, his cock pressing against her stomach.

She giggled, her hands roaming around his shoulders and biceps. *Home.* She was his safe haven, his comfort zone beyond all the comfort. His home.

"You're insatiable, *Thor*! Is that *hammer* of yours ever relaxed?"

"Rarely." He smirked.

Shaking her head, she returned to the kettle and made them both a cup of tea. "Okay, big boy, here is your tea," she said, pushing one cup across the counter. "Go sit over there because I want to tell you everything and I don't think I'd get through it if you're too close."

Reluctantly, he walked around and climbed onto the breakfast stool.

"I met David three years ago at a fundraiser. He dazzled me. He was… I don't know… sophisticated, cultured and handsome. I fell in love."

Art squeezed the hot cup, burning his hands, but it was nothing compared to the scorching of her words.

"Or I thought I did. Now I know I fell in love with the lifestyle he offered. We got engaged and that's when things started sinking in for me. Perhaps even before, but I ignored my intuition, feeling guilty for even thinking I wanted more from life. I mean, for fuck's sake, I had it all. He'd provided all I needed and beyond. So I stuck around. But I couldn't fool myself into appreciating things when there was no joy. We fell into a routine. Work, fundraisers, obligations with his family.

"Somewhere down the road, I gave up everything because none of my world fit into his. The breaking point came when he demanded I give up my café because his future wife should take care of his household as her primary focus. And so I sold my business, which was the last straw, I guess. I didn't find joy in my new life as David's fiancée. Because that was all I became. His fiancée. So, to answer your question, yes, all my things are still with him, but they were never mine. I didn't want to take them." She sighed and took a sip of her tea.

The regret and shame in her eyes weighed heavily on his chest. "Can I come closer now?"

She nodded. He walked over and took her in his arms. "I grew up in a trailer park and I lived in my car for six months before I turned eighteen."

Vi sighed into his chest, sending shivers down his spine.

"I have money now. A lot, so I know how tempting and dangerous abundance can be."

"Thank you," she whispered. He lifted her chin, frowning. *Thank you?* "Thank you for telling me, Art. And for listening, and hopefully not judging. And for responding with what I think were three full sentences."

He shrugged. "Now I know you're with me because I'm rich."

"Totally." She giggled.

He laughed, scooped her up and dropped her on the counter while exploring her mouth. Vi's confession, however, left him uneasy. She'd shared with him, exposed her skeletons, and made his secrets more significant because he still kept them.

"It's good I've got a present for you in the car," he said.

"Art, I don't need gifts. In fact, if my past is any indication, I don't want them. Clearly, they can fog my mind and heart." Red stained her cheeks.

"Don't compare me to him." He was annoyed.

"You're nothing like David. I was slowly dying with him and you, my sexy Thor, make me feel alive." She raked her fingers through his hair. "With David, life was planned and predictable. Nothing I need to fear with you."

"So I *can* get you gifts?" Shit, he'd already bought her several today.

She sighed. "As long as you give me more of yourself. I don't want things. I want you, Art." His mind misfired and he seized her lips again. *Home.*

"We better get going." She breathed against his mouth but didn't push him away. They made out for a moment longer because he couldn't get enough. There was never enough of her. He missed her when she was away and he craved her when she was around.

Violet Holland intoxicated him, filled his bloodstream with desire. If someone had told him two months ago that a woman would cloud his mind, he would have laughed.

"Let's go, babe," he said. There was a lot of house warming to be done at her new place, anyway. He'd fantasized about a few surfaces with Vi on them already.

She pushed off the counter. "The suitcases are by the door already and I have a box in my bedroom."

"On it," he said and strolled toward her room. He entered, picked up the box and walked outside. Their eyes locked and he realized his mistake. *Fuck!*

Even with the entire room between them, she stepped back, her eyes wide. "How do you know that's my room?"

17

He closed his eyes and exhaled heavily. "Vi…"

This was fucked up. She was clearly freaked out and he realized he couldn't lie to her. He didn't want to. He could keep things from her, but lie straight to her face? Impossible.

"How, Art? You've never been here before." Tears pooled around her eyes.

He took two steps, but she raised her arms, stopping him. She was so far away and only getting further. And once he told her, she would be unreachable, the gap between them devastating.

"Hot water freezes faster than cold water." His heart pounded, and his brain felt like a whirlpool swirling around, drowning him. Automatically, he reached for the one thing that always anchored him. Data. "The average drunk driver drives under the influence over eighty times before being arrested for the first time. A chef's hat has exactly—"

"Cut the shit, Art. Tell me!" Her voice echoed around the room, tightening his throat, his stomach, his heart.

"I hacked into the security here."

"When? Why? How?" She fought the tears. "And don't you dare give me one-word answers."

* * *

VIOLET DIDN'T WANT to cry, but his words punched her hard.

Art swallowed several times. She could almost hear his molars grind.

"Before our first date when you asked me to wait one month." His eyes filled with remorse and a plea. "I needed to see you, to know you were okay."

"So you stalked me? How did you even know where I lived?" This was so screwed up. A tiny voice in her mind whispered the romantic portrait of his betrayal, but the sense of violation was louder.

He pinched the bridge of his nose and sighed. "I hacked your phone and CCTV cameras around the patisserie."

She covered her mouth with her palm, but a gasp escaped. He'd watched her! The whole time, he'd watched her! She walked to the sofa and sank into it because standing suddenly consumed too much energy.

"Babe, I couldn't stop thinking about you and I know I shouldn't have…" He bit his lip.

"That's right. You got that right, Art. You shouldn't have." She stood up. "Get out." She couldn't even look at him. How dare he?

"Vi—"

"Just get the fuck out of here, Art. I need to… I can't." The hurt was raw and bitter. The betrayal crawled under her skin, sucking out all the good and joy this man had brought to her life. "Please go." She sat back down, closed her eyes and put her face into her palms.

She'd been happy only minutes ago. How could things change so much so quickly? She trusted him. She actually stupidly trusted him.

He hovered for a moment longer, overpowering her senses. Hell, she was already missing him. Yet his presence currently cut through her like a knife.

"Go!"

Finally, she heard the click of the door and let a sob out. Her energy drained, she dropped sideways and let herself cry into the pillow on the sofa.

Shivers of cold jerked her body. Her joints and muscles hurt. She must have cried herself to sleep. Vi sat up and shook like a wet dog. She wasn't sure how long she'd slept, but it certainly didn't make her feel better. No clarity or understanding presented themselves.

A man she was falling for was a voyeur with a complete disregard for her privacy.

Though his eyes, when he'd confessed, told a different story. His remorse squeezed her heart, making her feel his wounds as her own. He knew his actions were not acceptable, which was a step up from the one-espresso socially clueless man. She believed his intentions were… well, not exactly innocent, but they weren't malicious.

What a mess.

Violated.

Robbed of her privacy.

Exposed.

Her heart hurt and a heavy, lead ball rolled around her stomach. She missed him so much already.

Maybe it was for the best. Now he could leave and protect himself from the Da Bonno people.

Would he go somewhere else now? He'd said last night he wouldn't leave without her, but maybe he'd change his mind now that she'd sent him away.

Weeks ago, Vi wanted to start afresh without being entangled with someone else. Now she had her chance, but it made her sick. Why? Why? Why had he done that? Why couldn't she simply laugh it off?

She called a taxi, collected her things and made

her way downstairs. She stopped in front of the building and froze. The very familiar large SUV parked at the curb challenged her determination.

Art opened the door and stepped out.

She closed the distance between them in a few shaky strides and placed the box on the ground. "I asked you to leave."

"I couldn't." His voice inflicted pain and infuriated her at the same time. She didn't want to feel sorry for him.

"Did you watch me naked? Sleeping?" The accusations flew free from some deep corner of her brain she'd been avoiding. "I feel so fucking exposed."

A couple walking their dog stopped, staring before they rushed along.

He stood there. Not agreeing, but not protesting either, which just about broke her heart. Suddenly, she realized she wasn't only angry, disappointed and sad. A fear stubbornly reigned the messed-up emotions, coiling around her bones. A fear they wouldn't be able to fix this. A fear she was losing him.

"I fucked up," he said finally, his ice-blue eyes riddled with misery so honest she wanted to hug him. "I'm sorry."

"Have you read my emails? Listened to my conversations? Did you jack off staring at me?" She spat the words, causing pain, both of them suffering.

"I didn't read or listen. I didn't even Google you

or run a background check. I'd have known you were engaged if I breached your privacy that way," he said, clenching his fists.

She glared. A big part of her wanted to forgive him, but she would lose a part of herself. And she didn't want to go there. Not again.

"I was monitoring your location and every day I confirmed that you got home safe. I've been jerking off to a fantasy of you since the day I first saw you. And I never watched you sleep on camera. I've stopped checking the footage since we've gotten together. I watch where you are, a red dot on a map, because it makes me feel better. I can't breathe without you, Vi."

He exhaled heavily, looking exhausted from the sheer number of words he'd spoken at one time. And their meaning probably.

Her taxi arrived. This was the most honest and seriously messed up declaration of affection she'd ever imagined, but Vi needed some distance.

"My taxi is here. I need to think about it all. Give me your new number. I'll call you," she said and picked up her box.

Art retrieved her suitcases at the building's entrance. The driver got out and helped her load everything. Every breath, every heartbeat, every swallow or blink of an eye required more effort than usual. As if her body was giving up, slowly succumbing to the agony that seared through her. An agony he'd inflicted, so why did it feel like she was the one breaking them?

"Give me your phone," Art demanded. When she handed it to him, he typed something in but didn't return it. Instead he walked to his car, then came back with two boxes. He opened a plastic pouch, pulled out a pink phone cover and wrapped her phone in it.

"What's that?" She took her phone. The new case sparkled with crystals, and was kind of cute. Not black, for sure. "Are these diamonds?"

"So we don't mix up our phones anymore," he said with a sad smile. He searched her face and she desperately wanted to give him something to hang on to, but she couldn't. Hell, she had nothing to hang on to.

"Thank you." The emotions clogged her throat.

"I also got you a tablet, so you can present Chrysal's art to the galleries," he said and Vi lost the ability to think, speak or breathe. A tear rolled down her cheek.

"Don't you dare be nice to me now. I'm so hurt and confused," she said and hurried to the taxi.

Art put the tablet in her lap and closed the door.

* * *

Vi unlocked her new apartment, her excitement stained with the absence of Art. She wanted to step confidently over the threshold, cherishing the new beginning, savoring the significance of the moment.

But she ended up stumbling through the door while balancing the box in her hands.

Even in her deflated state of mind, she had to admit her new home was amazing. And lonely. The orange and purple colors of the sunset beamed through the large windows, but her eyes focused on the shadows. The place was empty, just like she was.

The front door opened up to an elevated platform with a coat hanger on one side and a copper railing—imitating the exposed pipes, a key feature of the apartment—on the other side. Vi dropped the box and rolled her suitcases in.

She took the three steps down and collapsed on the last one, sitting with her chin in her hands. A kitchen with cement counter tops and copper industrial lights hanging on ropes from the ceiling seemed like the only livable space as the rest spread out unfilled.

She needed furniture. Like a bed. Even the kitchen with its swanky appliances was only an illusion since she had no dishes yet.

Vi checked her watch. If she hurried, she could buy some basics. Plates, cups, groceries and an air mattress would help her feel less lost.

The intercom buzzed.

What? Who would even know she was here?

She pressed the button.

"We have a delivery for Violet Holland." The black-and-white image of two men stared at her from the monitor.

"Oh, okay." *Shit, how do you operate this thing?* There wasn't a key symbol on the pad. She tapped the screen a few times, but the selection of icons made about as much sense as the rest of her life. None.

"Hold on a second, I'll come downstairs." Great! If Art was here, he would have known how to use the intercom. *Stop it!* She narrowed her eyes at the screen. Was he watching her now?

She shook her head and went downstairs.

"What is it?" She peeked over the delivery man's shoulder.

"Bed, mattress, breakfast table and chairs." He shoved a delivery slip under her nose.

"I didn't order anything." But the document was clear. Paid for by Art Mathison. *Fuck!* "I don't want it. Take it back."

"I can't take it back. You can return it with the receipt, but you have to go through the customer service," he said, unimpressed.

She puffed air into her cheeks. "Come on in then." She had no energy left to fight him. And having a bed was too appealing right now. She was going to pay Art back. Damn him and his thoughtful gifts!

It turned out he had paid for delivery and assembly, so Vi spent another hour with two strangers putting together the most amazing brass bed frame and a small round copper table with two chairs. The furniture fit the place perfectly.

Vi apologized several times that she couldn't offer them a glass of water. One of the men ended up drinking from the faucet while Vi wished the floor would swallow her. At least she wouldn't see them ever again. Though she might visit the store—the pieces were exquisite.

Once they were finished, she ran out to get a few dishes, plus new sheets and towels. She made her bed. Everything was done on autopilot in a detached state because she couldn't stop thinking about Art. This moving day was the worst ever.

She showered and climbed under her new sheets then held her phone for a moment, contemplating. She wanted to share this with him, but she couldn't simply forget what he'd done.

Her finger hovered above the screen and then typed.

Vi: How much do I owe you for the furniture?

The floating dots showed his immediate response. It warmed her inside.

Art: It's a housewarming gift.

God. She was torn. She wanted nothing from him. It felt too much like what got her sucked into the vortex of David, but deep down she knew it was different. And it was a thoughtful gift. Her apartment felt less lonely and empty because Art had organized it all. If the spying fiasco hadn't happened today, they would have received the delivery together and he would be here with her, testing the new bed.

Vi: Thank you.

Art: You're welcome.

Damn it! This was painful. The desire to call him was tamed, but only barely. And she was pretty sure he was hoping she would.

Vi: Good night, Art.

He started typing. The pain of the day had accumulated in the thumping rhythm in her temples. She didn't want to feel like this and she could change that. Forgiveness was, however, a tricky deed. Would she give him too much control if she gave in now?

Art: Don't go yet.

I don't want to, she thought.

Vi: I'm tired.

And I have to feel miserable and lonely because you drove us into this impasse. She didn't type because there was no point. It was hard to get him to talk in person, let alone in a text message.

Art: I miss you.

She sighed and he sent another message.

Art: I'm really sorry.

Tears freely rolled down her cheeks. She wasn't even upset anymore, just really sad. He fucked up, and they were both clearly suffering because of it.

Vi: I know you are.

She didn't want to sleep here alone, but she needed to be strong. This was her new beginning. Oh, damn it.

Vi: Can you promise me you will never ever invade my privacy again?

Art: I swear.

She was probably giving up too soon, too much and too irrevocably, but she didn't want to be this miserable.

Vi: I don't want to be alone in this big bed.

Art: I can be there within an hour.

Vi: Drive carefully.

* * *

ART PARKED on the street and rang the bell for 7B, his stomach suffering from self-inflicted anguish.

"I'm coming." Her voice spread warmth through his body and increased the anguish situation at the same time. Why was she coming down? Wasn't she planning to let him in?

When she appeared on the other side of the glass, he staggered. At the sight of her, but also at the realization. It sank in with an irrevocable clarity. He loved her. He loved this woman.

"Hi." In a black tank top and pink pajama pants she looked sexier than ever, and so adorable.

"Hi," he rasped. The air seemed in low supply as the lump in his throat grew bigger.

"Come on in." She stepped back and walked into the lobby without looking back.

Okay, she let him in. That's good. "Isn't the intercom working?"

"I haven't figured it out yet." Her eyes darted in all directions, trying to avoid him. As they rode up, the soft hum of the elevator engine echoed, emphasizing the heavy silence between them.

She unlocked the door and gestured for him to enter first. He stepped around her. If he brushed her skin accidentally, he wouldn't be able to keep his hands off her and it was the most important thing right now to let her lead. To let her be in control.

After he'd left her this afternoon, he'd spent two hours in the gym working out and then sparring with Luca. He'd punched Luca so hard, the poor bastard bruised along his jaw. They shouldn't have fooled around without protecting their heads, but sometimes the voice of reason took a day off.

Even with all the physical exertion, he was going crazy. When she'd messaged him, his hands shook so much he could barely type. The depth of suffering he'd experienced because he loved this woman was ridiculous. But he wouldn't change it. In retrospect, the stupid cyber stalking was destined to get him in trouble, so it was suffering he'd deserved.

She closed the door and they stared at each other

for a moment. The air zapped with chemistry. With pain and want.

He clenched his fists, stopping himself from pouncing. She tapped her foot. Not the best sign, but he was here and he wouldn't leave this time.

She exhaled heavily. "I can't do this."

18

THE BEAT of silence that followed almost deafened him.

She licked her lips. "First, I need you to look me in the eye and promise again."

A stream of relief slowly seeped through his worry. Not yet flushing it out but bringing hope. "I swear I'll never invade your privacy like that."

She dashed to him, hooking her hands around his neck. He captured her lips, the softness of her body against him taking some of his pain away immediately. *Home.*

They kissed hungrily, pouring all the anguish and frustration into the dance of their lips and tongues.

Art counted to a hundred in his head because he needed to let her determine how far he was allowed to go.

When she pulled away, she took his hand and

walked him through the empty space. "Let me show you our new bed."

"Wait." He stopped them. "Just to make sure, the promise concerns the cyber space only, because I plan to invade you with all I've got."

She laughed. "Get out your hammer, Thor."

SEVERAL HOURS LATER, after they thoroughly christened the new bed and slept some, they were sitting at the new breakfast table and Vi was scrolling through old chats in the dark web where other hackers discussed his accomplishments.

It was time to tell her who he really was, but telling the story didn't sit right with him. Too many words and too many opportunities to say something wrong, to fuck it all up. But she deserved to know the truth, so he'd shown her. Honestly, not all of it was completely true, but it painted a close enough picture.

"You were behind the cable automated payments fraud? Oh my God!" Vi put her palm over her mouth and read on.

Art feared she would be scared and throw him out, but watching as her eyes lit up with excitement while she fought her moral objections was kind of adorable.

"I remember the scandal. For years, they didn't realize people didn't pay their bills because they appeared as paid every month. You did that?" She shook her head as if appalled, but he could swear there was admiration in her voice.

"I wanted to help my neighbors at the trailer park," he said.

She smiled. "That's kind of sweet."

Wearing his T-shirt, she looked edible.

"Yeah, it exploded the year after I sold the code." The assholes had paid him a hefty price, but they were too greedy, abused the system and got caught.

"So you helped your neighbors and then made money from that program? Is that why you're rich?"

He chuckled. "Definitely not." She held his eyes, still looking excited. Never had he imagined finding out the truth—or some of it—about him would thrill her.

She raised her eyebrow. "Let me read on." She swiped her elegant fingers on the screen, biting her lip.

"Can you at least take the shirt off?" He leaned back in his chair, pleased with its comfort. When he'd ordered the breakfast dining set, he worried it would only look nice in this space. So many things complemented the interior design but lacked the functionality. It would have sucked if he'd given her useless furniture.

"Behave, mister. I will not have my boobs spread at my new table." She shook her head and read on.

"Since I have custody, I want them free." He

smirked.

"You have custody of my boobs?" She laughed.

"Of course, I do." He loved making her laugh—a beautiful sonata for his ears only.

She narrowed her eyes, pursing her lips to suppress a smile. "How so? They are my boobs."

"We've established already that I love them more than you do." He shrugged and she burst out laughing again. That sound was a drug. If only he could program a code that would make her laugh constantly.

"Do I have custody of your dick?"

"No fucking way." He snickered. "I love my dick."

She threw her head back and cackled, the song of it echoing in the empty space. And then she surprised him by pulling the shirt over her head and throwing it at him. *Home.*

"That's better." He stood up, trying to distract his dick. "I need coffee."

"Oh my God," she yelped.

"What?" He stopped on his way to the cupboards.

"It says here, you and someone named Venus are responsible for crashing several major websites. Holy shit." She looked at him wide-eyed. "Did you really? Why?"

He pretended to search the empty cupboards. That wasn't his proudest achievement.

"Art, I don't have any coffee or a kettle." She stood up and followed him. "Did you really do that?"

He turned and leaned against the counter. "Yes."

"Why?" She stepped between his legs. She put her hand on his chest and he closed his arms around her waist.

"For fun." He shrugged.

Her eyebrows shot up. "You lost them a lot of money."

"I didn't think or care about that. I wanted to prove I could." This would disappoint her.

"Wow, and prove you did. Is it horrible that I'm impressed?"

"No, that's a relief. Though you probably shouldn't be." He leaned down and kissed her. She moved her arms up around his neck and her stomach growled. "Okay, woman, let's go for breakfast."

"What if someone sees you?"

"We'll be okay." He winked. She was his. She was with him. All that other shit could wait.

"Let's order in." She wiggled her hips, her lips teasing his.

"Good thinking. You could stay naked," he said.

"So who is Venus?" she asked.

Fuck. That was the last thing he wanted to discuss. "Another hacker."

Before she could ask another question, he pivoted them. He lifted her to the counter and spread her legs. She sighed and wrapped them around his waist. *Home.*

* * *

THEY MADE LOVE, ate breakfast and made love again.

"I like this one," Vi said and showed the tablet to Art, showing him a sofa. They were back in bed. It should have been frustrating that they weren't able to spend time in town, but Vi was happy they could be together without facing the world. She understood it wasn't realistic to stay cooped up, but somehow, without the interference of reality and external influences, their closeness deepened and broadened.

She enjoyed having this beautiful, flawed man all for herself. Well aware she'd been living in avoidance the last months, she decided a few more weeks wouldn't change much.

"You should get it." He kissed the top of her head. She was nestled against his chest, choosing her new furniture, feeling peaceful. Amazing. Happy.

"Maybe I will, but I'd rather go and sit on it to make sure it's comfortable," she said. "Can we go tomorrow? I have one more day off."

Vi had run out earlier to check on the patisserie, but Erica had everything under control. Carla was returning in a few days, but Vi didn't want to think about not having a job. Or an idea of what to do next.

Art had helped her hire a photographer to take professional photos of Chrysal's art, but even if she could sell his paintings, it was a far cry from a career. But perhaps it could be a start.

"We'll see," he said and kissed her again.

"You don't want to be seen. I understand," she said. Perhaps she wasn't as pleased with their situation.

"When Carla comes, we'll go away," he said.

"What?" She pulled away. "What do you mean away? Where? For how long?"

"Vi, I can't stay around," he said.

"But you said you wouldn't leave without me."

"Exactly." He sat up straighter.

She scrambled to the other side of the bed, covering herself in the sheets. Why had he simply decided this? She needed to figure out her life here, not run away and hide somewhere.

"I told you about David and how he monopolized my life and now you just spring this on me and I should shut up and follow?"

"Stop punishing yourself because you fell for a prick." He stood up. "This is different."

"How is it different? You've decided for me. I need to stay and find a job or start a business. I've just signed a lease on this place. You want me to leave and hide? I thought when you said you wouldn't leave without me, it meant you wouldn't leave." She stood up now, pulling on his T-shirt.

"Vi, this is a question of safety. We'll stay at my house in the Dominican Republic and return as soon as this is over." He pinched the bridge of his nose.

"If I left with you now, it'd be the same story.

You'd own me." Anger spread through her like lava. How could he not understand this?

"We can fly commercial." He shook his head. He was exasperated? Really?

"What?"

"Jesus, Vi, so you can pay for your flight." He spread his arms in frustration.

They glared for a moment. There was another way to see this, she realized. Nothing—aside from the lease—was holding her here and they could be free over there, not hiding in one spot all the time. Her temper had flared up because he'd announced it rather than discussing it with her.

"Art, I don't want to argue." She sighed and took a step toward him. They stood at the foot of her bed, so close yet so far from each other.

"Yet here we are." He exhaled heavily.

"What is that supposed to mean?" She crossed her arms, tapping her foot. He was so infuriating.

"It's just a fucking vacation. You keep hiding behind this made-up responsibility. Covering yourself in black. Avoiding joy at all costs. Sacrificing yourself for your dead friend, for your former fiancé, for Carla. There is a threat to my life, and if they linked you to me already, probably on yours. You have nothing to hold you here right now, but you still use that as an excuse. Perhaps you don't want to be with me. Certainly not as much as I want to be with you."

He stormed out of the room.

"Art…" She followed him. "Stop. Of course I want to be with you. I want to be with you so much, it scares me."

He stopped in the middle of her empty living room. The light illuminating his perfect body accentuated the anatomy of his sculpted torso and narrow hips. He lowered his head at her words. Vi stopped, desperately wanting to say she loved him. She loved him?

"When you *announced* that we're leaving—announced, not discussed—a warning bell went off and I felt… I don't know, your words triggered something. I fucked up with David. I ended up losing myself, so I guess I'm simply more careful with my independence. You didn't deserve my reaction, but I completely deserved to hear what you think about me…"

She closed the distance between them and hugged him from behind. He covered her hands with his on his taut stomach. Wanting to inhale some of his strength, she pressed her cheek against his back and closed her eyes.

He thought she was hiding, avoiding joy. He thought she was weak. Pathetic.

She wanted to tell him she loved him, but his long —longest thus far—speech had stopped her. He said he wanted to be with her, but perhaps he worried about her safety. His words suggested otherwise, but the thought numbed her anyway. A seed of doubt bloomed.

Her arms dropped. He turned around, kissing her on the forehead.

Before they could say anything else, both their cell phones rang. They scattered, a bit too eager to answer.

Vi grabbed her phone from the counter and Art disappeared into the bedroom. "Hello," she said.

"Violet, hi. It's Lena speaking. Thank God, you're okay," Lena said, her voice trembling.

"I'm fine. What's going on, Lena?"

"I was walking around the patisserie just now and someone must have broken in."

Vi's eyes widened and her brain went blank for a moment, suspended in the air, trying to grasp the reality. "What do you mean?"

"The window is broken and everything inside seemed trashed. I called the police. You should come," Lena said.

"Of course, I'll be right there," she responded and hung up.

When she turned, Art stood outside of her bedroom. Their eyes met. "Luca has been reviewing the CCTV in front of the patisserie to see if they returned and they had," he said, confirming Lena's words.

"Lena called the police. I need to go." She wanted to leave immediately, to escape the painful aftermath of their argument. At the same time she felt leaving right now would set their relationship back by a mile. All the trust and intimacy lost.

"Luca is downstairs. He'll get you there and wait. We'll talk later," he said, and Lena wished the "talk later" wasn't part of the plan.

Art sat down on the chair, and perhaps she made it up but it felt like he took a wide berth around her to get there.

Vi sighed and rushed to the bedroom to get dressed. When she emerged, he was still sitting there, his face in his palms.

"I don't know how long I'll be. I'm assuming the police will have a lot of questions." She stood in the doorway, afraid to move closer, but unwilling to leave without some type of contact.

He stood up and hugged her. "I'm sorry. Be careful." What was he sorry about? About Carla's place? Or the words that hurt despite being true?

"I'll have Luca with me." She tried to smile and rushed out.

* * *

ART PACED AROUND THE APARTMENT. She'd been gone for four hours and he'd only gotten three messages from Luca, mostly telling him to relax. The footage had confirmed it was Taworski's men, one of them the driver from the other day.

He wished this hadn't happened. He'd brought it

to her doorstep and now her friend's place was destroyed and Vi was probably in danger. If they'd made the connection to him. And they probably had. Why else would they have trashed the place?

The timing couldn't have been worse. Right after their argument. He shouldn't have pushed her. He shouldn't have said all those things. He hated conversations.

Fuck, instead of telling her he loved her, he hit back with her own insecurities. It wasn't his place. She was the most generous person he'd known and he'd thrown it into her face. Fuck it! Words were always a weapon and he was never good with them.

Time stretched to eternity and Art was going crazy. The heavy feeling on his chest grew, suffocating him under the rollercoaster of thoughts that were spiraling out of control. If he only gave up Simone to the Bureau, this shit would go away. But even an arrogant prick like him couldn't betray Simone—anyone really —like that. He couldn't be so dishonest. A hypocrite.

His job for the Bureau set him free, put his past deeds above the law. Helping to arrest Simone would be different. Her illegal activity wasn't worse than his and while he was set free, she'd rot in jail. Despite all the shit she'd ever done to him, the hurt she'd inflicted, he couldn't inform on her.

He sent another message to Luca, but this time no response came. Shit! Where were they?

He circled around the living room for the thousandth time, but it didn't lessen his anxiety. The emptiness of the apartment only added to the hollow feeling spreading beyond his chest.

He scrolled the news on his phone, hoping to get some information, and he was considering hacking the police computers when the click of the key pulled him toward the landing by the entrance.

Vi and Luca entered. She was pale and looked beaten. Art took the three steps in one big leap and gathered her into his arms.

"I'm so sorry, babe," he said, not knowing how to help her, wishing he could.

"I'm exhausted," she mumbled against his chest and pushed him away, trudging to the kitchen.

"Let me make you some tea," he offered, remembering she had tea when stressed out.

A ghost of a smile passed over her face and she sat down at the table. "Thank you."

"When sleeping, sea otters hold hands," he said. *Shut up, asshole!* He filled the single pot she owned with water since she didn't have a kettle yet.

"I'll have tea as well." Luca plopped into the other chair. "The police claimed the footage had been erased, but your recording still clearly shows who it was. Taworski lost track of you there and now they wanted to… I don't know, find you under the counter there?" He shook his head.

"Send a message?" Art shrugged, leaning on his hands against the kitchen island.

Vi was staring into a blank space in front of her. His chest hurt. How was he going to make it better?

"Carla and Charlie are flying back. I called them. They are catching a flight from London as soon as possible and should be here by tomorrow evening. We'll wait for them and we'll tell them everything," she said, her voice removed and flat.

Art put the tea bags into the cups, trying to stop his hands from shaking. He poured the boiling water and set the pot back. The silence too loud in his mind.

"I don't think *everything* is the way to go, but we should show them the footage. They need to know the Da Bonno family is behind it. It's his family after all, isn't it?" Luca said.

Vi nodded but said nothing. Art put a cup in front of her and leaned down to kiss the crown of her head. His favorite scent of coffee and caramel filled his nostrils.

"I'm going to take a shower." Vi stood up. "I'll finish my tea later." She briefly touched his arm and walked away. Her absence robbed him of his lifeline, leaving him abandoned and lonely.

"Is it about the break-in or has something else happened between the two of you?" Luca asked.

"What do you mean?" Art didn't feel like discussing something he didn't quite understand.

"She was distant, quiet in the car on the way

there. I'd expect anxious or nervous, but she was… I don't know, sad," Luca said, the words splitting Art's heart in two.

"We argued before and I said things," he confessed. "Never mind now, we need to figure out this shit. Perhaps I should call Scully and send her the footage from the break-in?"

"You could, but I don't think she would care. Her bosses defined the target and it's not the Da Bonnos." Luca took a sip of his tea.

Art collapsed into the chair. It still carried the heat of Vi's body and it made him feel oddly closer to her. Water ran in the bathroom, and he wished he could be there, holding her.

"We have three options: give the data to Taworski, set up Simone so the Bureau proceeds on using the data finally, or go to the Dominican and hope that both cases move forward without our involvement," Luca said.

"I don't like any of those options." Art sighed. The shower turned off. He imagined her stepping out and wrapping herself into a towel. She was so close, yet distant.

"What's wrong with the Dominican?" Luca frowned.

"Vi doesn't want to go," Art said.

"We are going." Her voice came from the other side of the room. "Let's leave as soon as I debrief Carla."

19

"WHAT A FUCKING MESS!" Charlie repeated for the hundredth time. Carla and her husband had arrived late in the afternoon the following day. Vi and Lena had met them in front of the patisserie. The yellow police tape prevented them from going in, so they had retreated to Carla's apartment.

Carla was speechless, completely out of character for her. Vi couldn't help but feel responsible for her friend's misfortune. If it wasn't for her relationship with Art, nothing would have happened. They were standing around the kitchen island and Vi was considering how to tell them about everything.

"We'll rebuild, sweetheart." Charlie pulled Carla into an embrace. "I promise."

"I'm so sorry, Carla," Vi whispered. "I'll clean up everything and I'll contribute to renovations. This is all my fault."

"Stop it," Carla said and pulled away from her husband. She put her hands on her hips. "You didn't do it."

"But it was related to me," she said and they all turned to her, gaping. "I met a man and someone is after him. They connected him to me and I think they either wanted to send him a message or believed he might be there."

"Who?" Charlie snapped.

"Your family," Vi whispered.

Carla gasped, covering her mouth, and Lena reached to put her arms around her shoulders.

"I don't believe that," Charlie snapped.

"There is footage," Vi said, hoping she wouldn't have to admit where she had it from. "There is someone downstairs who could show you."

"Who? Why is he downstairs?" Charlie threw his arms out and then dragged his hand down his face.

"Charlie, don't yell at Violet," Carla urged, placing her hand over Lena's, searching for comfort.

Standing on the other side of the island, Vi felt cold and alone, but she deserved that.

She had barely spoken with Art since their argument. She had gone to bed last night and pretended to sleep when he came to the bedroom. This morning, he and Luca had spent hours reviewing footage and searching for someone online while Vi faked a headache and stayed in her bed until it was time to meet Carla.

Charlie picked up his phone.

"Who are you calling?" Carla asked.

"Get the footage," Charlie ordered Violet, and she took her purse and turned to leave. "I'm calling Rocco," Charlie told Carla, his voice significantly gentler.

Vi went downstairs to find Luca, who had followed them from the café to the apartment, and he returned upstairs with her.

"This is Luca. He works in personal security." Vi wasn't really sure how to explain or introduce him. This was so painful. Not only did she feel personally responsible for Carla's loss, but she knew she had to leave soon and things with Art had come to a tipping point.

Luca nodded his greeting and showed Charlie and Carla the footage.

"How do you know these men were sent by Da Bonno?" Charlie asked.

"My client…" Luca cleared his throat and searched Vi's face as if to confirm how to talk about Art, "has been threatened by a man, Phil Taworski, and we linked him to Tony Da Bonno."

"I remember Phil. I can't believe Rocco wouldn't warn me if they were going to hit our place." Charlie ran his hand over his face and toward a cabinet in the corner. "I need a fucking drink."

"Rocco is Charlie's cousin, Tony Da Bonno's

son," Carla explained. "You're a horrible host, darling. We all need something stronger right now."

"Not me," Lena said. "I need to pick up Sarah in half an hour."

"Thank you, Lena, for everything. You've been so helpful," Vi said and hugged the woman, but gratitude was only half of the reason. Vi needed comfort and none was currently available. Lena squeezed her tight and Vi burst into tears, surprising herself and everyone else.

Carla rushed over and the two women tried to console Vi, only making her cry more. She wasn't even sure why she was crying, but it wasn't entirely about the break-in. She wanted to drag Carla to a corner and tell her everything, but that would be selfish. Her best friend had her own set of issues to deal with.

The doorbell distracted them all and Charlie went to open the door. The man who walked in looked as though he'd just come from a magazine cover photo shoot. He gave Charlie a one arm hug. Carla approached him and they kissed on both cheeks.

"Wow, he's hot," Lena breathed, surprising Vi. But damn, she was right. Styled messily, his curly hair reached below his ears, adding a bad boy vibe to his sophisticated clothes. He had a couple of days of stubble covering his square jaw and the darkest eyes Vi had ever seen. His three-piece black suit without a tie increased his carefree sex appeal.

"Ladies." He sauntered toward them. "I'm Rocco," he said and kissed Vi's hand and then Lena's. He didn't smile, but his eyes sparkled with mischief. This man with his broad shoulders and bulging biceps was trouble.

"Nice to meet you, Rocco," Vi said, trying not to glare. He was involved in Art's trouble, after all.

"I'm afraid I have to go now," Lena said, swallowed hard and tripped a few times as she rushed to the door and left.

"Okay, asshole, this is not a social call," Charlie snapped. "Could you explain why our patisserie is trashed?"

"Hey, no need for name calling." Rocco raised his hands in mock surrender. "What are you talking about?"

"Have a look." Charlie beckoned his head to Luca, who promptly played the footage.

"He's hot," Vi whispered to Carla.

"He's also a bad bet, managing all the family brothels and being groomed to step into Tony's shoes," Carla said.

"Hot and dangerous. It was funny how Lena stumbled out of here," Vi said and Carla leaned her head on her shoulder, reminding her of the damage she'd attracted. "I'm sorry about everything. Art, the man I'm dating, I guess, though it's very complicated, didn't want this to come to your doorstep."

"Oh, *amiga*, stop apologizing. You helped me big time so I could go away, and while I don't like the return, it's not your fault. If anything, it's his." She gestured toward Rocco who was now scratching his chin, frowning.

"These are Taworski's men. The asshole has been trying to replace Papa for a while, but we paid little attention," Rocco said. "Why would he trash your place? It makes no sense unless he just wanted to cause trouble, the dickhead."

Charlie raised his eyebrows. Luca cleared his throat and gave Rocco an abbreviated and somewhat manipulated version of the truth.

"So you're saying your client has something Taworski wants because it could give him an upper hand over my father and that he found out she is…" He spoke about Vi as if she wasn't there, but tossed her a wink. "…dating your client, so he tried to send a message?"

Luca nodded. The air between the two of them was tense. Luca stood with his legs wide, glaring, and Vi wondered if he was going to punch Rocco.

"Can I have the footage?" Rocco asked and Luca pulled the tablet closer to himself. Rocco raised his eyebrows and scratched his chin with his thumb and index finger. "Listen, fucker, I don't know you and I have no reason to help you out, but since my cousin and his lovely wife are involved, I'll take care of Taworski. If you're telling the truth and one of the

men in that video will sing, Taworski is no longer a
threat to you."

* * *

ART WASN'T sure how to break the silence that hung
heavily between him and Vi. She was watching the
countryside pass as Luca drove their rental car toward
the coastal house. They had barely spoken in days
and he was going crazy with nothing to do but stare at
her. Wearing her poignant sentiment, she was still
breathtaking.

He'd held her hand the whole flight and she'd let
him, but she'd remained quiet. Deep in her thoughts
or avoiding the conversation. It was killing him to be
this close but so isolated from her at the same time.

They pulled onto the dirt road leading to Art's
villa. The local guards were already waiting for them
and opened the gate promptly. Vi turned in her seat,
watching the gate close, and something gripped his
stomach. She didn't think he was imprisoning her,
did she?

The car stopped on a gravel lot in front of the
house and Art squeezed her hand. What else could he
do? How to cross the bridge when he didn't know
where the dynamite was hidden? An explosion would
be better than the Arctic wind currently separating
them.

"Wait in the car," Luca ordered.

He conferred briefly with the two local guards and entered the house.

The silence in the car suffocating him, Art tapped his fingers on his thigh. "Sculpture, music, painting, and architecture used to be Olympic sports between 1912 and 1948." Why was it that every time he wanted to say something that mattered, shit came out of his mouth?

"I didn't know that," she said and looked at him. "Why are you nervous?" It wasn't as much a question as an accusation.

"I'm sorry, Vi," he said.

"For what?" She searched his face. She'd been pale, tired and so fucking sad, it was breaking his heart and he needed to fix it.

"For the patisserie, of course, but mostly for making you come here," he said as Luca opened the door.

"All clear," Luca announced and she ran out of the car.

"Vi," Art called after her and she stopped, probably realizing she didn't know where to go.

"I'll go to the town to get supplies." Not losing any time, Luca jumped into the driver's seat, promptly leaving them.

Vi stood facing the house, trembling. He approached her as if walking on the ice that was cracking around them. The short distance stretched in the confusion he felt. Finally, he wrapped her in his arms and buried his face into her hair. *Fuck. What was going on?*

"I don't want to be your burden," she whispered, her voice shaken with tears.

"Burden?" He squeezed her tighter. What was she talking about? How could she think that?

"I know you're feeling responsible for my safety," she said. "For some strange reason, you've been feeling responsible for me since you saw me crying that first day at the patisserie. Or maybe even since the mugging."

"You wouldn't be hiding if it wasn't for me." He turned her gently around.

"Well, you said that I'm hiding, anyway. From life. From joy. Clearly you think I'm broken…" Her voice cracked and she blinked as if blinded by a flashlight.

Fuck me! The realization of his utter failure to comprehend the situation almost knocked him over. He placed his finger under her chin and tilted her face to him. He met her watery eyes. "Babe, you're not broken. You're the best thing that ever happened to me. I grew up not really having a home and I found one with you."

"But you said—"

"I love you, Vi." He touched her forehead with his.

Her eyes widened and for a moment he feared it was the worst thing to say, but he couldn't hold back any longer. The last two days had been agony. He cupped her face and wiped her cheeks with his thumbs. He realized he didn't even care if she said it back because speaking the words already released the chain squeezing at his heart.

She raised on her tiptoes and kissed him gently, sighing against his lips. "Show me the bedroom, Thor."

20

HE LOVED HER. He loved her.

The tension of the past days melted away with his words. Vi squealed as he lifted her and walked her to the house. They didn't make it to the bedroom, but she didn't care. She needed him inside her, she needed him to take the pain away.

Art put her on a counter or a table—she was too focused on him to be sure. Yanking his T-shirt over his shoulders, Vi pressed her hands to the warm skin of his chest for a second and inhaled deeply to calm herself. This was everything she wanted.

He pulled her dress up her thighs and pushed her onto the hard surface. The cold stone made her shiver delightfully.

"Babe, I can't take it slow, I need you now." He ripped off her underwear.

"Take me," she whispered as he spread her legs

and tugged her to the edge. He placed her heels up next to her butt, opening her for him. She held her breath, fearing she wouldn't be able to take him this way, but before she could think further he slid into her in one powerful thrust, shocking her with his size. His intensity. Her need to surrender.

"I love the feeling of you," he growled. Staying still for a moment, he allowed her to adjust to him. He circled his thumb over her clit, shooting waves of pleasure through her, and she moaned with anticipation. Then he slid deeper.

"That's it, babe."

Finally he started moving, the frustration of the past days crumbling with each thrust. It was hard and fast. Pain mixed with pleasure. Desire peaking, robbing them of all reason, all care. Replacing feeling with raw need.

He pumped into her and she took it. The force of their union redeeming.

A sheen of perspiration covered them both as the room filled with the sounds of their flesh, of their hunger, of their devotion.

She was getting closer but didn't want to get there yet. Not yet. Not so soon. She moaned and closed her eyes.

Art changed the angle, placing her legs over his shoulders. "Look at me," he ordered.

Her lids heavy, she pried them open and met his eyes and her breath hitched. It was there. In his eyes, she found the proof of his love. He meant what he'd said.

And she hadn't said it back. She had to say it now.

"Art—"

An earth-shattering orgasm rippled through her, stealing her ability to speak. Art jerked inside her as his own release took over and they both rode into the bliss of the aftermath, clinging to each other as if they were bouncing through the rapids on a whitewater raft.

Art pulled her to sitting, allowing them to connect even closer. Vi wrapped her arms around his shoulders, desperately seeking all the contact their bodies could draw.

Still deep inside her, he kissed her forehead and gathered her tighter, craving the same nearness.

Out of breath, shaking and embracing, they stayed in each other's arms, connected on the most intimate level, unable to move away.

"Art," Vi whispered against his shoulder.

"Hm," he groaned.

"I love you too."

* * *

ART'S HAND on her thigh—a simple touch—communicated directly with her heart, sending rippling tingles down her body. He was driving, a simple joy they hadn't had a chance to fully experience since their first date.

They were heading to Santo Domingo. Art's villa was in the middle of nowhere and they had stayed there for three days now, but today Art had insisted they go shopping.

Vi didn't really need to get out of their bubble of love. The days on the island cruised in a comfortable, lazy beat. Art fussed around her and fulfilled all her wishes before she'd even asked. They swam, ate, drank and made love. Most of the time, they acted like horny teenagers.

Luca kept making fun of them, but Vi could see he was happy for his friend. She'd gotten to know him better and understood now that he was more than a bodyguard. He wasn't only Art's buddy to talk shit, drink and hang out with. He genuinely cared about Art, and Vi was grateful they had him around. He also mixed a mean margarita and marinated meat to perfection.

But most of the time, she and Art were alone, exploring new corners of their intimacy. Deepening the feelings they now declared openly.

"What is it we need to buy?" she complained. "I thought your money could get anything delivered to you. I enjoy staying in. I don't want to share you with anyone or anything."

He gave her a lopsided smile. "New clothes."

Despite her protest, she had to admit it was nice to

get out without being driven, guarded or hiding. Freely enjoying their time together outside of four walls—however luxurious—was a new concept, and Vi realized it was actually a welcome change.

"New clothes?" She giggled. "Have you run out of clean underwear?"

He raised his eyebrow, deadpan. "For you."

"For me?" She frowned. "I don't need new clothes."

"I disagree." He squeezed her leg.

"What is wrong with my clothes? And besides, we're naked most of the time, so you don't even know what clothes I own." She folded her arms across her chest.

"They are black," he said.

"Oh," was all she managed. *Shit*. He was right. Wearing black was simple, easy. It provided cover. For the body she didn't love. And against the attention she wanted to avoid. She hadn't even realized when it had become a uniform that represented all her vulnerabilities.

They parked the car and Art rushed around to open the door for her.

"I'm paying for everything," he said and seized her lips before she could argue. She tried to wiggle free, but he had her in a tight grip. His lips insistent and so hot on hers, Vi gave up and leaned into the kiss. Art skimmed her back with his large hands and squeezed her butt. "Let's go." He grabbed her hand.

"You're not paying," she said, clutching his fingers.

"We'll see."

A wide commercial avenue vibrated with vendors, tourists and bright colors. Art dragged her to the first boutique and as soon as they entered, Vi knew this was higher end than her usual brands. This was David's level of elegance and luxury. And apparently Art's. She stopped in her tracks at the entrance and he tightened his grip on her hand.

"How can I help you?" asked the shop assistant, a beautiful woman with her black hair in a high ponytail and her eyelashes so thick and long they must have weighed half a pound.

"My girlfriend needs new clothes." Art pulled Vi closer under his arm and kissed her temple. *Girlfriend.* For a moment, the declaration made her forget she didn't want to be there. She like being the girlfriend. His girlfriend.

"What's the occasion?" The lashes fluttered and brought Vi out of her palpitating heart, back to her head.

Ambush. That's how it all felt. "Art, I don't think I—"

"Shut up, woman." He smirked.

The woman stepped back, those lashes fluttering again.

"Art, I swear to God—"

"Get three new dresses and I'll make it worth your

while when we get back," he whispered darkly, his breath on her ear sending goosebumps down her spine.

"Are you offering me sexual favors?" She tried not to laugh.

"Two orgasms for each dress that is not black." He bit her lobe and she gasped.

The shop assistant hovered, straightening hangers beside them, avoiding their show of affection, but unwilling to let go of a potential commission.

"You got yourself a deal, but I'm paying." Vi strolled toward a green dress that caught her attention.

"My girlfriend is a pain in the ass," Art said loudly, sighing with mock exaggeration.

Vi smiled to herself. This could be fun. She needed a bit of color in her life.

Three hours, five dresses, three skirts and multiple new tops later, Art groaned and dragged her to a small restaurant with simple plastic tables. "I'm starving."

"Let's eat and then go look at shoes," she teased. Well, not entirely, because she did want new shoes to go with her new clothes. This had been more fun than she'd anticipated.

"Yeah, and we need several gallons of water," he murmured, frowning at the menu.

"Whatever for?" She giggled.

"Two orgasms per dress." He raised his eyebrows

and Vi burst out laughing.

"I love you, Arthur Mathison." She reached above the small table and kissed his cheek. "Thank you for bringing color into my life. And for letting me pay. Though I should start saving now. When the condo board realizes I didn't pay six months in advance, as they believe, I'll be pressed for rent."

He cleared his throat and studied the menu. "Oranges are a hybrid of tangerines and pomelos. They aren't naturally occurring fruits."

"Art?" She adored when he spit random facts, but it was his tell as well. "What are you trying not to tell me, but you should?" she asked.

The server came and they ordered the special of the day. The aroma coming from the kitchen promised a salivating experience.

"Promise not to get mad," he said, tapping his fingers across the table as if he was on his computer.

"What did you do?" *For fuck's sake. What now?* They had been so happy.

"Remember the orgasms I owe you." He tried to tango around the topic.

"Art." She raised her voice and eyebrows.

"I hacked your application." He grabbed her hand, his grip so strong she yelped.

"You're hurting me," she snarled.

"And you are going to run away."

She glared. "Art, you did this before the promise to never invade my cyber privacy. Loosen the fucking grip. I will not run." He let go, but didn't remove his hand, keeping his palm over hers on the table between them. "I'm mad at you, but we can't run away every time something comes up. God, why? Why did you do that?"

Her pulse pumped in her temples at double speed. She knew the answer. She was mad, but she loved her new place. The way she'd gotten it didn't sit well with her, but her desire to live there overrode her moral trepidation. Shit, the man was a bad influence.

"You deserved the place," he said.

The waiter brought their drinks.

"I feel like a criminal." She took a sip of the cold pop.

"I'm the criminal. Besides, no one will ever know." He rubbed his thumb on the back of her hand.

"Geez, Art, did you actually pay the six months' rent or did you do what you did with the cable bills? Whatever that was." She closed her eyes, bracing for the answer.

"No. Of course, I paid."

The server stepped between them to deliver the meals and Vi wanted to strangle him over the constant interruptions.

"That is only marginally better, Arthur," she scolded.

They ate in silence. Art rarely started a conversation anyway and she needed some time to reconcile the fraud she was now a part of. She had to admit it was kind of romantic, but so wrong. God, why couldn't she fall in love with a taxi driver or a chef?

Halfway through the meal, Art reached under the table and put his hand on her knee. It felt like a tickle, rather than a grip, as if he was afraid she would swat him away. She didn't. She still glared at him, inhaling her food along with her feelings, but she let him stay connected to her because… well, she loved him, with all his faults and complexities.

After lunch, she dragged him to several shoe stores, just to torture him and he took his punishment with grace, grinning. She let him pay for two pairs of shoes and purchased two more herself. This shopping trip made a serious dent into her savings, but she couldn't let him pay for everything.

He carried the bags to the car and opened the door for her. She raised her hand and cupped his cheek. Anxiety laced his eyes.

"Thank you for taking me shopping. Now take me home. You have a debt to pay, Thor." She traced his jaw with her palm, drifting behind his neck, and then she tugged him closer and captured his lips.

At first surprised, he staggered a bit, but recovered quickly, pushing her against the car and deepening the kiss, their tongues dancing. She dug her nails into his shoulders and hooked one leg around his hip. His erection poked her stomach and Art groaned, sliding his hand up her thigh. He gripped her hipbone as if trying to stop himself from exploring further.

Suggestive whistles from a group of teenagers snapped them out of it and they rushed into the car.

Art drove out of town, the chemistry hissing between them. Vi needed the angry sex and she knew he needed the redemption. As if reading her thoughts, Art turned onto a dirt road and stopped the car.

"Back seat. Now," he growled.

And just like that, he delivered the first two orgasms he owed her before they even returned to the villa.

* * *

"Look, these photos are great," Vi said. They were lounging on the side of the pool and she was reviewing the photos of Chrysal's art. She'd hired a photographer who worked with Chrysal to prepare a high-quality portfolio. The pictures Chrysal had taken with his phone didn't do justice to the life he rendered on the canvas and Vi feared it wasn't possible to capture his genius for a digital portfolio.

"As good as it gets," Art murmured and closed his eyes, drifting.

"Are you tired, love?" She poked his ribs. He must have been. The nightly performance was taxing. Vi herself was sore and tired, but the arrival of the pictures re-energized her.

Art didn't answer, breathing evenly. Vi smiled, left him to rest and walked inside.

The living area of the house wasn't big, but it was luxurious. The rustic tiles on the floor changed their color with the moving sun, reflecting on all the white surfaces around—the U-shaped sofa and a glass coffee table. The open concept room extended to the kitchen with its marble countertop and white cabinets.

She plopped down on the sofa. This had become her favorite part of the house, aside from the bedroom. She would sit here, enjoying a bit of shade and watching the waves on the horizon. How wonderful to live in a warm enough place to have a wall of floor-to-ceiling windows that remained open even during the night.

Vi flipped through the pictures, her heart fluttering with excitement and trepidation. Art had forwarded her contacts for three galleries. He'd been their client and they would entertain meeting her based on his recommendation, but the rest was completely on her. This would be a great start, but she hesitated to make the move and reach out. Something in that approach didn't sit right with her.

Given she wasn't sure how long they would be stranded on the island, it was hard to fully entertain all possibilities. She had still enough money from the sale of her café, but that wouldn't last forever and she didn't want to rely on Art's generosity all the time. It was a point of friction between them, so they kind of avoided an adult conversation about dealing with expenses. Mostly because Vi knew he would simply refuse to take her money.

Their time on the island had been bliss and she didn't want to dwell on the reality of shared life. They were stuck in paradise and it was good for now. No need to poke into things. While the circumstances were unfortunate, it was almost as if the universe had granted them a honeymoon rehearsal. Not that she expected a proposal, but what they had right now was a honeymoon fantasy.

She put the tablet away and admired the view.

The blue ocean spread across the horizon. How dramatically her life had changed. She used to be engaged to a man who she thought she loved and who didn't even love her back enough to stay away from prostitutes. She'd given up on her own life for that man. Well, if she was honest, she'd given up on life even before that, grasping at things that felt comfortable and easy.

Nothing was easy about her life now and she wouldn't change it for anything. Art, with all his quirks and often arrogant behavior, was a kind man who adored her. He spoke little, but he showed her in many ways daily how much she meant to him, starting with daily deliveries of caramel swirl cheesecakes since they'd arrived here.

He pushed her out of her comfort zone, forcing her to explore self-love by small deeds. He'd forced her out of her black clothes. He'd encouraged her to pursue the art business. The day after they'd arrived here, she'd received a package with several books on art history and art business and management as a gift from Art. She'd been reading every chance she had.

Unlike David, who cheated and formed her into his own picture, Art was loyal and supported her to build her own mosaic of self.

How did she get so lucky? Not even the uncertainty of the future could cloud the overwhelming feeling of belonging. He'd told her she was his home. He was hers. She had been wracking her brain to come up with a gift she could get him. To show him her love the way he'd been showing her. But nothing seemed worthy, original or good enough.

Art sauntered in. "Hey, babe," he said sleepily. His swim trunks hung low on his hips, the sculpted V with ripped abs hers to admire. This man was too perfect.

"Did you have a good snooze?" She stretched her arm, inviting him.

He joined her on the sofa, kissing her. He pushed a strand of hair behind her ear, his eyes full of mischief and something more serious. "Beautiful," he drawled.

She smiled at him, reaching out with her hand to stroke his cheek. She brushed his jaw with her thumb and he fisted her hair gently. They kissed lazily. There was no rush. No urgency. Only the liquid happiness and the sunset on the horizon. Vi had never been so happy.

"What have you been up to?" he asked, nuzzling her neck.

"I have been chilling here and admiring this place. It really is an amazing house, Art." She snuggled closer.

"And you didn't want to come here," he murmured against her hair.

And suddenly she knew what she could give him. Remembering their first date weekend, she jumped up and ran to the bedroom.

"Where did you go?" he called after her.

Hastily, she retrieved a pair of her new red high heels. She put them on and shed her dress and bikini.

She rushed back but stopped behind the sofa for a second and exhaled, trying to regulate her heartbeat. She then sauntered to stand in front of him.

His eyes widened as he scanned her naked body, his gaze stopping at her red stilettos. The corner of his mouth curled up a bit and his eyes slowly skimmed her curves, leaving goosebumps in their wake. His appreciative scan completed, their eyes locked finally, and she straightened her spine. No shame. No hiding.

"You're right. I didn't want to come to this paradise. Maybe you need to punish me," she said, her core already trembling in anticipation.

Art exhaled sharply and smiled as a dark promise flickered through his eyes.

21

Death should never be a reason for joy, but the death of Phil Taworski brought a sense of freedom to Violet. They had found out five days ago, but had taken the opportunity to spend a few more days in paradise before returning home.

Luca had stayed in touch with Rocco Da Bonno, who confirmed Taworski had been working on his own, behind Da Bonno's back, and he'd paid the price in the form of an accidental overdose.

While relieved the immediate threat had been eliminated, Vi had a hard time reconciling the events that led to their freedom. She wasn't stupid and she understood that Taworski would have been punished for his betrayal even if it wasn't related to them. Yet somehow she felt responsible for his death.

She tried to push the thought away as she walked from her apartment toward Sweet Temptations. It felt a bit like they had left the joy and sun in the Dominican Republic. Chicago welcomed them with an overcast sky, making it difficult to cling to the glow of their time away.

They had landed last night and Art went to his house that morning. He hadn't been there for many weeks and he wanted to prepare it for her visit tonight. She was going to see his personal space. His home. It put a stupid smile on her face. Somehow, this signified a new form of closeness and trust.

"Good morning," she greeted everyone as she entered. The patisserie missed its former charm. Carla had tidied up as much as possible and reopened, but the place had lost its soul, desecrated by people who no longer lived.

"*Hola, amiga,* look at you all tanned and smiling." Carla gave her a hug and they sat at her usual table. "How was your trip?"

"It was wonderful." Vi smiled and exhaled with joy. "I'm in love," she whispered.

"*Mierda*! The last time we sat here you were engaged to another man. I'm so glad to see you happy." Carla stood up. She returned with a bottle of Prosecco and two glasses. "I had this in the back for special occasions."

"This is hardly a special occasion," Vi protested, spying the chipped wood on the counter. "I'm sorry it impacted you in this way."

"It's alright. This place was special because this is

where Charlie and I truly began, but I've decided to relocate. Charlie has been looking for a new location. We'll create new memories and new beginnings." Carla curled up her lips in a sad smile. She popped the bottle open and poured them both a generous glass. "Now let's celebrate new beginnings regardless of the circumstances." She raised her glass. "Tell me about *him*."

"Do you remember the computer geek who would sit here for hours and drink one espresso?" Vi asked and bit her lip, smiling.

"No way," Carla shouted and promptly put a hand over her mouth. "You vowed to get rid of him."

Vi giggled, took a sip of her bubbles and told Carla everything.

"*Dios mío*, what a story. But it seems you found your soul mate and the passion you were missing." Carla squeezed her hand. "Well, I guess this place started with my love story and it's ending with yours. Oddly, it makes me feel better about everything."

"Are you sure you don't want to close for a month or two and remodel?" Vi asked.

"No, I'm looking forward to a new project, actually. You know what the worst thing is? I'm kind of glad the asshole is dead." Carla dropped her voice.

"I know what you mean. My feelings are suspended between relief and outrage or fright," Vi confessed.

"Well, Rocco doesn't seem concerned at all and I

don't think we could have changed the sentence, so it's best not to think about it." Carla downed her glass and promptly refilled it.

They sipped in silence for a moment.

"Before I forget, I have the paintings in the back. One of them got a dent in the middle, but the other three remained intact," Carla said. "It was a great idea to display art here. I might consider it for my new location."

"I'll pick them up later. I'm considering representing the artist." Vi reached for the glass, unsure what to do with her hands, avoiding Carla's eyes. She wasn't even able to tell her friend she'd already offered him representation.

The idea of stepping into the unknown made her anxious. She did not know what she was doing and heaps of self-doubt buried her determination. Who was she to manage artists or double in art dealing?

But Carla didn't seem shocked in the least. "You should open your own gallery. You have some capital from the sale of your café and you certainly have an eye for talent and promising pieces."

"I don't know about that," Vi said quickly, but the idea of her own gallery awakened something in her that sent her stomach fluttering.

"What? You helped me choose all the art in my apartment."

Violet had forgotten about that. Or rather, she

remembered helping with decorating, not with art acquisition.

"And I not only get compliments all the time," Carla continued, "but we had offers from Charlie's clients who are art collectors to buy some of our pieces. I'll tell Charlie to look for a space for you, too."

"I'm not sure if I'm up for it, but I guess it wouldn't hurt to look at potential locations. Just for fun, anyway." Vi hesitated and at the same time couldn't wait to share this development with Art. Would she be able to pull it off? Her own gallery?

"Great!" Carla beamed.

Vi finished her glass, took a coffee to go and left. She had an afternoon of pampering in front of her. This visit with Art seemed like the second first date and she wanted to get ready for it.

The late spring sun tickled her skin as the warm breeze played with her hair and Vi took a detour on her way home, enjoying the waterfront. Was Carla right? Could she, a former coffee shop owner, enter the world of art without being laughed at and considered a fraud?

She sat on a bench and watched the waves and the seagulls forming a perfect backdrop for her current mood. If she worked hard and believed in herself as much as Carla or Art, she could try. And if it ended up a disaster, she would simply force Art to return to the Dominican. She laughed inwardly, basking in the sun and her happiness for a moment longer.

She walked up to her building, the smile still warming her from the inside out.

"Violet," a woman said, pushing off a short wall of bricks that lined the path to the entrance. She was tall and skinny, kind of unhealthy looking with her pale complexion, but there was beauty in her features. Her dark indigo hair fell straight to just above her shoulders. Bangs cut above her eyebrows framed her face in a square kind of way, but it was her eyes that captivated Vi's attention. The woman glared at her with dark eyes that shined in a weirdly magical way. A raven.

"Yes. Who are you?" Vi asked. The smirk on the woman's face sent eerie goosebumps down her spine.

"I'm Simone, Art's wife."

22

THE BLOW KNOCKED the air out of him. Art doubled over and stumbled, but quickly recovered, straightening up again. He barely evaded a hook to his jaw by tilting his head backward and Luca's hand swiped through the air. He was getting it from every angle today, unable to concentrate. The next punch connected with Art's helmet so hard he staggered sideways and bounced into the ropes enclosing the ring.

"What's wrong with you today? Are you weakened by *love*?" Luca chuckled and took off his gloves, patting Art's shoulder.

"Fuck you, asshole," Art snarled. He didn't like the beating, but his mind wasn't in it. Boxing was the best way to clear his head, but its benefits eluded him today.

"What's going on, dickhead? I thought you were

bringing Violet home tonight. Are you shitting your pants at the significance of that?" Luca grabbed a bottle from the corner of the ring and gulped down the entire thing, squeezing the plastic in his hand and tossing it into a bin in the gym's corner.

Art stared at him. *Significance?* "What are you talking about?"

"Well, the only other woman you've brought home was Simone." Luca lifted the rope and jumped from the platform.

Art followed him. "Talking about Simone…" He cleared his throat, the words lodged there painfully. "She tried to contact me."

Luca stopped. "That's never good news."

"I'm going to talk to her." Art wiped his face with a towel and hooked it around his neck.

"Why?" Luca asked, but the reason dawned on him immediately. "You're serious about Vi." He nodded in agreement, frowning as if already assessing the level of threat. "How did she contact you?"

"We used to have this code and a secret message that would appear on several servers to know the other one needed to talk. I'd forgotten about it, but she used it today." They walked upstairs into Art's kitchen.

He pulled two bottles of water from the fridge and they drank.

"Is she the reason you fought like an amateur today?" Luca smirked.

"Asshole." Art rolled his eyes. "I need to take care of this once and for all."

"You do."

"I'm worried." Art pinched the bridge of his nose, trying to focus.

"About?" Luca emptied his bottle and tapped to open the trash.

They stood in the middle of the rectangular kitchen. Luca leaned against the fridge while Art rapped his fingers on the counter.

"Every time I've hidden something from Vi it's backfired. I don't want her to know about this," Art said, part of him realizing it was a terrible decision.

"So you want to hide something from her again?" Luca raised one eyebrow. "I advise against that. You should have told her about Simone already."

"Not helping." Art dropped his head. "I'm going to shower and then reach out. I want you to be present. I need a witness."

"You're going to commit a cyber murder?" Luca snickered.

"You're so witty, fucker." Art pushed off the counter and went upstairs to his bedroom.

Luca was right—he should have told her sooner. But how did you tell someone that you were a rehabilitated criminal, the Mafia was pursuing you and oh, yeah, you were kind of married. Fuck! It was too much, but perhaps he should have ripped the bandage off all at once, not rationed the disappointment.

The hot water helped him relax a bit. He wanted to focus on Vi's visit tonight, but he couldn't. Not yet. Though even as he stepped out and dried himself, he was imagining how Vi would look pinned against the glass wall of his walk-in shower.

He wanted to ask her to move in with him, and he would even sell this place if she wanted to live elsewhere. This house used to be his oasis, but it wouldn't be without her. His home was with Vi.

But Simone had to be dealt with first.

He rubbed a towel over his wet hair and skipped shaving to save time. Dressed in gray sweats and a white T-shirt, he walked downstairs. Luca was humming in his room, so Art sat down at the edge of the U-shaped sofa that dominated his living room. He put his head in his palms and waited.

What did Simone want? Since he'd gotten the message, he focused on what he needed from her, but she'd contacted him. What if she was in trouble? Was the Bureau closing in on her? Was she going to ask for his help? What would it cost him?

"Ready," Luca announced and they headed to Art's office.

It was a large room with two glass walls. Art's original idea had been a brighter office to combat the stereotype of dark, dingy basements where his kind of work often happened. It had turned out the sun's reflection really was a bitch, so he'd had shutters installed.

He punched a switch by the door and the humming of the engine echoed around the room. Within a minute, the two glass walls were covered and the room sank into darkness, the only source of light the three screens on his desk.

He sat down while Luca leaned against a cabinet behind him, the monitors clearly visible to him. Art typed a message and they waited. She responded within minutes and Art sent her a secured connection for a video call.

"Darling Art, how are you?" Simone sang, beaming. "Luca, of course you're with him. I've always been jealous of you."

"Cut the shit, Simone. What do you want?" Luca snapped. Art leaned forward in his chair. Despite her cheerful confidence, she didn't look very good. New lines weaved her forehead and shadows circled her eyes.

"Right to the business I see. Are you going to speak for Art?" Simone glared into the camera. All the feelings he'd ever had for this woman had distilled into pity. There was a time once when he'd thought he loved her, but that had been an illusion. She was a master manipulator and he'd let her play him. He felt sorry for her now, but that didn't resolve his problem.

"What do you want, Simone?" Art asked, tapping his fingers on his thighs.

"I want the data you harvested from Miller."

"I didn't pull anything from Miller."

"Don't insult my intelligence, Art. It was done and only you could have done it. With that imbecile Taworski gone, I've lined up a new buyer. Perhaps buyers. A little bidding war would be fun." She smirked.

"Yeah, it would if you had anything to sell," Luca responded, leaning forward, flattening his hands on the desk next to Art.

"I'm pretty confident I'll have the data to offer." She smiled, not moving her gaze from Art's. His fingers tapped his thighs faster than ever.

"Okay, let's say I have the data," Art said and Luca turned to him, frowning. "Sign the damn papers finally, Simone, and the Miller goldmine data are yours to sell."

Luca pushed off the table, groaning, then stepped to the side and shook his head, but Art ignored him. He needed her to finally divorce him and this was his chance. She'd refused for seven years. It hadn't mattered before, but now he needed to be free.

"Well, well, well, what a reasonable price, but I want to remain Mrs. Mathison. We had our disagreements over the years, but once I'm rich, we can reunite and play happy family. I still love you, Art. I always will. We belong together," she drawled.

"Shut up," he snapped. "Sign the fucking papers, Simone, or I swear—"

"I'm not signing anything. I want the data. I'll contact you in forty-eight hours with the instructions.

In the meantime, enjoy the footage, darling," she said and the screen turned to static.

"What footage?" Luca dashed to his side.

A link pinged on the screen and Art clicked on it. It took him a second to understand what he was seeing, but as soon as comprehension hit his cortex, violent shudders swallowed his body, twisting his organs in agony.

"Fuck!" Luca punched the desk, sending a set of pens flying.

Art looked up and ran his fingers on the keyboards. A few strokes and he zoomed in, refocusing the image of the footage. He touched the monitor, stroking Violet's face on the screen.

* * *

Twenty-four hours of anguish. Or was it less?

Vi paced around the empty room. It couldn't have been more. Or was it? Was someone looking for her? Where was she? The unanswered questions roamed in her head aimlessly, driving her crazy. But not as mad as her helplessness. Despair oscillated around, drowning her, and then bursting her into survivor mode intermittently.

When they'd pushed her in here, the pungent odor of mildew hit her nostrils, but now it seemed scentless and airless. Was she going to suffocate? What was this room, anyway?

Her knee throbbed from the tumble she'd taken when they shoved her down the stairs.

Simone and a bulky man had forced her into a nondescript truck and covered her eyes with some fabric. They'd driven for a long time, but it felt like they'd ridden in circles. They definitely hadn't taken the highway. Chances were she was still in Chicago. Was that a good thing?

The air refused to fill her lungs. She doubled over, resting her hands on her knees. People did that when they were hyperventilating, didn't they? Why? It didn't seem to help one iota. She sucked the air in short bursts and eventually got a hold of it. She breathed, but it didn't come naturally. She was stuck in a cold, empty room with a boarded window, and even breathing required thoughtful concentration.

Slowly, the inhales started leading to exhales more organically and Vi straightened up again and resumed her pacing.

The smell and the incoherent glimpses of insignificant details on the way from the truck suggested she was trapped under ground level. She was in a basement, probably. As if it even mattered.

The door was bolted.

She'd spent hours pounding on it earlier.

Or maybe it was minutes.

The concept of time had disappeared with her freedom.

They had taken away her watch, her phone and

her shoes. The last seemed random, since she was wearing flats with no shoelaces. Cold feet were the least of her problems.

She cycled through several emotions—fear, anger, frustration, anxiety—but at the end a heavy sense of hopelessness had overridden everything else.

The single bulb hanging from the ceiling blinded her. She'd drifted, but every time her sleepy limbs had slumped deeper into the hard cement floor, she'd jerked awake. Sleep deprivation seemed effective in subduing her because she didn't have the energy to pound on the door anymore.

Tears rolled down her cheeks.

Stop it! I can't lose my shit.

The bulky man who'd overpowered her in front of her building had brought her bread and water, but for the first time in her life she had no appetite.

The only glimmer of hope was the camera in the corner of the ceiling. Had Art hacked it already? Was it even possible? Did he know she was missing? He must have been looking for her.

Her feet blistered from the pacing, the pain distracting her slightly from her circumstances.

She wiped her tears angrily. None of this hurt as much as the fact that Art was married. He'd lied to her. He'd told her he loved her while he belonged to another woman. How would she ever trust him again?

A sharp needle-like pain shot through her foot into her injured knee and Vi slid down to the hard, cold floor. She looked up, wondering if Art was watching her already, trying to find her. Could she send him a message somehow? Could he hear her?

She had no idea where she was, anyway.

Approaching footsteps drew her tired brain to the present. The lock clicked and Vi scrambled to her feet. For a second she considered running, but she slumped against the wall, barely standing on her feet, when she saw her visitor.

Simone entered, pulling a chair behind her. A twisted gesture of hospitality? Before she closed the door, Vi glimpsed the muscle who had been doing all the manhandling for her captor. He was guarding the door, making sure she wouldn't... what? Overpower Simone?

Simone placed the chair by the door and sat down. Vi almost chuckled at the absurdity of the situation.

"I thought I should introduce myself properly," Simone said and crossed her knee over her other leg in a graceful move. Vi leaned against the wall. She winced, the needles in her knee and foot demanding attention, but she remained standing. It might be unreasonable, but she felt more in control when she stood across from Simone.

"How much did Art tell you about me?" Simone asked, her voice laced with confidence. Something shuddered inside Vi. He hadn't told her anything.

Her silence must have confirmed just that because

Simone smiled slowly, like the backstabbing bitch she was. "I see. I guess he assumed you're not the mistress type."

Vi started counting in her head, desperately trying to keep Simone's words in the distance. Without meaning. Without significance. Yet, they were cutting through her heart and she had nowhere to hide.

One. Two. Three.

"He wouldn't have told you we're planning a family together, would he?" Simone rolled her lips and paused.

Four. Five. Six.

"The thing is though that our work got, temporarily, between us." She shrugged.

Ten. Eleven. Twelve.

"As soon as he comes to his senses, I'll let you go. I don't care about Art's sloppy seconds." She smirked, leaning forward. She rested her elbow on her knee and cupped her chin between her thumb and index finger. She cocked her head, studying Vi as if she was a strange object.

Eighteen. Nineteen. Twenty.

"But it seemed he cared about you enough and I got his attention." She smiled, but her words would freeze hell.

Twenty-five, twenty-six. Just shut up, bitch.

"Even if he sees something special in you, you can never understand his world. Only I can. I'm as good as he is." She wiggled her fingers, pretending to type.

She was a hacker. "Perhaps better. We need each other in a way you could never offer. Viking and Venus, we can rule the world."

Venus? Another hacker, he'd told her. Vi's stomach constricted, the acid of Simone's words burning a hole in her heart. She'd specifically asked him about this woman and he didn't tell her. Was it all a game to him? A puzzle to solve and then he'd be done?

"What do you want from me?"

"Nothing. You're the incentive for Art to do the right thing." Simone stood up and wrapped her long fingers on the top of the backrest, spinning the chair around, ready to leave.

"If he loves you, why would you need me to entice him?" Pushing Simone was probably the worst approach, but Vi had nothing to lose and provoking the woman gave her a sense of having the upper hand. A false sense, but more empowering than the hopelessness surrounding her when she was alone here.

"Men rarely know what's best for them, and Art needs guidance in real life."

He needs acceptance, not your judgment. "So what's the plan here?" Vi crossed her arms over her chest.

"That's none of your concern really, but it will *all* be over soon. I just wanted to get to know you. To see what he sees in you. And now I know."

"What would that be?" Vi asked, willingly running into a minefield.

"You're a princess in need of a knight. From what I've found out about you, your life fell apart recently. No doubt he met you when you were in distress. Art's weak point is his need to save others, to solve their problems. Look at his loyal sidekick, Luca. He almost didn't survive his wife's death, but Art took care of him.

"Art can't take care of himself, so he overcompensates by taking care of others. It's almost hilarious how he could sense what others need, but is absolutely clueless when it comes to his own needs. His care could suffocate and you're not strong enough to survive it."

This woman was deranged, but that didn't lessen the impact of her words. Art had saved her from the robbery and had demanded her reason for crying when he'd seen her the first time at the café. If she wasn't homeless, unemployed and heartbroken back then, would he have noticed her?

"Well, let's hope Art cares enough about you now to deliver the data I need."

* * *

WHAT WERE THEY TALKING ABOUT? Art stared at the screen. Vi had her arms across her chest and was standing her ground. Not letting Simone bullshit her. *My girl!*

Simone had left the video stream on and Art hadn't moved from his computer.

"You need to stop watching." Luca barged into the room and with him entered the light. The sound of the shutters rolling up drilled into Art's tired brain.

He blinked a few times and covered his eyes with his forearm. "Stop it!"

"No. You haven't slept in over twenty-four hours. If you want to help, stop staring at her and start thinking and acting." Luca kicked his chair, sending Art rolling toward the window. "I called Rocco Da Bonno on the off chance she contacts them about selling the data. You should do your magic and try to find her, not sulk here, asshole."

Art dropped his head and pinched the bridge of his nose. The fear was paralyzing. At least if he watched her, he knew she was okay. Under the circumstances. He should do something, but the numbness spread from his limbs to his brain.

"Snap out of it, Art. She needs you. She needs you now," Luca urged.

She needed him. His Vi needed him. He rubbed his face and moved his chair back to the computer.

Earlier he'd tried to ping Vi's location by tracking the video stream, but he'd taught Simone well and it was a dead end.

Art stared at the keyboard, his brain computing endless data, all of it useless in this situation. He couldn't focus. He had nothing.

"Perhaps we should get the Bureau involved?" Luca leaned on the desk, placing his hand on Art's shoulder.

"Let's try to talk to Simone again." Maybe if he tried to track her while she was online, he'd succeed. "What did you tell Da Bonno?"

"I told him the woman who worked with Taworski had kidnapped Vi and that she was going to sell the data Taworski wanted," Luca said.

Art raised his eyebrow. "And he didn't ask for more clarification? Do we even trust him? What if he wants the data and doesn't give a shit about Vi? Give me his number. I'm going to hack his phone," Art said, suddenly empowered by the simple action. One step at a time.

Luca scribbled the number on a yellow sticky note. "I kind of trust him. He helped with Taworski, but you're right. We know shit about him."

Art glided his fingers over the keyboard. The familiarity of the work slowed down his frantic heart rate, but the hollow sense of loss still reigned over him.

Luca's phone rang. "Speak of the devil." He answered with the speaker on.

"The bitch called," Rocco announced. "She called my father directly, but I was with him and I took over. I'm meeting her tomorrow."

"She agreed to meet you in person?" Luca asked.

"You better thank me, asshole. I told her I only

pay cash, untraced bills. She must be desperate, because she agreed. I'm assuming you want to join me for the meeting?" It was midmorning, but club music played behind Rocco.

"We'd be watching from a distance. She knows me. We don't want to spook her," Luca said.

"I'm not giving her my money…" Rocco hissed, short of breath. He panted and then let out a strangled yelp. Was he getting a blow job? Fuck! Art rolled his eyes and Luca chuckled.

"Money is not a problem," Art said.

"Who is this?" Rocco asked.

"Sorry, it's Art. I didn't realize the two of you haven't met yet," Luca explained. "Send me the meeting details."

Rocco inhaled sharply again. "Why should I pass on the data, gentlemen?"

"I have it on good authority that most of Miller's country-wide business ventures will be in the need of new management shortly. Even if you've got the data, you won't have enough time to use them to your advantage," Luca explained. Art lowered his head and pinched the bridge of his nose. What a fucking nightmare!

Luca hung up and sighed.

"I need to call Scully, don't I?" Art said.

"Let's think for a moment. Simone has a potential buyer and she seems desperate enough to meet because she needs money. Is she going to meet with

Rocco without having the data to sell?" Luca scratched the back of his neck.

"If she is so desperate, she could try to fake it," Art said.

"Yeah, but if he doesn't bring money and stall, we could follow her and find Vi."

Art's computer chimed. "I'm in Rocco's phone." He reviewed the history.

Luca checked his phone. "And he's just sent me the details of the meeting."

"I know, dickhead," Art snapped, pointing at his monitor.

"You better sleep off your fucking mood." Luca pushed off the desk and walked to the door.

Art looked at Vi who now sat on the floor. So alone. So unreachable. He stood up and silently asked her to hang in there.

"I can't sleep. Let's spar."

* * *

"I need to use the bathroom."

Vi stepped forward as the man entered to replace the food tray. She'd spent another night here. She couldn't have been sure, but the tray of bread meant it was the morning. They brought the poor excuse of a meal three times yesterday, but then there was a long pause. This was a new day and damn it she wasn't feeding her despair anymore. At least not until she tried to escape.

The man beckoned with his head toward the door. He was large, not tall, but bulky, with a shaved head and a thick neck. He was in his forties or older and his expression remained impassive. Vi had yet to hear him speak. She wondered if he was hired help or if his involvement and relationship with Simone were more significant.

She shuffled into the dimly lit hallway. They had let her use the bathroom next door. A closet-size room fit only the toilet itself and a small, bowl-size sink. There were no cabinets. Nothing to search for something useful.

She reached for the doorknob, her heart pounding. She wasn't sure how to act for this next part, so she remained turned to the door. Not facing her captor increased her confidence by an insignificant margin. In her current situation, it was plenty. "I need to wash up. Isn't there a full bathroom here?" She turned slowly to face him, half expecting he would shove her into the small closet.

He narrowed his eyes, but didn't refuse or show signs of aggression, so she pressed on. "I have my period."

He scrunched his face like he'd swallowed an insect. He even jerked his head back as if he could catch her bleeding. Growling, he scratched his neck.

Vi's heart sprinted, all her nerves in overdrive. His

decision-making stretched for eternity, though it really lasted only seconds. She licked her lip and swallowed, all the slight gestures magnified in her mind as an invisible clock ticked loudly in her head.

He grunted again and shoved her toward the stairs without a word. She stumbled, briefly losing the concept of walking, overwhelmed by the surge of excitement that she'd made it upstairs. What was she going to do there? How was this a good thing? Could she simply use this trip to the bathroom as an exploratory mission? What if she had no other opportunity? She was walking freely, well, minus the large man following her. She should take her chance now.

With a renewed determination, she took the last step that led into the kitchen. Her eyes darted around.

A door leading to the backyard was only two steps away. Was it locked?

If she tried, it would be the end of exploration.

A knife on the table. At first, she didn't even register it. It was within her reach, but before she could even contemplate what she was capable of, the large hands pushed her into a hallway with another set of stairs.

And the front door at the end of it. She longed to reach it, but he shoved her forward to the steps.

She tripped twice, but somehow reached the upper landing. Thick-neck pushed her through a door into a small bathroom. He picked up the garbage bin, opened the cabinet above the sink and dumped everything into it. He then opened the bottom door and shuffled things around, clearly looking for a potential weapon. Just as she'd intended.

He looked around one more time and left with the garbage bin.

As soon as the door shut behind him, Vi collapsed on the toilet. There was nothing here left to help her escape. She dropped her head to her knees and fought a sob.

After a moment, resigned, she used the toilet and washed her hands and her face. She turned on the shower, for show. She wasn't on her period and while she felt filthy and uncomfortable in her own skin, she had no desire to shower. The room had an undescriptive air. There were no fresh towels, only a single hand towel hanging by the sink. It wasn't even damp. Did they not stay here with her? Was she here alone apart from the few times they came to her prison?

Where was Simone? She might have been in one of the rooms upstairs, but wouldn't she wonder what was going on? If Vi was alone with Thick-neck, this could be her chance. She wasn't strong enough to fight him. It would be a stupid, futile mission. Tears broke as the familiar despair returned to her bones.

Vi stopped the water and opened the door. Thick-neck stood there.

"What's your name?" she heard herself asking. *Why?*

He beckoned his head toward the stairs.

Vi limped her way down, her legs heavy. She hadn't even looked at the front door. She almost wished she was back, locked in her bare prison because this failed mission drained her and left her numb, more hopeless than before.

No one was coming for her. And soon not even Thick-neck or Simone would come. The thought propelled something unexpected just as they were turning into the kitchen.

Vi threw herself forward and grabbed the knife. She pivoted and without aiming she launched forward.

23

The blade sank deep and dull pain of the impact radiated up her forearm. His eyes widened, and his mouth hung open.

Vi staggered backward, staring. The knife handle stuck out of his neck, and blood swelled around it. Vi's breath was coming in short bursts, her legs wobbly.

The horror of the scene penetrated her mind, and she sprang to action. She dashed to the door and swung it open. *It's open. Oh my God, it's open.*

She ran, half-expecting Thick-neck's hands on her any minute. She took a turn around the house and found herself on the street.

Large maple trees lined the pavement of a residential neighborhood. Vi looked up and down the street and then ran toward the sounds of traffic.

She reached the main street of a neighborhood

that felt vaguely familiar. She was still in Chicago.

Small children were crossing the road with three young women in reflective vests. Two elderly men sat on a bench in front of a small coffee shop. A bus pulled to a stop. The life flowed effortlessly here. No one paid her any attention.

The sweat dripped down her back and her knee pulsed with pain. Had she really escaped? Was she free? She brushed the hair off her face and paused for a moment.

Vi noticed a cab and stretched out her arm. The car pulled to the curb and she jumped in, shutting the door with a bang. She looked in the direction of the idyllic street that housed her prison, but she couldn't see anyone. She uttered a sigh of relief.

"Where to?" the driver asked.

Sweet Temptations was the first name that came to her mind. She could find refuge with Carla and figure out what to do next. Run? Police? Art? *Married Art.*

She slumped deeper into the seat, the adrenaline still jerking her nerves. Looking down into her lap, she burst into tears. There was blood all over her hands.

ART TAPPED his fingers on his thighs, but the pretend keyboard did nothing to soothe his nerves. Luca leaned back in the driver's seat, his elbow on the window and his head resting on his fist as if he was bored. How could he act so casually?

They were parked across the street from a diner where Rocco sat leisurely, his arm across the backrest of the chair beside him. He looked so relaxed and arrogant that Art wanted to punch his face. Simone's back seemed tense, but perhaps it was just Art's imagination. There was no way to tell from this distance.

He had to give it to her, she was courageous to show up here not having anything to offer. She'd promised Rocco to bring a sample of the data, probably banking on the hope he would be gullible enough. She must be really desperate, being this reckless. On the point of stupid. And Simone Lecroix was anything but stupid. What had happened to her?

"She is leaving." Luca perked up and started the engine.

Art slid the laptop from the dashboard and consulted the screen. He was tracking all the phones in the vicinity, but there was no way to tell if he'd managed to find Simone's in the group. They were going to follow her, anyway. Not her online footprint, the actual person. Art felt like a fish out of water, but Luca was the expert here and Art had to hope Simone would lead them to Violet.

Simone stepped out and Rocco followed her. He walked her to the car she'd arrived in, but before she opened the door, he grabbed her and pushed her back against the car.

"What the fuck?" Luca craned his neck as if he could hear what was happening.

Art frowned.

Rocco leaned closer and Simone tilted her head to escape him. She nodded frantically and even from the distance Art saw something in her eyes he'd never seen before. Fear. She was desperate and scared. What was going on?

Rocco pushed off and walked away with a satisfied smile. Simone dropped her head and when she looked up, the familiar mask of haughty confidence was back. She hopped into the car and took off.

Luca pulled into the traffic, keeping a safe distance while not losing sight of her.

On his tablet, Art clicked on the window streaming from Vi's prison. "She's not there," he said, raking his fingers through his hair.

"That's a long bathroom break," Luca kept his eyes on the rear of Simone's SUV.

But it was what he hadn't said that lay sour in Art's stomach. Had they moved her? Where was she? What was going on?

Luca's phone rang and he answered on speaker.

"She gave me a USB key," Rocco said, "and we agreed I'll be in touch once I review if it's worth the trouble. She's scared. Just in case you fuckers lose her, I put a tracking device on her." He sounded very pleased with himself.

"Thanks." Art pushed out the word while wanting to strangle the asshole.

"What's in it for you, Rocco, I wonder," Luca said.

Art raised his eyebrows. Not that he didn't want the answer, but this was the last place and time to have this conversation. Owing a favor to Rocco Da Bonno was probably worse than any threat they'd faced yet, but Art didn't care. As long as Vi was safe.

"Oh, I'm having fun with this, but nothing is free. I'll collect when the time comes. Go save your girl." He hung up.

Art looked at the map on his screen. All the phones he'd hacked earlier continued blinking in the diner's vicinity. "I didn't get into her phone," he said.

"Good that Rocco has a tab on her, then."

"I hate the asshole." Art pinched the bridge of his nose. Never had he felt this powerless. The fear had him paralyzed. He watched the SUV and a jolt of anger surged through him. He opened a program on the laptop and sent an encrypted message.

Simone pulled into a residential street and parked in front of a semi-detached brick house. Luca stopped half a block behind her on the other side of the street. She dashed to the front door of the house and entered.

"Should we simply go in?" Luca asked, but Art was already opening his door. He sent another encrypted message from his cell phone and strode toward the house, his heart hammering against his ribcage. He clenched his fists. Open. Close. Open. Close.

Without thinking, he knocked on the door, but there was no answer. Luca peeked through the window and gestured toward the side of the house.

Art nodded. He pounded on the door again, while Luca rushed around the corner to the back of the house.

Why wasn't she answering? Was Vi here?

He was about to pound on the door again when it burst open. Art's eyes met Simone's. She glared, her arms twisted behind her back where Luca was holding her as she wiggled, trying to get free.

"Let me go, you, asshole," she snapped.

"Where is she?" Art growled as he entered and shut the door behind him.

"How did you find me?" She kicked Luca's shin.

"Cut it out, bitch." Luca growled and pivoted her, pinning her to the door, her back to them.

"Where is Violet?" Art howled.

"Let go of me." Simone tried to get free from Luca's grasp.

"Fuck it." Art moved into the house, looking for the access to the basement. He needed to find her.

Blood.

Body.

The things registered in a disjointed manner. It took only a microsecond to confirm the body wasn't Vi's. Even that insignificant fraction of time knocked the breath out of him. What the hell happened here?

Simone's and Luca's voices carried as they verbally assaulted each other.

"Come over here," Art called and Luca appeared almost instantly, with Simone struggling and practically under his arm.

"I almost tripped over him. What happened here?" Luca halted at the entrance to the kitchen.

"Apparently your girlfriend is a murderer," Simone snarled. Luca covered her mouth with his large hand and she must have bitten him because he swore. He carried her over the body to the table in the middle of the small kitchen.

Art spied the door and the staircase and was in the basement in two large strides. The door at the end of a short hallway was open. The room Vi had been held in, the room he'd known every inch of from staring at the grainy footage, was empty.

Vi was gone. He peered in the other door, a tiny bathroom. She was gone and there was a large man lying on the floor in the kitchen.

Art returned and found Simone tied to the chair. Her lips pursed, she sat there like a petulant child, her expression annoyed. She was fucking annoyed by it all.

Luca leaned above the body, pressing a towel to the man's neck. "There is still a pulse."

"Call 911 and let's get out of here," Art said.

Luca pulled his phone.

"What about me?" Simone looked up. "There are people after me, Art. I need your help. I need the money to leave and hide somewhere. We can find a nice beach in the Pacific and live there together. We can be big and important again. Imagine all the shit we could do."

"Who's after you?" he asked, not even sure why he cared. Perhaps he needed the validation for the message he'd sent earlier.

"Some bad people in England and maybe in Italy. And I'm pretty sure the FBI is closing in on me as well." Simone tried to sound nonchalant about it all, but sweat trickled down her forehead as her haunted eyes flitted around.

"I'll get you somewhere safe. You won't like it, but it's the best thing, Simone," Art said.

They glared at each other. "What did you do?" Her voice hedged between horror and threat.

"The ambulance is on its way," Luca interrupted. "What do you want to do?" He stayed on his knee, pressing the towel to the wound of the still body.

"I want to find Violet." Art continued glaring at Simone, silently saying his final goodbye.

The sirens wailed outside.

Luca nodded. Even though his friend did not know what the endgame was, he trusted Art. "Go to the car and I'll be there in a moment."

Art left the door open for the paramedics and

casually walked to his SUV to avoid attention. He got into the passenger seat.

With a few clicks on his phone, he found the closest CCTV was up on the cross street. He started reviewing the footage.

His beautiful Violet had escaped. His strong girl fought a man twice her size. While he was still worried where she was, his heart filled with pride. She was a survivor.

A black sedan pulled to the curb in front of the house, drawing Art's attention from his phone, and two suits got out. *Where are you, Luca?*

When they were in the house, he got out of the car and walked to the driver's seat.

"Leaving without me, asshole?" Luca's voice startled him.

"Fuck, how did you get out?" Art asked and returned to his side of the car.

Luca got in and started the engine. "I used the back door. Wasn't that Scully?" He pointed in the direction of the black sedan.

Art said nothing. Part of him regretted that the agents got the messages he'd sent earlier and got here in time. Confirming Simone Lacroix's identity as Venus for them was the worst form of betrayal, and he'd hoped he was right and she was safe now. Safe in prison soon.

"You did the right thing," Luca said.

The right thing felt pretty shitty.

24

———

"WHERE COULD SHE BE? Should we go to the patisserie or to Carla's?" Art paced in front of Vi's building.

"Calm down and call Carla," Luca said. "It won't help us to drive around and in the meantime she might come home."

"I don't have Carla's number." Art kicked a pebble. He needed to punch something or someone. He was so worried. What if something had happened to her after she'd run away?

"Why don't you stay here and I'll go check the other places. Keep the laptop and try to find her on the CCTV footage." Luca walked to the car.

Art wished he was able to think as clearly as Luca. A clusterfuck of emotions rendered him useless. As Luca returned with Art's laptop under his arm, a car pulled in and Art's heart jumped in his chest like a spooked horse.

Charlie Da Bonno opened the door and his wife and Vi got out. Carla kept a protective arm around Violet's shoulders.

She was safe.

She was here.

Her gaze landed on him and the fear he'd been feeling for the past two days intensified. Worried about her life and wellbeing, Art had pushed the repercussions of Vi finding out about Simone to the back of his mind, but Vi's face said it all. She was devastated. She was hurt. And he'd done it to her.

Charlie and Carla's icy looks confirmed he was the guilty party here. Even unwelcome. *No. No. No.* This couldn't be happening.

Luca looked like he wished they were anywhere but there and gave him a sympathetic glance.

The Da Bonnos walked Vi toward the entrance and Art stepped in front of them.

"You're safe," Art whispered, the emotions catching in his throat.

Their eyes locked and the pain in her eyes punched him in the guts.

"I killed a man." She sobbed the words.

"No, babe, he is alive." He reached for her hand, but she recoiled. She didn't want his touch. And because he was a man on the run, she couldn't even go to him after her escape. She didn't know where to find him, where he lived. He wasn't there for her when she needed him.

She'd recoiled.

She frowned and he explained, "We found him and called an ambulance."

She nodded. "I'm tired." She started toward the entrance.

Carla glared at him, but Art still turned and followed them. Uninvited.

In an awkward silence, the five of them squeezed into the elevator. Vi, pale and disheveled, avoided his eyes. She stared in front of her, her expression ripping his heart into pieces.

They entered the apartment. "I'm going to shower." She walked to her bedroom.

"What the fuck?" Carla put her hands on her hips. "Your wife didn't like you cheating, so she kidnapped Vi?" She raised her eyebrows.

"I'm sorry." Art stared into the space where Vi had disappeared.

"Oh, so he's sorry. Well then, let's open a bottle of champagne and celebrate the happy ending." Carla shoved his shoulder. "You know what she's been through?"

Art lowered his head. There wasn't much he could say, but he was sure as hell not explaining it to the feisty brunette. He wished everyone would leave, so he could help Vi shower and hold her in his arms, so she could rest and forget the ordeal. But she didn't want him here any more than she wanted to be trapped in that basement for two days.

"Sweetie, please sit down and let the fucker be." Charlie practically dragged his wife to the table and pushed her into a chair.

"Charles Da Bonno, don't you dare manhandle me. I'm so freaking mad and you don't want my wrath to turn on you," she snapped, and he ran his hand down his face and sat beside her, resigned.

"I think I want to be alone." Vi's voice got their attention. She was wearing black yoga pants and a hoodie, her hair lying in damp strands. She looked smaller. And beautiful.

"Please, Vi, let me explain," Art pleaded, already drained from the uphill battle he feared he'd already lost.

"I'm exhausted, but let's get it over with." She walked back into her bedroom.

Art looked around. Carla glared, Charlie seemed uninterested and Luca nodded, encouraging him to follow. And follow he did.

Vi stood by her bed. "You're married," she stated. No question there.

He nodded and stepped closer, his foot hovering in an effort to avoid mines. She stopped him with her arm, not allowing him into her space. Impenetrable walls surrounded her and his lack of access cut right through him.

"Why are you still married?" Her face was blank. It was as if she'd granted him an opportunity to explain but didn't really care. They were having a conversation he wasn't a part of. Or rather, she wasn't. How could he get her to understand? Forgive?

"She didn't want to sign the papers," he answered truthfully.

"I wish I could believe you."

In his life, he'd been on the receiving side of many punches. He'd once ended up in the hospital after an illegal boxing match. Nothing compared to the pain her words inflicted.

"My divorce proceedings started six years ago."

He'd tried. He wanted Simone out of his life for much longer than he'd ever wanted her in it. She'd never loved him. She'd loved the lifestyle. Simone was a thrill seeker and she craved the attention Art's skills got him in the hacker's world.

He'd taught her a lot. She was smart. But not smart enough to hide her cheating. Or smart enough to care and cover up the evidence that she'd been selling Art's codes behind his back. He wished to tell the story to Vi, but right now it didn't seem important anymore. Simone was a past mistake. Vi was Art's future. *Home.*

"Why didn't she sign?" Vi said wearily.

"She had a condition I couldn't comply with."

This conversation wasn't going in the right direction. He hated that they were even having it. He hated that it was his fault. He should have told her sooner. He'd avoided the topic and now he was going to pay the price. Just how high?

"Elaborate," she snapped.

"She wanted a child."

She jerked her head back as if avoiding a physical hit.

"She would divorce you only if you had a child with her? That's the stupidest thing I've ever heard."

"Agreed."

They glared at each other. Silence was just as unbearable as the conversation though. As was the coldness Vi exuded. He needed to hug her. Perhaps they should talk tomorrow. After they'd caught up on sleep.

"You didn't want children?" Her question surprised him.

He shook his head. Why would he want children with a woman who'd betrayed him countless times? Especially since she wanted a child only to stay connected to him forever. To torture him. Get his money.

"Of course not."

Vi nodded, tears glistening in her eyes. She dropped her head and exhaled heavily.

She looked so fragile his heart ached. She was slipping away from him in slow motion and he didn't know how to reach her. How to make it all better. He needed to hold her and help her forget, but she didn't want him to console her. She looked at him as if he were a disease. He touched her hand, but she recoiled again.

"Simone sent me a direct stream to that room you were in. Vi, I almost died watching you. I'll never forgive myself for putting you in that position."

"Art, she is a narcissist. She's sick. I understand where she was coming from. You couldn't have changed how she behaved or what she did to me." Vi turned away.

"Let's go back to the Dominican Republic and take some time to heal. To forget." Their days in paradise seemed like a distant memory now.

She looked at him, those caramel eyes a shade darker. "Oh, I need time to heal for sure."

"Let's leave," he said with a sliver of hope. "Let me hold you."

"I need to heal because you hurt me. I will not heal with you hovering around, pretending we can be strong together," she cried.

"Vi, please, don't—"

"You lied to me." The accusation was final, leaving no room for atonement. This couldn't be happening.

"I didn't tell you because it didn't matter. I haven't seen her in seven years," he said. He wished he could search for the right words online, program a code that would help him explain and fix things, but this was the real world. A world that was crashing down on him.

"You're married. You made me into the other woman." She spoke with difficulty, but with icy determination. The suffering deepened the shadows on her face as she held her arms clasped around her waist. "You made such a fuss when you found out I used to be engaged, and all the while there was Mrs. Mathison who, based on what she told me, is still planning her future with you. Every time I offered a bit of myself... every fucking time I trust you a bit more, you show me I'm in this alone—"

"That's not true—"

"How is this supposed to work if you don't trust me?"

"I trust you," he stammered.

"So then what? You don't *respect* me enough to share *this minor detail* about yourself?" She shook her head, tears streaming down her face.

"I fucked up, Vi, but I love you. I've loved no one more than I love you."

"I don't think I can love someone without trusting them. And I don't trust you. I get it, your lifestyle requires secrets, but you didn't let me in and I will not stay on the outside. I lived in a relationship that was an illusion orchestrated by David, and I don't want to make the same mistake again.

"You've been buried in virtual reality for too long

and I hope, for your own sake, that you may one day find a place in the real world. But for the first time in my life, I'm going to put myself first. You accused me of hiding and sacrificing my own joy for others. And I will not do that anymore."

Her words gutted him, a sharp knife slicing up and down his insides. The pain was immobilizing. He started pacing because the alternative was to jump her and force her to reconsider.

"The odds of giving birth at the first minute of a new year are around one in 526,000. Roughly the same as the odds of getting struck by lightning."

"Art," he thought she whispered.

"Niels Bohr received the Nobel Prize for the structure of atoms and was given a perpetual supply of beer piped into his house." He continued to pace, mining his mind desperately for something useful to say. He needed to shut up.

"Art," she might have said again. His brain stopped as he felt the warmth of her palm on his bicep. He froze, afraid to move. Her small frame quivered behind him, her breath on his back.

"A solar eclipse ended a six-year war when the sky suddenly darkened during a battle between the Lydians and the Medes in 585 BC and soldiers took it as a sign to cease fighting," he recited softly.

If she only stayed there for a moment longer, he could almost see the light at the end of the tunnel. *Just don't leave, Vi. Don't leave, please.*

"You need to go now. Please, Art," she whispered and stepped away. The heat of her palm left his arm and the coldness bruised him. Her soft footsteps disappeared somewhere in the house.

He stood there waiting for his death, unaware of time or space as the hollow in his chest slowly claimed the rest of him, spreading like mercury.

He was marginally aware of sounds coming from the living room and then heavy footsteps approached and a strong hand gripped his shoulder.

"Let's go, Art." Luca's voice destroyed the last brick of hope and Art dropped his head and followed his friend outside like a broken man on death row.

THE DOOR CLICKED CLOSED behind him and Vi limped back to her bedroom. Her legs gave in before she reached her bed and she collapsed to the floor. The pain squeezing at her chest erupted and Vi howled like a hurt animal. The agony coiled around her limbs and bones, penetrating her entire body like acid.

He didn't trust her enough.

It didn't matter that he regretted it. And she knew he did. His regret wasn't enough to mend the broken bond.

His breakdown earlier was as hard for her as his

betrayal. He hurt her, yet she couldn't watch him suffer.

He had another life outside of their relationship. A life she didn't know about and he didn't show her. She couldn't forgive that. She'd learned her lesson with David and she would not blame herself for what had happened. It wasn't her fault. But how would she let go of someone who completed her like Art had?

Curled in a fetal position, she bawled, forgetting about the people in the living room, knowing she would never stand up again. What for?

She told him she was going to focus on herself, but that didn't seem like a feasible concept. She couldn't find joy in an empty world, could she? And the emptiness in her heart was so palpable she doubted it could ever be filled.

She wrapped her arms around her knees and cried and cried, hoping for catharsis or redeeming sleep. As her wails turned into hiccupping sobs and images of Art's destroyed face kept flashing in her mind, attacking her from all directions, she abandoned her search for relief. She would live with the pain and grief, but live she had to.

Pushing herself to all fours took all the effort she had, but eventually she stood up, meeting Carla's eyes. Her friend stood, leaning against the door frame, waiting, holding space for her.

"I need to leave Chicago. As soon as possible and

without a trace." Vi barely recognized her own voice. "Can you help me?"

Carla frowned with concern. She inhaled and opened her mouth, but then closed it as if deciding against whatever she wanted to say. She nodded, pushed off the door and wrapped her arms around Vi's shoulders.

"Let's talk to Rocco."

And Vi wept again. Not because of the painful emptiness inside her, but because of her friend's kindness. Carla didn't ask questions and didn't try to interfere. She supported her the way Vi needed right now.

Vi wasn't strong enough to stay and a persistent whisper in her mind insisted she was making a mistake. But she needed to leave to find herself. She would no longer base all her decisions in consideration of others.

She would go somewhere new, rebuild, though her heart would stay here.

* * *

VI STIRRED AND JERKED UP, coldness wrapping around her.

"Hello, sleepyhead," Rocco drawled. "You're the worst company. Either moping or sleeping. Not much fun, Purple."

"Sorry. Where are we?"

"Not close enough, sadly. We've just left Ohio behind. You only slept for twenty minutes or so."

When Charlie had called his cousin two nights ago, he was thrilled to drive Violet to New York. He was planning to go to NYC and didn't mind driving. As he'd put it, the trip was off the books for him as well. Vi wasn't sure what that meant, but she appreciated the ride.

They had stayed over at a hotel near Cleveland and set out driving this morning again. Vi had a burner phone to call Carla once they'd arrived and one suitcase. She'd withdrawn all her money and Rocco was going to help her open an account under another name. She was going to disappear without a trace. And she hoped she could forget as well. The latter seemed unimaginable right now.

Carla had worried. She'd tried to talk Vi out of leaving. She'd insisted Vi should rest and get over the trauma of the kidnapping first, but Vi worried she'd cave. She needed to get as far as possible from Art otherwise she'd simply forgive him. And he would withhold information again and she'd lose herself in a circle of finding excuses.

Her determination to end things with him didn't mean it was easy. She'd left her heart in Chicago and was moving forward on autopilot. She'd survive. She must. There was no other option.

"I don't really understand women, but why are

you leaving if it clearly makes you miserable?" Rocco asked.

Yesterday, after they had left Chicago, Rocco didn't really ask many questions. He'd hit on her shamelessly, but she'd figured that was just his natural modus operandi. Carla had pestered Charlie all morning, worried they couldn't really trust Rocco, but he'd reassured them his cousin was trustworthy.

Vi had a dash of doubt when they'd arrived at their hotel last night and Rocco had said, "Let's share the room, Purple. I'll help you forget him."

But he hadn't pushed it and gotten them separate rooms. Not that she'd managed any sleep.

"His life is too complicated and he's kept things from me. It hurts that he didn't trust me enough. And I can't trust him anymore, either."

"Maybe he wanted to protect you," Rocco said. "There are things in my life I wouldn't tell a woman I cared about because it could cost her her life."

Vi shivered at his suggestion. "It wasn't like that."

"How do you know?" He raised his eyebrow.

She didn't and that was the point. There were too many secrets. "Anyway, I don't need protecting. It's too late for us." Saying the words broke something inside her. She looked back as if she could see Art behind her.

Was she making a mistake?

She owed it to herself to start anew.

"So you're available?" He winked and Vi

laughed. He was ridiculously persistent. Her own laughter startled her. She hadn't laughed since they'd left the Dominican Republic. *Damn it*. Just the realization broke the dam again. Vi turned to the window.

"What are you going to do in New York?" Rocco asked.

"I'm going to try selling art. Maybe find a job at a gallery." She failed to even out her voice.

"I can help you with that." If he heard the hitch in her voice, he didn't comment.

"I'm not laundering money for you." She shook her head.

"Hey, what's up with the assumptions? I'm offering legit help. Though the other option would make you more money," he said nonchalantly, as if they were talking about selecting furniture for a new apartment instead of suggesting potential criminal activity.

"Okay, sorry I assumed. What kind of help?" She turned to him, folding her leg under herself. God, she needed a good night's sleep in a good bed.

"I have a friend who moves in art circles. I'll introduce you to him and he might help you network," he said. "I also called in a favor and I have an apartment for you for the first two weeks. You're on your own afterward."

"How will I repay you, Rocco?"

"I'll come to collect at one point, Purple. Or it can

be a barter that will satisfy both of us." He winked again and she rolled her eyes.

"Rocco Da Bonno, you're an incorrigible flirt."

"And proud of it." He smirked.

They continued to drive in silence for a while. The highway slowly shortened the distance toward her new beginning and moved her farther away from the man who no longer was her future. Lost in her thoughts and regrets, exhausted and disappointed, Vi wept.

25

"So, what do you say?" Violet asked, feeling slightly excited. Or as thrilled as she could achieve in her current state of mind, which really wasn't much.

Chrysal looked around, his eyes sparkling with excitement. At least one of them was able to fully enjoy the anticipation of the big day.

Vi wished she could simply sink into the joy of her accomplishment, but the shadow of her grief and loss persisted deep down and bubbled to the surface regularly no matter how much she'd tried to move on. And she'd done it all. She'd cut her hair and got some lowlights that matched her eyes.

She'd found a bright apartment to ensure she spent her time in an environment that prohibited sulking. She'd dived into work and kept herself busy. But despite it all, three months later, her wounds didn't show any signs of healing.

Rocco had set her up with a respected art historian. It turned out Rocco was an art investor himself and he was known and probably feared enough to call in a few favors. With his help, Violet had opened a small gallery in Soho and was about to hold her first exhibition for Chrysal. She enjoyed the work, but her soul remained buried in shadows of her past.

A thousand times she'd wanted to return to Chicago and spread her digital footprint. Was he even looking for her? She regretted destroying her phone before she'd left. She didn't have Art's phone number. She hadn't had a chance to see his house before she'd left. She even considered flying to the Dominican Republic. Perhaps he'd gone there. Though based on the news, he didn't need to hide anymore.

A week after Vi had arrived in New York, news about Simone's arrest broke, followed shortly by several charges that brought down Miller's Holdings and their multiple illegal operations. Simone, a.k.a. Venus, got the credit for mining the data that brought Miller down. She was *rewarded* with several charges for her previous crimes and ended up in prison.

Rocco was pleased with the market opportunities the arrests opened up for him. His new business ventures brought him to New York often and he never failed to take Vi out for lunch or dinner.

They'd formed an unexpected friendship. She was grateful for his help and once she'd given him a chance, she realized there was a decent, funny person under all the bravado. He kept hitting on her and she kept laughing him off, but he remained respectful and she'd grown to like his company. He was her only link to Chicago which made seeing him masochistic, self-inflicted torture. He reminded her of what she'd left behind.

Who she'd left behind.

"I don't know how I'm going to thank you, Vi," Chrysal said, looking around the gallery like a kid on Christmas morning. Curated to tell the story of his work, the canvases hung on white walls, ready to speak to visitors, critics and collectors.

"Just enjoy your week here and on Friday we'll sell out, okay?" She winked.

"What if no one shows up? What if they hate the pieces? What if I don't sell anything—"

"Stop right now, Chrysal. I showed your art to a few people already and I can assure you the reception has been very positive. Selling it is my worry, not yours. Enjoy yourself," she said and hugged him before he left.

Vi picked up her notepad from the small counter in the corner. She had to check the current RSVP count and reconfirm the numbers with the caterer, but otherwise things were more or less ready for the show.

"Well, well, Purple, you look radiant." Rocco's voice surprised her.

He wore a charcoal three-piece suit with a yellow

tie and looked very attractive. If her heart wasn't broken and also forever taken, and if he wasn't an ultimate player, she would be a lucky bitch alongside this Hottie McHotterson.

"Rocco, I didn't know you were in town." She kissed his cheek.

"It wasn't planned, but the business was gruesome and all the girls I called were only available later, so I'm stuck with you. Or the strip club, but I need to eat." He winked.

"How can I refuse such a flattering invitation to spend time with you as the back-up of your back-up and only slightly better than a strip club." She laughed.

"Strip club is better, especially since you're stubbornly refusing my advances, but I don't like the food there." He wrapped his arm around her shoulders and she chuckled again.

"Let's go feed you then."

They grabbed a table in a trendy bistro across the street from her gallery. Vi enjoyed coming here and sometimes she'd even come alone. It had a simple, minimalist decor and the chef was a magician.

The waiter brought their drinks. "Carla and Charlie are coming on Friday. I delivered your regards and the invitation."

"Oh, that's wonderful. Thank you," Vi said. She couldn't wait to see her friend. She'd stayed away from emails, still using the library for all her business, and she was using a burner phone, hoping she could stay off the radar

They started reading the menu and Vi felt Rocco's eyes on her. "What?"

"Don't you think he deserves to know?" Rocco asked and Vi's heart jumped to her throat. Instinctively, she touched her stomach.

"Your silence confirms you're not bloated."

Well, that was crass.

"It's none of your business," she snapped.

"I agree, but it is his. Call it men's solidarity, but I don't like you keeping this from him. I don't even know the asshole, but, Purple, you haven't moved on since you arrived here, and I saw him and he's even worse than you." He took a sip of his whiskey.

"You saw him?" Vi leaned forward as if she could smell Art just by association.

"If that's the most significant information you found in my brief speech, that's telling by itself. Yeah, he's been fighting a lot and he looks like shit."

"What do you mean, fighting?" Vi now wrapped both her arms around her stomach.

"Boxing mostly. Illegal fights. He won me some good money too," Rocco said casually.

Vi gasped and her hand flew to her mouth. Art was hurting. "He told me he didn't want children when I saw him last."

"So the fucker knows about this?" Rocco clenched the glass.

"No, he doesn't, but that doesn't change the fact he said he didn't want children." Vi fought back tears.

"What can I offer you today?" the waiter interrupted.

Vi looked up, startled. She had lost all her appetite. Art was fighting, getting himself physically hurt. Because of her? She couldn't trust him anymore, but if the last three months were any indication, it might just be easier to learn to trust again than to keep trying to forget.

Especially since the little person growing inside her was a constant reminder. Rocco was right—Art deserved to know, but Vi hadn't been strong enough to tell him. Hell, she didn't even know how to contact him.

"We'll both have the sea bass special." Rocco took over the ordering after the waiter shuffled uncomfortably.

Vi smiled awkwardly and nodded.

"Look, Purple, I don't know in what context you discussed the subject, but just because he didn't plan to have a kid, it doesn't mean he wouldn't step up. You want the little one to have no father?" Rocco was annoyingly reasonable today.

"I have to launch Chrysal's career first, and then I'll consider my options."

* * *

THE GLOVED HAND connected with the side of his neck and Art stumbled. He ducked to avoid another jab, shifted his foot slightly forward. Left hook. Right uppercut. His opponent staggered and Art punched his face. Again. And again.

The referee blew his whistle, then firm hands gripped Art's arms as he tried to swing again. He shook off whoever was restraining him and threw another punch, the crush of bones vibrating down his arm. Droplets of sweat and blood sprayed around as Art swiped his arm upward again, connecting with the opponent's chin.

The audience's roar killed the sound of the referee's shouting and whistling. Two people dragged Art away, into his corner. He more felt than saw Luca next to him.

The sounds deafened him, the lights blinded him, pain licked at all his limbs and muscles. His knuckles throbbed. But none of it made him forget.

None of it helped him move on. There was no amount of fighting that could help him relax. Help him sleep. He was dying slowly every day, but somehow he was still alive. Numbness and darkness were his only company.

Luca pushed him out of the arena. The yelling softened a bit as they walked down a dark hallway toward the exit.

A man shook Art's hand. He was the manager,

wasn't he? Yes. He shoved a roll of money into Art's hand and patted him on the shoulder.

"I'll be back tomorrow," Art said. His left eye had swelled already, but he could still see out of the right fine.

"You can't keep coming here every day. You're going to get yourself killed," Luca said as he pushed the door open.

"Promise?" Art didn't joke. They stepped out of the dimmed arena and he squinted, attacked by the sun.

"Art, fuck, let's go to the island. Or let's look for her, but you can't go on like this."

Luca was right. He couldn't go on like this. But there were no options. Without Vi in his life, he was lost, so this was the only way.

"Gentlemen." They turned toward the voice. Rocco Da Bonno stood by the exit. He wore a suit and looked all smug as always. Art wanted to punch him too.

Luca walked back and shook his hand, but Art kept walking. He didn't want to talk to this fucker. He didn't want to talk to anyone. Well, that wasn't true. He wanted to talk to Violet. If he only could see her one more time.

"Hey, asshole, she is not doing well either," Rocco called and Art stopped in his tracks. His pulse increased, nearing a heart attack. He whipped around and narrowed his eyes.

Rocco walked closer, his hands in his pockets. Luca jogged to stand next to Art, ready to break up the fight. Or to attack.

"I mean she's hot as fuck…" Art shifted his weight and raised his arm, but Luca stepped in front of him. "And I'd prefer having her for myself—"

"Fuck you, asshole," Luca growled.

Rocco raised his hands in a mock surrender. "Easy, tiger. I was saying, she's not doing very well and maybe you should grow some balls and go see her."

"I don't know where she is." Why was he even responding to this guy? But as much as he didn't want to breathe the same air as Rocco, he wanted to continue this conversation because clearly Rocco fucking Da Bonno knew where Violet was.

"I'm not at liberty to disclose her whereabouts, but if you can't find her, then your fame is all smoke, no whistle." Rocco raised his eyebrows.

Art launched forward, but Luca restrained him. Their eyes met and Luca shook his head. In disapproval. In disdain. Or just in disappointment.

Why did this fucker know where she was?

Art shook his head. "She doesn't want to be found."

"Seriously, man, I don't get what she sees in you. It's like you have no imagination. Run into her by accident. I'll give you a clue. There is someone she's in touch with. And it's not only me."

"Carla doesn't want to talk to me," Art said. He'd

tried to talk to Carla, but she went batshit crazy and threw him out.

"It's not someone close to her. It's more professional than that. Anyway, thank you for the performance today. You won me big." Rocco patted Art's shoulder and sauntered away.

"What the fuck was he talking about?" Luca shook his head.

Professional? Art inhaled. "Let's go home. We have art to buy."

26

"You sold out," Vi said and laughed. Chrysal raised his glass and smiled shyly. The evening had turned out a spectacular success. Positive energy pulsed through Vi's veins, making her almost happy. The lingering pain persisted in the back of her mind, squeezing at her heart, but she was proud. She'd done it. She'd completed her entrée into the art world in style and class.

People mingled around her small gallery. The glass front wall reflected the cleverly lit paintings into the dark street. The lounge music mixed with hushed conversations and occasional laughter completed the atmosphere of the opening night for Chrysal's first exhibition. And he'd sold out already. Vi couldn't help but smile to herself.

"I'm so proud of you, *amiga*," Carla squealed behind her. "New York is at your feet."

"I don't know about that," Vi said with a laugh. It was wonderful to see Carla again. She'd missed her friend very much, and their lack of communication made things difficult.

New York was her new beginning and things had come to fruition tonight. Vi wished she could enjoy them fully. Without the shadow of what wasn't. She rubbed her belly mindlessly and then dropped her hands quickly. To not draw attention to the little baby bump, she wore a flowy red dress tonight. She didn't want to share the news with Carla yet.

Rocco was right, Art deserved to know. What would it do to their nonexistent relationship, that was the big question.

"Congratulations." Charlie kissed her cheek.

"I'm so glad you both could come. How is it going with your patisserie?" Vi asked.

"We found a great space. It's closer to the water-front. I'm reopening soon, hopefully," Carla explained and Charlie rolled his eyes. She swatted at him but left her hand on his chest. "He doesn't want me to work so much."

"I don't want you to stress so much anymore." Charlie pulled her closer and kissed her temple.

Jealousy squeezed Vi's stomach. She excused herself and wandered off to the bathroom. Everyone was so happy. Why couldn't she be?

She stared at her reflection in the mirror. She would have been married to David by now. That would have been worse. Okay, glass half full. She was better off now. Crippled by a broken heart, but better. She stroked her stomach gently.

"We're going to find your daddy soon." *And I hope he will accept you.*

Vi reapplied her lipstick and dragged her feet out to continue playing the hostess.

The room still buzzed with excitement. Chrysal was giving an interview in the corner and Vi's assistant was taking billing and credit card information from customers. The guests chatted and enjoyed themselves while Vi leaned against the wall and smiled. Life was good. It wasn't perfect, but it was good enough. Her heart might remain broken, but there was enough to fuel the drive every day.

A few guests started saying their goodbyes and the event was winding down when the door opened and Rocco strolled in with two tall models. "Purple, sorry I'm late."

He spanked his companions, sending them into what was left of the crowd. He squeezed Vi's shoulders and kissed her on both cheeks.

"You almost missed it." Vi laughed. "We sold out." She couldn't help but smile.

"I'm not surprised." He opened his arms and Vi stepped into an embrace. "Congratulations, Purple." He held her for a moment and then his hand slid down her back and he cupped her ass.

Vi swatted his hands away and stepped back.

"Stop it, you deviant." She widened her eyes and shook her head.

"You can't blame a guy for trying. You're fucking hot. Is that idiot of yours here?" Rocco looked around and grabbed a flute of champagne from the catering table.

"What do you mean?" Vi couldn't breathe properly.

"I spoke with him and gave him all the clues without breaking the promise to never disclose your where-abouts. I thought the smartass would have figured it out by now." Rocco gulped down the glass and took another one. "These are warm already." He scrunched his face as if drinking acid but drained the second glass too.

"You spoke with him?" she whispered, her hands moving protectively to her tummy.

"That's what I said, Purple. Keep up." He rolled his lips as he openly checked out every woman in the room.

Art hadn't found her. Which meant he wasn't looking. Tears stung her eyes.

"Cheer up, Purple. This is your night. He hasn't been fighting since we spoke though. Good thing. He almost got himself killed. Who is that girl over there?" Rocco asked and finally looked at Vi and froze, realizing the effects of his words.

"Did you make her cry?" Carla appeared from somewhere and everyone turned in their direction.

The feisty brunette didn't pay attention and opened her mouth again.

"Let's keep it civil." Charlie squeezed his wife's arm. She glared at him but didn't speak.

"I'm sorry. I'll be right back." Vi rushed to the back room, which was really a small storage area, currently full of catering boxes.

Two of the staff looked at her, startled, and stumbled to return to work.

Vi covered her face with her palms and sobbed. Fucking Rocco. Why did he have to waltz in here with his *well-meant* information? It was easier if she blissfully dreamed about Art. What he was doing, if he was as sad as her. But now she knew he wasn't looking for her. He didn't find her. He didn't care.

The door clicked open and Vi wiped her tears angrily.

"*Amiga*, you love him still." Carla wrapped her arms around Vi. "You need to talk to him. It's been three months and you're not getting any better. You're having this amazingly successful night and you can't even enjoy it. That's not the way to live. Haven't you punished yourself enough?"

"He didn't try to find me," Vi said, sobbing.

"Then go find him. You told him you don't trust him. You told him to go away. And he stayed away, respecting your wishes," Carla said.

She'd also asked him to never invade her privacy

after the cyber stalking fiasco. Was he respecting her wishes? To regain her trust?

Vi dashed back to the room. Rocco was talking to the girl he'd checked out earlier. "Call him." Vi pulled his sleeve.

Rocco's eyes widened. "Excuse me." He kissed the girl's hand and half of the women in the room swooned. "I'll be right back." He pulled Vi to the side. "I don't have his number."

"You were in touch when all the business with Taworski was happening," she insisted. Her heart thumped in her ears as if she was submerged underwater.

"I have Luca's number." He pulled out his phone.

Vi clenched her fists and bounced. Please. Please. Please.

"He's not answering." Rocco shrugged.

"Try again," she snapped.

"Okay, okay." He rolled his eyes and dialed again. Almost immediately, he frowned. "The fucker sent me to voice mail."

Vi rushed to the back room, grabbed her coat and purse. She fidgeted with her keyring. *Come on. Come on.* The keys slipped and fell to the floor with a clang. Shit. She picked them up and dashed over to Carla.

"Could you please lock up and pay for the catering? The small key is from the cabinet in there." She pointed toward the back door. "This one is from the small safe—"

"I'll figure it all out. Where are you going?" Carla squeezed Vi's hands.

"I'm going to find him." Vi turned.

"Now?" Carla asked, but Vi was already by the door. She swung it open and turned. "Rocco, send me that number."

HE WAS TOO LATE. She'd moved on.

Art stretched his legs out and crossed them at his ankles, effectively blocking the path for anyone else. Announcements echoed around him as the passengers rushed to their gates. The cacophony of all the sounds pulled at the nerves in his brain. He wished he could get a private plane organized, but it seemed catching a commercial flight was a faster alternative. In retrospect, waiting away from this teeming place would have been safer. He was going to punch someone soon.

She'd moved on. The image of Rocco Da Bonno's hands squeezing Vi's butt had been fried into his mind for eternity. Now, the last time he'd seen Vi would forever be this horrendous picture. And he hadn't even seen her, all wrapped up in Rocco's arms.

The fucker had told him she was waiting and miserable and he'd jumped at the idea like the needy, hurt puppy he was. But she'd moved on.

He was full of pride when he'd stood across from

the gallery. Her gallery. She'd done it. The room was full of people. He hated crowds, yet he wanted to be there with her. But the balloon of excitement had popped as soon as he'd crossed the street and saw her in Rocco's arms.

"Do you want a drink?" Luca kicked his leg.

Art shook his head.

"I still think you should have gone in." Luca nudged him with his elbow.

"To punch the fucker in his face and destroy her event?" Art deadpanned.

"What is his fucking game anyway? Why did he talk to you last week, encouraging you to find her? Maybe you didn't see what you think you saw." Luca leaned forward and rested his elbows on his thighs.

Art shrugged. He hated Rocco. He should have punched him when he had the chance. But that wouldn't get him Vi. She had a new life now. And all the regrets were his.

The glimmer of hope he'd been nursing for the last few days had dissipated in the blink of an eye. It set him back to the nothingness he'd felt before. Or probably beyond that.

Luca's phone rang. He pulled it out and raised his eyebrow. "It's Da Bonno."

Art puffed air into his cheeks and closed his eyes. The nightmare continued.

Luca ignored the call and the phone sounded again. He rejected the call.

"Fuck it, Art, let's go for a drink."

Too many drinks, too long of a flight and an endless ride later, the gate of Art's villa slid open and they rolled to a stop in front of the house that had brought him so much joy. He stumbled out of the car and fumbled with the keys. Finally, they pushed inside.

The sea glistened under the full moon and the underwater lights of the pool created an idyllic atmosphere he'd loved. He looked at the sofa and remembered Vi in her stilettos. She'd only been here once and now the whole place was soaked with memories of her.

Luca pulled two bottles of beer from the fridge and they walked outside.

Art plopped into a lounge chair. "I need to sell this house."

"You love this house and if you think it would make her disappear from your head, you're stupid. It won't. Sam had never been here and I still imagine her everywhere. But I can tell you, the memories blur with time."

"I'm fucking selling the house," Art growled.

She was done with him. Nothing made sense anymore. Ironically, when he'd met Violet, she was practically homeless and jobless and now she was thriving and he was dying.

"Let's just go off the grid for a week and then we'll see." Luca yawned. "Fuck them all. We can just use the burner phone to order food and booze. Time to forget, my friend."

They watched the water in silence. Luca's breathing soon turned regular and Art stared.

The numbness in his mind returned in full force. If he couldn't focus on work, he had nothing left. Only memories of a woman who made his heart beat at double the speed. A few short weeks of happiness. He'd fucked up and she'd moved on.

He wasn't worth her forgiveness.

* * *

How DID you find someone who didn't want to be found?

Vi unlocked the gallery and pushed the door open. It had been two weeks since the opening night and people were still coming to see Chrysal's pieces. She'd gotten him two more commissions and it was time to look for another artist to add to her portfolio, but Vi couldn't focus. The sense of loss blurred everything else.

She'd gone to the yacht club in Chicago, but they'd claimed no Arthur Mathison had a membership with them. Rocco had sent his men there, but even with their questionable persuasion techniques, he'd come back empty-handed. He'd taken her to the illegal boxing match and pressured the manager, but Art had signed up under an alias and the only contact information they had for him was Luca's number. She'd dialed Luca's number for a week, getting his voice mail, before she'd given up. She'd sent several messages, but they went unanswered.

Vi trudged through her art space and got to the back room. It was now her office and a storage room. Wrapping material lay in the corner. She would deliver Chrysal's art to its new owners in the next couple of weeks and she needed to replace it with something.

Vi sat down at her desk and checked her email. She'd received several submissions from new artists, but nothing had caught her attention yet.

Her phone rang and she rummaged in her bag.

"Hey, Purple, how are you?" Rocco asked.

"Devastated. Heartbroken. Lonely. Sad. Numb—"

"Okay, okay, you could simply say you're fine like the rest of us. Nobody asks how you are to hear the actual answer. Anyway, maybe I'll call another time."

Vi sighed. "What do you want, Rocco?"

"I heard from my contact at city hall. Arthur Mathison has no permanent residence or a property for which he pays taxes in Chicago," he said and Vi's misery hit a new level of desperation.

"Thank you for trying, Rocco. I guess that's it then. Art has spent his whole life living under the radar. I don't know any of his aliases, unfortunately."

"What about that place in the Caribbean? Maybe

we can find out who owns it. Look it up on the map and try to get the address. I have contacts down there," Rocco suggested.

"I'll do that." Vi perked up a bit. "I don't know why I deserve your help, Rocco."

"Oh, Purple, I'm simply hoping you get your closure soon, so I get my chance with you," Rocco drawled and she chuckled.

She hung up and opened the map site, trying to zoom in on the location of the villa. Why hadn't she paid more attention when she was there? As soon as she approximated the address, she texted it to Rocco and tried to immerse herself in work.

Two days later, she still hadn't heard from Rocco and her hopes faded more with each passing hour. She'd finished for the day and was turning off the lights in her office when the front door opened.

Normally she wouldn't hesitate to stay longer for someone who wanted to peruse the art on display, but today she'd had enough of everything and everyone. "We're closing," she said as she turned around.

Her keys fell to the floor and her heart stampeded to her temples. Disheveled but as handsome as ever, Art stood by the door, looking at her with his ice-blue hooded eyes.

They stared at each other. Energy zapped around them and Vi started blinking involuntarily.

"Art—"

He stretched his arm to silence her. "I know you

don't trust me. But trust is earned and I need the chance to earn it, Vi. I can't sleep without hearing you breathe beside me. Without feeling your body close. I can't breathe or think. I thought you made my life better, but I was wrong. You *are* my life. I need another chance to earn your trust. I know I suck at communicating and it seems to be an important cornerstone of a relationship, so please teach me."

He pinched the bridge of his nose and inhaled like he was holding his breath for all the words. So many words from him. Stunned, she couldn't form a sentence, but to her surprise he wasn't done yet.

"I learned to code at a library when we lived in the trailer park. I stole my first laptop. That's the one I used to code the cable bills scheme. I met Simone and she wanted to be as good as me," he blabbered rapidly.

Vi took a step closer, but he gestured again to stop her. He was panting now.

"I taught her and she was the first woman who considered me amazing. It was all smoke and mirrors, she just wanted to be the best. We married because she wanted to be like Bonnie and Clyde. We've done some amazing and very bad shit, but it was always my street credit that grew and she couldn't stand it.

"She cheated on me, betrayed me, took my work and declared it hers. We split seven years ago, but she refused to divorce me. She's signed the papers now. I'm officially divorced. I have three aliases. I'll forward you all the details about that. I hacked Miller Industries and for that the FBI erased all the cold files pertaining to me. Well, to my crimes, since they don't know who I am or where I am.

"That was the reason I was in the patisserie for several weeks. Many hackers tried to get into that system and I stupidly hung, on sneaking in at the exact time when the IT specialist went for lunch. He would leave at a different time every day, so I sat there, drinking one espresso—which I know now is an inappropriate behavior—and dipped deeper into their security. I believe I have no more secrets now, but if I remember anything else, I'll tell you immediately. Oh, yes, I—"

Vi dashed over to him and captured his lips, wrapping her arms around his neck. He didn't react at first, but his body took over quickly and he pulled her closer and deepened the kiss. Their tongues danced together in a desperate effort to make up for the lost time. The familiar touch of his large hands melted Vi's body.

"I wanted to tell you—" Art murmured, but she bit his lower lip.

"You'll tell me later."

He leaned into the kiss now, sucking and licking with the perfect amount of need and desire.

When they were completely breathless, he cupped her face and pressed his forehead against hers. She brushed her fingers across his whiskers, hungry for contact and intimacy. He was thinner, with shadows under his eyes. So much suffering they'd inflicted on each other.

"What took you so long?" she asked.

"I came for the opening and saw you with Da Bonno," he said. "I thought you were with him and I left."

"But you came back…" She failed to blink her tears away.

"We went to the Dominican and disconnected our phones. Rocco sent someone to the villa and forced me to answer his calls," Art said, his eyes narrowed as he tried to hide his annoyance.

"He did? He was helping me to find you. We threatened the yacht club and the fight club and someone at city hall and it was all a dead end because Art Mathison doesn't exist."

"It's my real name." He raised his eyebrow. "So you're not with Rocco?"

"Never." She shook her head. "Though he became a good friend."

"I hate him," he said.

She smiled. "Yeah, a lot of people do, but he got you to come." She kissed him gently.

"It pisses me off that I owe him, but you're worth all the debt in the world."

She nestled her cheek on his chest and sighed contently. They stood there for a moment. Her strong, beautiful, socially awkward but incredibly hot man was back.

"I've been waiting for you the whole time," she whispered.

"I've been wanting to track you down the whole time," he murmured, his breath warm in her hair.

"Why didn't you?"

"I promised to never invade your privacy," he said.

Like shackles, her defenses dropped, no longer restraining her. She squeezed her arms tighter around his waist. Oh, she wished it was just the two of them. The reality of the situation opened up an unhealed wound and Vi started crying.

"I'm here now. Sh, sh-sh-sh, babe." He stroked her hair, but his soothing voice and gentle touch propelled more grief and she bawled. He held her by the arms and pushed her back slightly, examining her. "Babe, what is it? Please don't cry."

"I'm-I'm-I'm…" Tasting the salt of her own tears, she couldn't get the words out through the sobs and fear.

"Vi, what's going on? What can I do?" His concerned voice tore her heart apart.

"I'm pregnant, Art," she finally pushed past the lump in her throat.

He dropped her arms, leaving her cold. The absence of his touch stabbed deep in her soul. She bit her lip, trying to stop herself from crying more.

He opened his mouth, but no sound came. He pinched the bridge of his nose and when he looked at her, his Adam's apple bobbed up and down several times before he smiled. "You-we-you and I?" He still looked stunned.

"I know you don't want children—"

"Bullshit." He cupped her face. "God, I love you!"

"But when we argued about Simone, you said you didn't want a child."

"With fucking Simone." He kissed her with a dominance that took her breath away. He wanted her with the baby. They had a chance. They could work. Hell, they had to work now. For the baby. And for the first time since she'd taken the pregnancy test, Violet felt grateful for the blessing.

"With you, I want to have at least five kids." Art stepped back and looked down at her stomach.

"Five?" She giggled. He looked at her now with awe. She took his hand and placed it on her belly. The love in his eyes coiled around every cell in her body.

"A baby's brain doubles in its size in the first year of life. When in water, newborns have natural aquatic instincts. They're born with three hundred bones, which is ninety-four more than adults. An average baby goes through approximately thirty-three hundred diapers in their first year of life," he sputtered.

"Art, let's go home now," she said.

"Of course." He kissed her again, his hands roaming down her back.

"Home. Now, Art." Vi slipped her hand into his. "I need you."

"I love you." He gave her that dark smile full of promise and a bit of threat, and her core tingled.

"I love you too, Thor."

EPILOGUE

"Art, stop it right now. Get off the phone and drive for God's sake," Violet panted, trying to deal with the pressure and pain. They had gotten to the car five minutes ago and Art had yet to start the engine.

"I'm downloading the up-to-date traffic data—"

"Drive. Now. Or I'm getting out and hailing a cab."

He looked at her, his eyes full of panic, but then he snapped out of it and finally turned on the ignition.

They zipped through the city as fast as possible, which wasn't fast at all. Why would her baby want to arrive in the middle of the day and not like other well-behaved babies who arrived at night when the traffic was reasonable?

Another contraction rippled down her spine,

squeezing her abdomen. "Art, I think I'm going to die."

"Breathe," he barked, but reached across the console and squeezed her thigh to balance the sentiment.

"What do you think I'm doing?" She panted and arched her back a little to adjust. Hell, who was she kidding—there hadn't been a comfortable position for her in weeks. "I'm scared."

"Over one hundred and forty million babies are born every year." He bolted through an intersection as the light switched to red, narrowly avoiding a collision. Horns blared through the neighborhood.

"Don't kill us now. Slow down, Art." Another contraction squeezed her insides. "Oh. My. God. Drive faster."

He didn't look at her, just tapped his fingers across the steering wheel.

They finally pulled in in front of the hospital and Art rushed out of the car. He helped her out and she smiled at him. Seeing the worry in his face melted her heart and sent it to an overdrive at the same time. This vulnerable side of him was so sexy. As the thought tingled her mind, the stabbing pain announced itself at the small of her back and she doubled over.

"Vi." He cried out and hauled her into his arms. His strength had no limits. He'd bulked up more in the last six months. The pregnancy-related anxiety had forced him to the gym twice a day. While she'd been working hard to pick up the momentum established at the opening night of her gallery, Art was fussing around her or finding his calm via a rigorous workout. He hadn't taken any new clients and wasn't really working, focusing his mind solely on Vi and the baby's well-being, loving her and suffocating her in equal parts.

"Sir, you can't leave your car here," someone called after them and Vi noticed that not only was the car in the no-parking zone, but the passenger's door remained open.

"Art."

He didn't look at her, just followed the path to the delivery ward, something he'd practiced several times. Now, clearly operating on an autopilot, she couldn't get his attention.

"Art," she cried. Nothing. She bit his biceps. Jesus, how could he carry her? She weighed more than a beached whale.

Her teeth stopped him. "We need to get there, babe. They could help." Her man was as scared as she was, which was oddly comforting.

She smiled and nodded. Fuck the car. She wanted the drugs first.

Two hours later, they were set up with monitors, an epidural and a nurse who had calmed them down. Somewhat. Art paced around the small room, and with each contraction he stopped and stared at her with pain in his eyes, as if mirroring her own agony. It should have been annoying since it was her giving birth, but somehow his own suffering gave her a false sense of sharing and she went with it.

The resident on call entered the room. "How are you doing, Ms. Holland?" The woman had her blond hair in a high ponytail and wore no makeup. She looked tired and Vi wondered how many babies she had delivered already during her shift.

"Call me Violet, and please tell me it's going to be over soon."

The resident probed her under the sheets while Art held her hand, practically cutting off her blood supply with his squeeze. At least it distracted her from all the other discomfort.

"You're doing great, Violet. A few more contractions and it's time to push." She smiled and patted Vi's ankle. She looked at the nurse. "Buzz me if anything changes." They spoke for another moment, but the conversation was drowned out by the adrenalin and other hormones surging through Vi's body.

Two contractions later, the nurse examined her quickly. "It's time, Violet. On your next contraction, you'll push for me."

On the next contraction, all the notes from the birthing class evaporated and Vi pushed and squeezed and held her breath, all at the same time. The pressure subsided, but not much had changed, leaving her breathless and deflated. She wasn't sure she could do this. No. She was quite sure she couldn't.

Art continued squeezing her hand, no longer pacing around, but focused on supporting her. At this point, however, she wanted to kill him for getting her pregnant in the first place.

The nurse, standing on the other side across from Art, encouraged her and pulled an oxygen mask from the wall. "On your next contraction, use this. We don't want you to hyperventilate."

"I always wanted to try that," Art said and the nurse giggled and handed him the mask.

Violet looked up. Above her, the nurse smiled at Art as if he was the god of sun, completely bathed in his presence, and Art put the mask on his face and inhaled. The two of them shared a moment as if she wasn't even there.

"What the fuck?" she growled, but before she could unleash her wrath, another contraction forced her to push. Art lowered the mask to her face and she swatted it away. "This is the last time I'm doing this. Ever," she spat through gritted teeth.

"I love you, babe." He kissed her forehead.

"I can't do this. I really can't, Art." The perspiration burned in her eyes.

He brushed the dampened hair from her forehead and smiled. Stupid dimples didn't work today. "You can, babe. I know you can. I trust you can."

"Will you stay with me?" she whimpered.

"I'm here." He leaned to sit on the edge of the bed.

"But here with me, looking into my eyes, not down there. I want you to see my…" She glanced at the nurse, who pretended not to be there, "pussy the way you always have."

He crushed his lips against hers, sliding his tongue in, his love seeping through. It would have been the perfect kiss if another contraction didn't wreck it.

Vi pushed for over an hour, the baby retracting back into her womb after every push. She was discouraged and disillusioned when the resident called for a doctor.

"Ms. Holland, I'll give you one more contraction, but then I'm recommending a C-section. The longer the baby is in the birth canal, the higher the chances of complications."

A guttural groan emerged beside her as Art squeezed her hand so hard, she was sure a bone must have cracked. She looked at him, the rush of adrenaline giving her the invincible courage.

"Art, there is no fucking way I went through hours of natural birth to end up with major fucking abdominal surgery. This baby is getting out now or—"

Her own roar killed her little warrior princess speech and she pushed.

"You're doing great," someone at her feet said. The next contraction came within a moment. "Wonderful, one more and the head is out."

She wasn't sure how long the next moments lasted, but the ice-blue eyes glued to hers provided so much strength and encouragement, she was unstoppable.

With the next contraction, several things happened. Immediate relief flooded her as the baby's head slipped free. Two more people in scrubs entered the room. A small cot with a lamp was wheeled in and pushed to her side, forcing Art to let go of her hand.

"What's going on?"

She didn't get the answer because the urge to push overpowered everything else. In the last effort, her eyes found Art who was staring between her legs. She'd feared he would only remember her like this and not find her attractive anymore, but what she saw in his eyes would forever remain engraved in her brain. Awe. Pure, honest awe.

Her beautiful man, hypnotized by the sight, took the scissors from the doctor to cut the cord and then looked up and locked his eyes with hers. I love you, he mouthed.

Another thousand exhausting moments later, sore, depleted and so fucking happy, she watched small baby Lucas peacefully sleeping on his father's chest. She would have never imagined her man could get any hotter, but her current view confirmed she had been so wrong.

"I love you. I love you both," she said.

Art looked up. "And we love you, Mommy." He winked.

"You promised to stay up here," she said, circling a hand around her upper body. "How will you ever go down there after…" She was being so self-conscious about this, and teary because of stupid hormones.

"Babe, I witnessed my son being born. It was the most beautiful thing in the world."

The warmth that spread through her body brought more tears on, but who cared? She was the luckiest woman in the world.

* * *

FIVE YEARS later

"Does your husband still hate me?" Rocco's carefree voice brought a smile to Vi's face. The man will never change.

Nor will their friendship. Somehow, in the middle of the heartbreak all those years ago, they forged an unlikely bond. Vi knew she could always call on the charming criminal to help her out if she ever needed it. Not that such a situation would ever occur since Art lived to protect her.

"Don't feel special, he hates any man who isn't him, especially when it comes to me." And now, true to his usual relentless routine, Rocco would say she should have chosen him.

"Yeah, probably. So are you pregnant again?"

Jesus. Looking through the front window wall of her gallery, Vi rubbed her still flat belly. Tonight, she'd tell Art. Rocco was joking, she knew, but there was no way she'd tell him first. Art will never forget Rocco was the first one finding out about her first pregnancy.

"What's going on, Rocco?" He didn't say she chose the wrong man.

"Why?"

Traffic rumbled in the background and Vi could almost picture his swagger down the street somewhere in Chicago. Water splashed around. Chicago probably suffered from the same weather as New York, punishing the streets and its citizens with a streak of rainy, gray days.

"Your flirting game is lacking," she teased.

The silence on the line was followed by a clung of the car door. "You might be onto something."

"Oh, no, is there someone special who finally grabbed your attention?" Now she was smiling.

"You could say that, but as much as I hate to admit it she seems immune to my charms. Maybe you should talk to her. You know, birds of the feather and shit…"

Vi laughed. "I like her already, but don't worry, Rocco, there are plenty of willing candidates."

She doubted Rocco would ever let a woman tame him. And with his dangerous lifestyle it was probably a good thing.

"You're right. After two weeks, I should just take a hint."

"Wait? What? You've been chasing a woman for more than a few hours? And she resisted? I want to meet her?"

"Don't be so dramatic."

"The first woman who said no to you? She deserves a medal!"

"Shut up, Purple." He sneakered. "But perhaps I should drag your ass here, so you can explain to her how much you regret not choosing me."

Who is this sassy woman driving Rocco crazy? Daring to tell him no? Start reading his story, ***Chased by the Billionaire here.***

Thank you for reading Chosen by the Billionaire.
For bonus Art/Vi epilogue type this link into your browser:
www.maxinehenri.com/chosen or scan:

CHASED BY THE BILLIONAIRE
EXCERPT

Rich barbecue smoke and humidity assaulted his nostrils when Rocco got out of the black SUV. The park buzzed with people. He surveyed his surroundings, spotting three of his men in black suits with earpieces immediately.

Seriously, they needed to reconsider the dress code. Who the fuck wore a funeral suit to a community event at a park? Especially on a summer day when Chicago miraculously migrated closer to the equator.

He wanted to shed his own blazer, but experience had shown civilians didn't respond well to the gun behind his waistband. Unlike his father's goons, at least he was wearing a black T-shirt and jeans. Not that it helped him feel more human. Fuck, it was hot today.

Families with children roamed around, playing

Frisbee, throwing balls, eating at long wooden tables brought here for the occasion. A local alderwoman wearing a summer dress took pictures with her constituents, her grin as corrupt as her beliefs and values.

Rocco exhaled heavily and strolled into the action. People stopped and either greeted him gingerly or turned away. Not that it bothered him. He was used to the fear, hate or awe his presence caused. He shook hands with a few men who enjoyed the afternoon with their families, taking time off from the jobs they worked for his family.

In this neighborhood, everyone was associated with the Da Bonnos. Either working for Tony Da Bonno, paying him for protection or plainly hating him—for all the bad things people believed the feared mobster had committed—while being scared of him at the same time.

A merry-go-round chimed to the side and children's laughter filled the humid air. This was Rocco's fifth event since the news about his father. Since his mother had decided to facilitate atonement for all his father's sins.

As usual, Penelope Da Bonno had found her own way to wrestle with God and persuade him to give Tony Da Bonno a get-out-of-hell-free card by immersing herself in charitable work. Not the same as before, supporting multiple causes. She no longer relied on hefty donations and glamorous fundraiser events. She actually got involved now. Grassroots. Today, she was serving food to the disadvantaged.

Seeing his mother ladling soup to people who didn't own a fraction of what her shoes cost tied a knot in Rocco's stomach. He'd respected her so much more when she was just writing checks.

She was here for one sole purpose: to redeem her husband. But as she stood behind the long makeshift counter, she wasn't able to regulate her facial expressions. His mother appeared bewildered at the sight of people who depended on the rations, as if she didn't understand how she had ended up here.

But the picture was disturbing for another reason, too. As he approached the table to greet his mother and sister, who had somehow been recruited to help as well, Rocco realized his mother had never served food to him. Not even when he was a child had she made him a sandwich or baked cookies. People had always been in the house to help with household chores and cooking.

A jolt of annoyance shot through him.

"Rocco, darling, you came." Penelope smiled and dropped what she was doing to give him a hug. She pulled him closer and kissed both his cheeks. Her usual scent of a heavy flowery perfume and vodka reached him.

"Look, Alessandra, your brother is here."

Alessandra sat on a nearby chair, not even pretending she gave a shit about serving those in need. She stumbled over and hugged Rocco. And, of course, she was drunk too.

"Let's get some food and coffee, ladies." He pretended things were normal. Well, they were normal. Normal fucked-up—typical for their happy little family.

"Darling, I still have work here." Penelope swatted her arm toward the line of people waiting to be served.

"Ladies…" He strolled behind the table and smiled at the other volunteers, who actually knew what they were doing and did it for more than their own selfish reasons. "Will it be okay if I steal my mother for a minute?"

He winked and got the reaction he was used to by now. All of them beamed at him, practically begging him to take his mother away. He suspected this was equally due to his charm—he'd learned to use it a long time ago and it worked like a Swiss watch—and his mother's lack of skills.

Not that serving food required special skills. But Penelope, with her glass of something bubbly or hard in her hand from the time she opened her eyes every day, was more nuisance than help to anyone.

He bought them burgers, water and coffee and sat them down at one of the large tables that miraculously cleared out as soon as they approached.

"You look very handsome, darling." His mother picked at her fries. He should have known she would consider it unbecoming to eat a burger, especially in public.

"Sure, Mom, Rocco is as handsome as ever. Probably because he doesn't have to spend his nights in a bed with someone he hates," Alessandra snarled.

Rocco closed his eyes and inhaled, ignoring the comment. A point of friction had always festered between him and his sister. She'd been forced into a hellish arranged marriage and he'd been saved by a series of unfortunate events from the same fate.

Though Alessandra might soon get her justice since, due to the current situation, the pressure on his nuptials had increased by tenfold.

Watching his mother and sister suffer and turn to alcohol in addition to his own brief engagement had led to his absolute refusal to ever get married. Women who married men like him either lived in fear of becoming widows or put up with infidelity.

That was the only pattern he'd seen. Both options were as appealing as drinking hot lava for breakfast. He didn't mind messing around, but he wouldn't sign up for hurting a woman.

"You should go home and get some rest, Mom." Rocco squeezed her hand and shoved the coffee closer to her. "I'll take you shopping sometime this week."

"I have several shifts in the soup kitchen and I don't want to be spending money."

This was the first time a shopping trip wasn't motivation enough.

"*I'll* be the one spending money," Rocco assured her. "And I'm sure you can still work your shifts." He stopped himself short from rolling his eyes.

"You can take me shopping. God knows *my dear* husband doesn't." Alessandra took another bite of her burger, eyeing it with a mixture of pleasure and disdain.

"Did the fucker take your credit card again?" Rocco's blood bubbled—not yet boiling, but close to the edge.

"Will you rearrange his face again? I don't mind, but last time it didn't look good at the church on Sunday when we play happy families." Alessandra dropped her burger and stood up. "I need wine." She stumbled away.

Rocco exhaled. The two women he loved—his mother and his sister—were the biggest pains in his ass. It shouldn't be this hard to take care of them and protect them, a role he'd been filling since their husbands had resigned from their positions. Fuck, he hated everything about this situation.

The pull of a dutiful son and brother played tug-of-war with his desire to simply mind his own business. It had been increasingly difficult lately to respect both his mother and his sister for their choices and lifestyle. Though he knew their options were limited by men like him.

Temperamental strokes of a guitar boomed from the speakers. Rocco turned his attention to the stage.

A girl stood in the middle, looking so small he assumed she was a child.

With her back to the audience, she held one arm above her head and the other on her hip. Holding the hem of her red dress between her fingers, she exposed a lean leg. This was not a girl, but a woman.

She started tapping her heels to the rhythm of the guitar, the beat throbbing in Rocco's chest. Stomping rapidly, she turned to face the people and his temperature increased while goosebumps covered his spine.

The movement of her petite, slender body was sensitive, profound. It tugged him to his feet and he was moving closer to the stage before conscious thought kicked in.

She had raven black hair tightly pulled into a bun at her nape. Her complexion was almost translucent, the contrast with her dark hair startling. Her small frame suggested delicacy, yet her dance was fierce. She was a warrior pixie.

Her percussive footwork and movements displayed pride, force and elegance, all passionate yet methodical, never missing a beat. Not that he knew much about flamenco, but he was lost in the emotional intensity of her body language.

Her hands, arms, and feet, her whole body, spoke in harmony and beauty. She was a vision, stomping her feet with drama while swaying her skirt sensually. The line between brutal and tender blurred within her dance.

Who was this woman?

The stomping increased, mirroring the growing crescendo of the music. His heart pounded as if he'd just finished a marathon. He wiped his palms on his jeans. His hands had never ever gotten sweaty. The music finished and the dancer stomped a few more times before halting in a beautiful pose.

Like a statue, she stood there with both arms up above her head and her face turned, showing her exquisite profile. She looked powerful and vulnerable at the same time, and he wished to have her like this under him.

Applause erupted, apparently startling her. She stared wide-eyed, as if only now realizing she had an audience for her raw beauty. She bowed too quickly and dashed from the stage.

"Maybe you should take me home. I have a headache." His mother's voice surprised him.

"Mom, I have things to do still, but James will drive you home. Let's get you to the car."

Rocco absently offered his arm to his mother, his gaze darting through the crowd. Where had the dancer disappeared to?

"Slow down," his mother complained as he practically dragged her across the lawn. He instructed the bodyguard, James, to take her straight home and practically ran back to the stage.

He circled around, but he couldn't find her. A boys' choir was getting ready to perform next. A clown juggled red balls. A group of girls practiced some choreography. But he couldn't see his dancer.

What the hell? Since when was she *his* dancer?

He approached a woman who was smoothing a choirboy's messy hair. "Where is the flamenco dancer?"

"Who? Vanessa? She's gone." The mother straightened her son's shirt.

"I think her car is that way." The boy pointed in the general direction of the parking lot and Rocco did something he hadn't done in a very long time. He ran. He actually fucking ran to catch a girl. A woman. *Vanessa.*

He reached the parking lot, his chest heaving as he scanned in all directions, praying he would find her. *Praying?* Heatstroke was the only explanation. He shook his head and was heading back toward the stage when a battered red Fiat that shouldn't be allowed on the road anymore passed by. A driver was a young man who seemed vaguely familiar, but it was the passenger that made his heart thump.

The flamenco dancer, Vanessa, looked up and their eyes locked. It was probably his imagination, but her lips curled up slightly. Before he could react, the car turned and disappeared.

Vanessa.

ALSO BY MAXINE HENRI

Untamed Billionaires Series

Tempted by the Billionaire (A Fake Relationship Romance)

Chosen by The Billionaire (An Enemies to Lovers Romance)

Chased by the Billionaire (An Age gap/Innocent Heroine Romance)

Stolen by the Billionaire (A Forbidden Love Romance)

Reckless Billionaires Series

Reckless Fate (A Second Chance Romance)

Reckless Desire (A Single Dad Romance)

Reckless Dare (A Fake Relationship Romance)

Reckless Deal (A Grumpy/Sunshine Bosshole Romance)

Reckless Hunger (An Age Gap Romance)

Reckless Bond (An Accidental Pregnancy Romance)

ACKNOWLEDGMENTS

First, thank you, dear reader, that you made it this far and you took a chance on a new author. I appreciate your time and plan to reward you with more steamy stories. It's only because of you that I can pursue my dream and spend my days escaping into the world of stories.

Thank you, Martin. I wouldn't have been able to focus on writing without your, at times hesitant :-), support. You're my soulmate and best friend.

Editor Jess, you made this book readable and pointed out logical issues, for which I hated you at the time, but this book is so much better because you somehow manage to understand what I want to say.

Thank you, Dan, for finding the typos and other mistakes. I really don't know how you spot them.

All the ladies in my writer's support group. You inspire me daily with your dedication, knowledge, wit and talent. I'm glad I have author friends because this job is lonely.

I want to thank Craig Martelle, one of the most generous bestselling authors out there, who selflessly creates space and opportunities for us, indie authors, so we can succeed.

And I'm going to loop back and thank you, dear reader, again. Because none of this would be possible without YOU!

ABOUT THE AUTHOR

Maxine Henri is a contemporary romance author who infuses her stories with steamy passion and complex characters. When she's not crafting stories that will have you swooning, she can usually be found sipping on a cup of black tea while reading a good book. Or traveling to new destinations.

Maxine believes that stories matter. They facilitate emotional journeys, inspire and entertain. And when it comes to books and fiction, stories are a great escape and probably the most beneficial addiction on this planet.

Her billionaire romances are the perfect escape, offering a taste of luxury and adventure. Maxine introduces heroes who may have a dark past, but are always balanced by a lighter side. And her leading ladies? They're strong, independent women who may be a little broken, but always find their way in life.

You can connect with her on any of these platforms:

facebook.com/maxinehenriromance

instagram.com/maxinehenriromance

bookbub.com/profile/maxine-henri

amazon.com/author/maxinehenri

Made in United States
North Haven, CT
29 December 2023

46712771R00232